LIARS' TABLE

D. K. WALL

All inquiries should be addressed to:

Conjuring Reality Media
65 Merrimon Avenue #1053
Asheville NC 28801
ConjuringReality.com

ISBN 978-1-950293-05-6 (Paperback)
ISBN 978-1-950293-06-3 (eBook)

Library of Congress Control Number: 2021917505

This book is a work of fiction. The story incorporates real locations and
entities, but all are used in a fictitious manner. The events of the story, the
characters, and the community of Millerton are products of the author's
imagination and purely fictional. Any resemblance to actual persons, living or
dead, is coincidental.

Cover designed by Glendon S. Haddix of Streetlight Graphics

ALSO BY D. K. WALL

The Lottery

Jaxon With An X

Liars' Table

Sour Notes

CONTENTS

To all the liars who have entertained me.

SATURDAY

1

I stood ankle deep in the morning dew, sipping my coffee and watching Belle circle the giant maple tree that centered our backyard as she sniffed for the perfect blade of grass to water. Once she completed her first task of the day—second if you count the stretch and fart in my bedroom that announced she was ready to herald the dawn, as reliable as any rooster I've ever owned—she focused on her nemeses, the evil squirrels chittering from their high branches. Much to her dismay, they once again refused to come down and play her games.

Her gait might not be as steady or her hearing as acute as they once were, but if a coyote hid in the weeds or a bear rustled in the shadows, she would bark and chase it away. This morning, though, she remained focused on the scampering tree rats.

The sense of wrongness I felt deep in my bones, much like a twinge announcing a coming storm, was mine alone.

Nothing visible lurked in the neat rows of corn stretching from the edge of our yard to the horizon. Our home had once been the main farmhouse, but Shelby and I scraped together the down payment forty-five years ago. The family that owned the surrounding land had built a new place across the vast field out by the paved road and were willing to sell their old place at a price we could afford. We were newlyweds envisioning a brood of kids filling its numerous bedrooms and playing in this yard. Things hadn't worked out as we had hoped, and now only Wyatt and I remained, his snores echoing out of the open windows of his upstairs bedroom.

The crops stretched into the distance, disappearing into the morning fog obscuring the North Carolina mountains rising on either side of the valley. The unseen creek burbled in the distance as it had for thousands of years. Birds squawked as they hunted and protected their families. The dirt road in front of our house faded into the mist, long before I could see the paved road it intersected. The church steeple marking the entrance to our cove was obscured. The faint whiff of the paper mill over in Canton hung in the air.

Clutching the warm mug in my hands, the one Shelby had given me years ago, I spun slowly on my heels, trying to identify the source of my unease.

My hammock swayed invitingly in the breeze, biding its time until my afternoon nap. A pair of unoccupied rocking chairs waited for the evening on the porch of the faded white clapboard house. Nothing but serenity stretched for as far as I could see, but I sensed something was out of place.

I sipped my coffee and willed it to fire my brain cells into wakefulness as I walked a wide circle around the house. The place was much too large for me to maintain anymore, certainly too big for only two people, but I couldn't give it up. My best memories were here.

My search under the shrubbery and in the shadows for any threat went quickly, despite entangling with spiderwebs woven overnight. Nothing ominous lurked in the yard, so I returned to my starting point and looked down the short driveway to the dirt road. Wyatt's dew-covered Toyota 4Runner sat parked in its normal place. Beside it was only a patch of oil on the gravel.

Then it hit me.

My car was missing.

2

Missing? Misplaced? Lost? Stolen?

My mind raced to accept what I was seeing as I stared at the empty spot where I had parked the night before. And the night before that. And so on. Except for the rare vacation, I had left my car in the same place for all these years. Same spot. Same car. Same house. Same wife. I was a creature of habit.

I didn't like things being out of place or routines being disrupted. Every morning, my car waited in its place for me to come outside and drive into town. No reason for it to be anywhere else.

Except this morning, the car wasn't here.

The exposed oil on the gravel taunted me. I rarely paid attention to it because my car hid it from view. Was the blot accusing me of poor mechanical skills because the engine leaked? *Maybe*, I argued silently with myself, I was a good mechanic because the car was older than my marriage. Neither was perfect, but both had lasted a long time. Both took work.

Just misplaced. Misplaced is temporary. Not gone. Gone is permanent.

I scanned my surroundings as if there might be a ton and a

half of metal hidden somewhere in the yard. No matter how much I looked, though, my ride was absent. This wasn't like looking for lost items in weird places in the house—a cell phone in the refrigerator, my wallet in the cookie jar, or Shelby's wedding band in a bag of flour.

I had once found my car keys in a dog food bag. I'd unlocked the door and rushed to feed Belle without emptying my hands first. Sure enough, I'd buried them in the kibble, discovering them only after searching the rest of the house for hours before thinking of the odd spot.

Good thing I hadn't left them in the crazy old dog's bowl. She had consumed stranger things in her life.

If not here, where?

Maybe I hadn't driven the car home. In my younger and wilder days, I'd partied as hard as everyone else. My car stayed overnight in the parking lot of a few bars while a more sober friend took me home.

The only bar in Miller County, though, was Sammy's Pub. I hadn't darkened those doors in weeks, and that was for his roast beef sandwiches and iced tea at lunch, hardly the start of a bender.

Besides, I wasn't the young buck I used to be. I hadn't thrown a good drunk in decades. Shelby never tolerated that junk from me, not even in our youthful times. She was no longer here to greet me when I came home, but her influence still guided me. I'd barely had a half-dozen beers in the last month.

Calm down. Think. Retrace your steps. Just like you did when you finally found those blasted car keys in the dog food.

Last night, like every night for the past two years, I had driven over to the Mountain View Nursing Home for dinner with Shelby. Beef stroganoff with carrots and peas and a dollop of banana pudding for dessert. I remembered it clearly. Soggy peas on an old woman's chin made an impression. She had stopped eating after only a few bites, so I had spooned it into her mouth. She forgot things like finishing meals. Or the day of the week. Or who I was. Or what planet we were on.

After I returned her tray to the food cart, we sat together on the couch, talking about nothing, which was all she could remember last night, until her bedtime, which came early in a nursing home. Once she was safely in her room, I came straight home.

Wyatt and I ate together at the kitchen table—another habit, except for the nights he had a better offer, and I ate alone. He was young and deserved better companionship than an old man, so I didn't begrudge him a social life. Last night, though, he'd cooked. I remembered because we took turns, and he was a better cook than me. We could both come up with food marginally better than nursing home beef stroganoff, but neither of us claimed to be a chef.

After our meal, I washed the dishes. The one who didn't cook handled the cleanup—house rules. Once everything was put away in the cabinets, Wyatt watched TV in the den. At one point, I heard him on the phone with one of his buddies. Nothing unusual about that.

I sat in my rocking chair on the front porch, swatting at mosquitos as the sun set over the mountains. Entranced as always with the natural beauty surrounding me, I didn't care that I had lived here forever, except for a few years when Uncle Sam put me to work. Mother Nature puts on the best show for those who pay attention, not that I've had much success convincing Wyatt it's better than anything on that blasted television.

Bats swooped through the air, gobbling up insects. The last light of day waned along the ridges to the west. A pack of coyotes yipped down near the river. The leaves rustled with the summer breeze. The smell of fresh soil lingered in the cool air.

Distant heat lightning flickered in the sky. No better art could be found in any museum, not that I had been to many.

When darkness claimed my surroundings and the lightning bugs took over, I woke Belle from her snoring slumber on the porch and sent her into the yard to do her nightly business. Then the two of us went to our room. I sprawled in the bed I'd shared with my wife until I couldn't care for her at home. Belle curled up on an old blanket in the corner. She was welcome to climb into the bed, but old habits and arthritis prevented that. I went to sleep listening to the muffled sounds from whatever show Wyatt watched.

Had my car been in the driveway when I turned in for the night? Despite the fact that I had sat not twenty feet away, I couldn't honestly say. I wouldn't have thought to look for it. Why would I? Surely, though, I would have noticed it was missing.

Had Wyatt seen or heard anything?

Despite Belle and I stirring about in the hazy light of sunrise, Wyatt's upstairs window remained dark. His snoring had settled to a heavy breathing, still obvious in the morning quiet. He never rose this early, preferring to stretch his sleep for as long as he could. His morning routine consisted of grumbling he was going to be late, scampering about the house, and racing out the door. For those few moments between his awakening and departing, he was little more than grunts, doors slamming, and feet stomping. Quiet wasn't his forte.

Confident he was still in bed and not watching me from his vantage point, I inched my way over to his 4Runner. Once he had straightened out his life enough to start earning a paycheck, he saved the money to make a down payment on that SUV, despite it being older than him and having over two hundred thousand hard miles. He needed something that could handle the mud and snow found on the construction job sites he worked. I tried to steer him toward an old Ford F-150—an

American-made truck, not some foreign vehicle—but to no avail. He didn't listen to me about that any more than he listened to anything else I said. I had to give him some credit, though, because he kept the thing running with lots of help from his mechanically inclined friends. As the oil spot attested, that didn't include me.

With a final stealthy glance up at his window, I placed my hand on the hood of his 4Runner. Cold. A thick layer of dew. Many nights, I had heard his car leave long after I had gone to bed only to return in the wee hours of the morning, but apparently that hadn't happened last night.

In his first few months living with Shelby and me, he had taken my car without permission a number of times, usually late at night and always when he was up to no good. I had even hidden my keys for a while, not that it slowed him down since he could hot-wire a car.

The truth, though, was he hadn't taken my car in years. His snores told me that was true of last night, too, because he was here, and my car wasn't—knowledge that didn't stop the doubts rising in my brain.

3

L ike most bad news, the phone call had come late at night. "We regret to inform you…"

The cold, impersonal voice on the other end of the line belonged to a detective with the Knoxville Police Department. Jessica's body had been found in a suspected drug house. She was probably a victim of an overdose, he said, but an autopsy would tell us more.

We had long expected such a call. We'd hoped and prayed she was doing well and living a good life, but we had feared it wasn't true. That soul-crushing confirmation of our worst nightmare via an impersonal phone call brought home the devastating reality.

We asked all the questions we had feared we might one day have to ask. Were they sure it was her? How long had she been living there? Was she a victim of a crime? How did we claim her body?

The more pressing issue, the detective advised, was what to do with her son.

That revelation, we hadn't seen coming.

TWENTY YEARS BEFORE THAT CALL, Shelby and I had been scrambling about the house, preparing for a normal day. I worked first shift in one of the factories, and she had a clerical job with the county. If Jessica missed her bus—again—one of us would have to drive her to school and be late for work. My earlier shouts up the stairs hadn't created any response, so I went up to her bedroom, knocked, and told her to get moving. I heard nothing, so I pushed open her door and surveyed the room. The bed was unmade, and clothes were strewn about. In other words, normal for a sixteen-year-old girl, except for the fact Jessica wasn't there. She had never been a morning person, so long experience told me she had snuck out the night before after we had gone to bed.

Our first reaction was anger, not fear. She'd snuck out numerous times to hang out with her friends or see a boy. We had both done the same a few times as high schoolers, so we could only feign so much indignation. Shelby called a couple of Jessica's friends, who denied knowing anything. Kids back then didn't have cell phones, so we had no way of leaving her a message.

We guessed she'd come home after school, pretending we'd just missed each other that morning. We agreed we'd ground her as punishment as soon as she turned up, not that that had ever had much impact on her behavior before.

When she didn't show up for school, everything changed. Shelby had stopped by to confirm she was okay, but the records showed her absent. Sharing our alarm, the principal and teachers asked her friends for information. No one admitted knowing anything.

She had broken up with her previous boyfriend a couple months earlier. He said the split was amicable, no hard feelings, and no, he hadn't seen her lately.

The police became involved. They searched her room and then our whole house and the fields around us. They dragged the poor ex-boyfriend in for questioning. They interrogated her friends, and some of them suggested there was tension at home. They pointed to a recent argument with her mother, though Shelby said it was just the typical thing.

The police asked us questions about our home life. The fact we hadn't panicked at the first sign she was missing was interpreted that maybe we knew more than we let on. They treated us more like suspects than victims. I grew angrier at them as each day passed without a clue of where Jessica might be or even if she was okay.

Out of the blue a week later, she called. She was in Atlanta. No, she wasn't coming home. No, she didn't need money. She had a job. No, she wouldn't tell us doing what. No, she wouldn't give us an address. She didn't want anyone to try to make her go back to Millerton.

A police detective was in our house when she phoned. She assured him no crime had happened. We were bad parents, she agreed in answer to his questions, but not criminal.

Having seen too many TV shows, she became convinced the police were trying to trace the call and hung up.

The police lost interest. She had told them she was safe and had left of her own accord. She was under eighteen and a runaway, but no crime had occurred. If the authorities happened to locate her, they would send her home, but did we realize how big Atlanta was? Did we know how hard it would be to find one girl? If she got arrested, that would change things, but otherwise it would be difficult. They never apologized for all the accusations they had leveled at us.

We reached out to shelters and groups in Atlanta that worked with runaway teens. Yes, they would keep an eye out, but the number of kids they saw was overwhelming. Their experience also made them curious and suspicious about why she had left home in the first place. Many of their kids were running from nasty family situations. Was something happening we weren't telling them? Had we hurt her in some way?

Despite being on the defensive again, we did our best to assure them otherwise. Maybe some believed us, because they warned that most teenage girls who run away to Atlanta turn to prostitution within forty-eight hours.

Panicked, we drove to the city and searched for her. We asked people at homeless shelters and soup kitchens if they'd seen her. We talked to kids hanging out in parks—other runaways who eyed us warily and hit us up for money. We gave them what we could spare.

We even asked hookers as they looked for work. We showed her photo to dozens—maybe hundreds—of people. No one recognized her.

The second phone call came a month later. Mobile, Alabama. She had met a guy. He was nice. That worried us, but she told us she had a job waiting tables, so that made us feel better.

Three months until the next call. New Orleans. New guy. New job.

Then six months passed until Dallas.

Then nothing.

WAS SHE ALIVE? Was she dead? Was she hurt somewhere and needed us? Maybe she had settled down and was happy, and the last thing she wanted was our interference.

Shelby wanted to look for her, but where could we start? Based on the few calls, she had moved first south and then west. Was that a pattern? Maybe she was headed to California.

Maybe she wasn't. How could we pick up her trail if we didn't even know which direction to look?

We considered hiring a private detective. Books and movies made it look so easy. We talked to one in Asheville, but he didn't give us much hope. The cost just to sniff around was well out of our reach.

The police were unsympathetic. There was little they could do. The best hope they offered was the off chance she'd be arrested, and they'd match her using records of missing persons. Once she turned eighteen, though, even that chance would disappear. The calls she'd made proved she had left voluntarily and wasn't in harm's way. How could we say she was missing when she had let us know where she was?

Months of silence led to years. We'd think about her, wonder where she was, pray she was happy, but we didn't have an answer.

Until the call from Knoxville.

AFTER GETTING THE NEWS, I'd gathered Shelby in my arms, and we wept. All those years of worrying and praying, and I was still surprised how hard the grief hit us. We weren't just mourning her death, though, but all those years of her life we hadn't been able to share. All the old doubts resurfaced. I replayed every argument, every time I hadn't been there for her, and every mistake I had made.

When the tears finally slowed, we stayed in each other's embrace and confronted the immediate problem. What were we going to do about her son, the boy we hadn't even known existed?

The detective hadn't pulled any punches and made clear his disdain. The boy was fifteen, so Wyatt had been conceived long after Jessica had left Millerton and long after our last contact with her. No one we talked to had a clue who the father might be. He was a tough kid with a checkered history with the police. Social workers in various cities had been involved. Courts had debated cancelling Jessica's parental rights, but there were no good alternatives to offer Wyatt. He had spent time in foster homes and juvenile detention centers, but Jessica had always been able to get him back.

When her body was found, Wyatt was sitting with her head cradled in his lap. Heartbreaking. He was high and had drugs in his pockets. Heartbreaking in a totally different way.

When the police asked him about other relatives, he could only shrug. He didn't have any more of a clue who his father was than we did. She'd mentioned us to him, but he'd never met us, and based on what she had said, he didn't like us. He knew only that we lived in some dead-end town that she'd sworn she was never going back to. He had no interest in meeting us. My heart couldn't break any more.

We cried through the night, holding on to each other and arguing, hammered with grief, confusion, and questions. How could Jessica have had a son without letting us know? What were we supposed to do with a complete stranger? On the other hand, how could we ignore his plight?

I pointed out that if we encountered a stranger with a police record and a drug addiction, we'd cross the street to avoid him. Shelby still wanted to embrace him. The things she didn't know about him didn't matter, she argued—he was her grandson. He was her family, even if I didn't think of him that way.

By midmorning, we were on our way to Tennessee in my Chevy Nova, the two of us still unsure what we were to do or even what we would be allowed to do. Did we have custody rights? And did we want them?

WE MET WITH THE POLICE, who made clear they thought of Wyatt as nothing but a budding criminal. We talked at length with a social worker who was confused and concerned about why we were so disconnected. Jessica had told her that her parents were dead. The fact that she was barely a year older than Wyatt when she had run away didn't help. Discussing what had happened two decades earlier opened up all those old wounds and put us in her crosshairs. Nothing we said seemed to make her more comfortable, but how could we explain something we didn't understand ourselves?

Somehow, though, the social worker relented later that afternoon. We had apparently passed her test, and we were rewarded with our first glimpse of Wyatt. His shaggy hair was dirty, tangled, and matted. His eyes were sunken and dull. His clothes were ratty and filthy. He was thin with stringy muscularity. He eyed us with as much doubt as we felt. One look at him, though, and Shelby insisted we try to care for him. She had seen the family resemblance in his face.

The details of the next few days were many but mostly unimportant. Wyatt was a minor, unable to live on his own. No one was claiming paternity or demanding parental rights. Jessica left no instructions of what to do. That left only a painful choice—Wyatt was in our charge or at the mercy of the state.

The decision was largely up to him since he could easily scuttle any agreement. With his open warrants and long list of arrests for minor crimes, the police wanted him locked up. He shocked us by telling the social worker he preferred juvenile detention, something he knew and understood, to us.

She explained that even after he got out of detention, he would be a ward of the state in a boys' home until he turned eighteen. At his age and with his record, few foster homes would take a chance on him. Only faced with that reality did he reluctantly switch his choice to us.

A JUDGE SIGNED off on temporary custody. Reports from a social worker assigned in Miller County and a guardian ad litem—a volunteer whose sole job is to represent the best interests of a minor—would determine the permanency of the situation. The open warrants would be purged if he stayed out of trouble until he turned eighteen.

The police released a canvas backpack—no bigger than a book bag a student uses in school. Scribbled on the back with a magic marker were the words *Wyatt Earp*. In response to my raised eyebrow, he shrugged and mumbled, "Nickname."

The bag contained everything he owned—two pair of underwear, a pair of socks, a pair of blue jeans, three T-shirts, a hoodie, and a single crinkled photograph of his mother and him taken a decade earlier. That, plus what he was wearing, was the entirety of his worldly possessions. Every piece of his clothing was filthy and riddled with holes.

He rooted through the bag and shot a look at the officer. "Where's my money?" he demanded, though with a far more colorful vocabulary.

The cop looked down at the printed inventory sheet. "No money was listed."

"I had cash in here."

The cop jabbed a finger at the sheet of paper. "That chicken scratch right there? Your signature says you agreed this list represented everything we confiscated. No money."

"It was there."

"Watch it, kid. No one here took anything from you. The junkies you lived with probably got it."

Wyatt's face reddened, and his nostrils flared.

I asked him, "How much?"

He turned to me, his eyes cold and hateful. "I don't know. Thirty, forty dollars."

I tilted my head toward the door. "Let's go. Not worth it."

His eyes flicked back and forth between me and the police officer. He snorted, grabbed his bag, and stomped toward the door. I followed him out the building and toward our car, where Shelby was waiting. When we were halfway there, he spun and got in my face. Even at fifteen, he was taller than me. "What if I took off right now? Ran? What would you do?"

I studied him and answered honestly. "Get in my car and go home."

The shocked look on his face told me he hadn't expected my reply, so I continued to push. "I'm not going to lie to you. You're faster than me, so I can't catch you. You know places to hide, so I can't find you. If and when the cops pick you up again, they might call me. I'd come get you then."

He rocked back on his heels and looked around the parking lot. I half expected him to jackrabbit. "And what if I get in the car? Then what?"

"We take you home. You'll get a hot meal, a shower, your own room, and a comfortable bed. Tomorrow, we'll get you some clean clothes and a picture frame."

He averted his eyes. Weighing his options, I guessed. "And after tomorrow?"

"Day at a time. Get you back in school. Maybe a part-time job. Help you figure out what you want."

"You'll have a bunch of rules?"

I shrugged. "A few. Clean up your language. Go to school. Stay out of trouble. No drugs."

He turned back to me. His face had softened. He looked less like a criminal and more like a lost little boy. "I don't know if I can do that."

"Which one?"

"Drugs. School. Language. Trouble."

"Nonnegotiable."

His tongue ran across his cracked lips. "I'll try."

"Then I'll help you."

We stood silently in that parking lot, sizing each other up. The choice was his, so I waited. He looked down at the tattered bag sitting between his feet. His words came out soft and resigned. "I don't want to end up like her."

I found a distant point on the horizon to study. I barely knew him, but I didn't want him to end up like Jessica either. My vision blurred as tears filled my eyes. "Then don't."

The two of us stood there, still unsure what to do. I should've hugged him, but I'd never been good at things like that. If I had, I'm not sure how he would have reacted. Would he have hugged back? Or would he have turned tail and run?

Instead, I asked, "Ready to go?"

He picked up the backpack and slung it over one shoulder. "Nothing left for me here."

WE DROVE BACK across the mountains to Millerton and gave him his choice of bedrooms upstairs. He picked the one with the best view, the same one Jessica had grown up in, the one farthest from Shelby and me.

That had been five years ago. I would love to say everything had been idyllic from there, but it wasn't. He wasn't accustomed to a curfew, but we didn't yield. He hated going to school, but we insisted. He didn't like chores, but we tied his task list to privileges around the house. His language was filthy, but we stuck to our rules.

The thing that almost broke us was chemical. I'd never understood addiction. Wyatt had seen drugs kill his mother. He knew the toll they took on his friends and others around him. He felt the lure in his own body. He said a thousand times he wanted off them.

But he kept going back.

Within weeks of him moving into our home, we knew we were in over our heads. We got him into a rehab program—no easy feat to find space for a fifteen-year-old. There were far too many teenaged addicts and far too few slots available. He completed the program and came out clean. He was using again a week later.

Shelby found the drugs stuffed under his new underwear in a drawer. She had been putting away his clean laundry, but he thought we were searching his room. He ran away that night but hadn't realized how long it would take him to hike out to the interstate. He reached the truck stop around dawn, just about the same time I realized he had left. I pulled into the lot as he was trying to hitchhike with a trucker.

I pulled up beside him and pushed open the passenger door. "Where are you going?"

"Back to Knoxville."

"I'll take you. Safer than a stranger."

He looked stunned. With a last glance at the truck driver, though, he threw his bag onto the back seat of my car and climbed in.

I shifted the car into gear and headed down the on-ramp. I aimed west and settled in for the ride. I was retired by then, so the only thing I was missing was the Liars' Table. I almost never skipped, but my friends would wait a day.

He didn't speak until we were almost in Tennessee. "You really taking me back?"

I shrugged. "If that's what you want."

Another twenty miles rolled by.

"She shouldn't have searched my room."

I explained about the laundry. "Besides, you shouldn't have drugs."

Fifteen miles.

"I'm sorry."

"Sorry to me, to your grandmother, or to yourself?"

Ten miles. We were approaching the exit to Gatlinburg and Pigeon Forge along with the hordes of tourists flocking to their vacations.

"Everyone, I guess."

"What do you want?"

The bridge over the Holston River, the border into Knoxville, loomed.

"I don't want to do drugs."

"I'll help you if you want it."

He nodded, his voice barely a whisper. "Please."

"Then let's go home."

A tear rolled down his face. I turned around at the next exit.

4

"Wyatt!"

I heard the crash of something falling in his room. Probably his alarm clock. He was always rough on them, even destroyed a few as if it was their fault he had to get up. In his early years before living with us, he had been as likely to go to bed at dawn as the other way around.

Mumbled cursing floated through the open window. His throat cleared, and he called out, "What're you yelling for? I'm not late."

Now twenty, Wyatt reminded me so much of his mother sometimes. Jessica had often accused Shelby and me of yelling when we hadn't been. At least, we hadn't thought so. I took a deep breath to calm my voice. "Can you come out here, please?"

In the quiet of the morning, I could hear every noise from inside the house. His bedsprings squeaked, and then his bedroom door opened. His bare feet slapped the wood steps as he descended to the main floor and crossed the den. The shriek of the screen-door springs announced his presence. His hair was a tousled nest of chaos. He blinked against the daylight. "Yeah, Grandpa?"

I cringed at that moniker. I didn't like being called that, but I was more distracted by the way he was dressed. Or, more accurately, wasn't dressed. That boy hadn't even bothered to put on pants. He was clad only in his boxers. "Aren't you worried someone is going to see you in your skivvies?"

Wyatt exaggeratedly looked around at our surroundings. No neighbor houses were within view. "Who's going to see?"

I needed more coffee before I debated him, not that I ever won no matter how caffeinated I was, so I tried a more reasonable approach. "Just get dressed before you come outside from now on, okay?"

He shrugged and opened the screen door to go back inside, but I stopped him. "Have you seen my car?"

He let the door clang shut, rubbed his eyes, and stared at the empty spot beside his own vehicle. He ran a hand through his disheveled hair and stumbled down the steps into the yard. "Where is it?"

I did my best to hide the exasperation in my voice. "If I knew the answer to that, would I be asking you?"

He padded out to the driveway, wincing as his bare feet crossed the gravel, and pointed at the oil stain. "It was right here when I went to bed."

"You sure?"

"I think so. Where else would it have been?" He did the same thing I had done—looked around the yard as if it might be under a bush or hiding in the cornfield. The only thing in the yard was Belle, hunched over and depositing her morning fertilizer. Wyatt shrugged and scratched his butt. "It ain't here."

I clenched my jaw in irritation and fixed my stare on him as he shook his head, his longish hair flipping across his face. He said, "Maybe a swarm of mosquitoes flew away with it. They were fierce last night."

Memories of his mother's teenaged sarcasm flashed into my mind again. I bit my tongue, something I should have done more of back then. "You have no idea what happened to it?"

His smirk faded into a chilly stare. "Why would I know anything?"

"I'm just asking, not accusing. You went to bed after me. Maybe you heard something. Saw something."

"I don't know a thing."

Ever the peacemaker, Belle jogged over and nuzzled his leg. He squatted to scratch her neck. She flopped over on her back in her not-so-subtle hint for a belly rub. He obliged.

"You think it's stolen?"

I looked at the bottom of my empty coffee cup. I really needed more caffeine. "What else could it be?"

"You going to call the sheriff?"

He no more wanted me to call the law than I did. I may have never felt the cold steel of handcuffs on my wrists like he had, but I still had my own disdain for cops. My experiences through Jessica and Wyatt told me all I needed to know.

Besides, I didn't want a patrol car coming down our road, raising a cloud of dust and announcing its presence. We didn't have many neighbors, but they would sure be entertained by a lawman's visit. The rumor mill would fly, probably with speculation that Wyatt had gotten into trouble again.

"It'll take them an hour to get a deputy out here. He'll look around, type up a report on his computer, and leave. Not like he can dust the gravel for fingerprints. I'll call them from Abe's."

"You don't have to do that on my account. I'll head into work before he gets here."

"It's not about that. I want to get into town."

Wyatt stood, much to Belle's disappointment. She pawed at his bare ankle to get his attention, but he ignored her.

"You could skip your breakfast club once. The world wouldn't end."

Rather than trying to defend my routine, I decided to use Wyatt's challenging adjustment to our rural lifestyle. Being stuck at the house was his biggest nightmare, so I knew exactly what would get his agreement. "I don't have a car. Too late for me to call C.J. for a ride, so if you don't take me to town, I'm here all day."

Belle, deducing no more attention was forthcoming, trotted up the steps to the porch. She waited by the screen door, casting an accusatory look in my direction to remind me it was breakfast time. I dutifully followed, calling over my shoulder, "Get dressed."

"No one's going to see me."

"I see you, and that's more than enough." I let the screen door slam shut behind me.

5

Wyatt dropped me off at the faded Abe's Market sign and raced off to work, late as usual. I walked past the old gas pumps—the kind without those fancy credit card readers that had to be turned on from inside with a wave if they knew you or a deposit if they didn't—toward the low, white-framed building. From outside, the unassuming building didn't look like much, but the bevy of vehicles parked out front hinted at its popularity.

Abe's father had started the business as a full-service gas station before any of us were born. During his high school years, Abe worked part-time changing oil, pumping gas, and repairing cars. People who couldn't afford the bills offered goods for barter—fresh produce from their gardens, canned goods of excess crops, butchered meats, and even moonshine brewed in illicit stills. The enterprising Morgans built display shelves and sold the goods—except the moonshine, which might have brought too much attention to their business—to the workers getting off shift from the factories at the industrial zone next door.

As the grocery business became more valuable than car

repairs, the building was expanded. Coolers were added for milk, juice, soft drinks, and eventually beer—once legalized, alcohol replaced the old moonshine business. Metal shelving replaced the creaky wooden displays for the groceries, now brand-name products from big distributors alongside produce from local farmers.

A new garage was built behind the business. The old bays were converted to a simple butcher counter. Later, that morphed into the deli that now served breakfast and lunch six days a week. The retired old men who used to hang around the garage took over a table each morning, drinking coffee and telling stories. Abe, in his late sixties like me and the rest of the gang, pretended to still run the store, but the third generation of Morgans did the heavy lifting. Abe did little more than watch over his empire as we friends gathered for breakfast, news, and tall tales.

I pushed through the front door, sending the little bell jangling its alarm. With a quick wave to Colette—Abe's daughter—behind the register, I stomped through the produce aisles to the deli in the back—run by Danny, Abe's son— without even a good morning to anyone else. A dozen of us gathered for breakfast, and I was the last through the door. The others glanced up as I approached, but Abe was in the midst of his latest tale. They returned their attention to him.

"I FOUGHT him with everything I had, but nothing worked. He was the strongest one I've ever tangled with. An absolute beast. I know you don't believe me, but he looked me right in the eyes and smiled. He wanted me to know he was winning.

"The longer the fight went, the more I struggled to stay upright. My arms burned. My hands tingled. My back screamed in agony. I was exhausted from the battle, and he seemed to gain more energy minute by minute. I was fading while he was growing stronger.

"I braced myself on the slippery rocks as best I could, but he had the advantage in the river. He reared back with a mighty yank, using every ounce of his massive size, and pulled me with the strength of a thousand mules. Go ahead and laugh if you want, but it's true. My boots skidded on the wet boulders. Rather than find solid bottom, my right foot sank deep into a hole. Icy water flowed over the top of my hip waders and filled my boot. My foot grew numb, making it that much harder to keep standing. I lost my balance and found myself flailing about, fighting to keep my head above the surface.

"No ounce of mercy was coming from him. He took advantage of my weakness and pulled again, dragging me deeper into the river. My wedged leg twisted. The pain shot up my spine. If the bone snapped, the battle would be over. I'd pass out from the pain, and he'd pull me under that raging water. Drown me right there. My life flashed before my eyes, just like they say it will. I thought of my poor Martha over there as a widow. My kids orphaned and trying to run this store without me. All of you, my precious friends, sitting around this very table with tears in your eyes. Go ahead and scoff, but you guys would miss me something terrible. I realized I had only one choice if I wanted to get out of there alive. I had to let go.

"If I didn't, I was going to meet my Maker. I wasn't ready to leave this world. I begged the beast to give me a chance, just the slightest opportunity, and I would leave him be.

"He answered me. Don't laugh, but I'm telling you he did. The most amazing thing I've seen in my sixty-eight years. That monster leapt out of the water. I don't mean he broke the surface. He came way up high, his entire body above the rapids. A beautiful sight to behold.

"He was the biggest one I've ever seen. I swear he was this long…"

ABE'S HANDS hung frozen in midair, marking the length of the lucky fish that had escaped, much bigger than any fish the men around the table had ever caught. If I was a betting man—not that I was—I would say bigger than any fish Abe had ever brought home for Martha to clean and fry.

That was the point of a good story, wasn't it? The fish that got away was always the biggest because no one could prove it wasn't. We were entertaining each other, not trying to win any accuracy award. Every man at the table knew better than to let facts impede a good tale.

Abe was one of our best storytellers, if I was honest, which was a funny thing to try to be at the Liars' Table. He was almost as good as C.J., not that we said that aloud since it was Abe's place where we gathered.

Interrupting one of his better tales made my rude entrance even worse.

Abe fixed his glare on me. "Would you sit your butt down until I finish?"

On any normal day, I would've slunk over to my empty chair and waited quietly, but it had been anything but normal so far. I broke protocol and interrupted with my announcement. "Someone stole my car."

The Liars' Table had rules—not written or formalized by committee, but everyone seated knew them. Order breakfast, or at least coffee, from Danny behind the counter before settling into your seat. Throw money into the pile on the table at the end of the meal to cover your bill. If you're short cash one day, make up for it when you can. Never sit in someone else's chair. Don't talk ill about another member at the table or their families, but anyone else in town was fair game. Banter was acceptable if you didn't take it too far.

But changing the subject when someone commanded the

attention of the group? That simply wasn't allowed. I had violated the sacrament.

"What the hell are you talking about, Purvis?"

A sharp voice rang across the store. "Abe! Language."

Most of our rules were self-inflicted and self-enforced, but Martha did not tolerate foul language inside the store. She stood in front of her display of flowers, which were picked fresh each morning from her garden at their house behind the garage and arranged neatly into bouquets. She proudly called it the "just because" section of the store, reminding all of us we should buy flowers for the women in our lives "just because," not only on special occasions. We secretly referred to it as the "I screwed up" section, though none of us was brave enough to say it so she could hear.

Martha planted her fists on her hips and tipped her head toward their teenaged grandson stocking shelves. Luke's face reddened at the attention as he tried to hide behind a tall shelf of canned goods. We knew he heard much worse at his middle school—probably said worse too—but we were smart enough not to contradict Martha. After decades of marriage, so was Abe. He turned his scowl back toward me, lowered his voice, and repeated his question sans profanity. "What are you talking about?"

Some men enjoyed being in the spotlight, regaling others with a fable. I've never been one of them. Most mornings, I sat quietly in my chair, bantering and laughing but rarely venturing onto center stage. As everyone's eyes turned toward me, I dropped my gaze to my mud-caked, scuffed work boots. My red flannel shirt hung askew, misbuttoned and half-tucked in a pair of dirty Wrangler blue jeans. In my rush to come tell them what had happened, I hadn't changed my clothes.

Sweat rolled down the side of my head and slipped under my gray-speckled beard. I ran my hands through my thinning hair, a nervous tic I tried to avoid since it left my hair standing in scattered directions, unruly and unbrushed, leaving me looking like some lunatic. I took a deep breath to calm my nerves. I wanted to explain, but all that came out under the pressure of their gazes was a repeat of my words. "Someone stole my car."

A hush settled over the table as they absorbed the news of such a crime in our small town. A murmured debate broke out. Was this more proof the world was going to hell in a handbasket? Or maybe the opening gambit to another fantastic and entertaining tale? The consensus settled on the latter, signaled by Levi's opening suggestion, his green eyes twinkling with mischief. "Maybe it was one of those Russian spies getting revenge for your CIA spy days."

I'd never told them I'd been a spook back in my military days. Once the stories started, though, I'd never denied it either. That tidbit had developed over the years, and I didn't object since it sounded more glamorous than the reality of a menial desk job. Now I was stuck with the lie even though I had never said it.

Tommy's booming voice, shaped by years of coaching football at the local high school, carried from the end of the table. "Always thought it was quite clever for the agency to have one of its secret agents masquerade as a lowly airman in the air force. Who would ever suspect an enlisted man lived a life of intrigue?"

"I don't think it was CIA." Harlow pulled on his handlebar mustache, a trademark habit when he was deep in thought. "Since he was air force, maybe he really worked in Area 54 and the aliens got their revenge by beaming up his old car."

Levi raised an eyebrow. "You mean Area 51, dingbat."

Harlow crinkled his face in confusion. "I thought it was 54. You're sure the aliens are at 51?"

"It was Studio 54 and Area 51."

"There were aliens at Studio 54?"

Tommy rolled his eyes. "Have you seen photos of that place? They were definitely alien. Disco aliens."

Abe grimaced. "Nitwits. It wasn't aliens." He paused until everyone looked at him. "It was Bigfoot that stole that car. After all, it wasn't his first visit to Purvis's house."

They laughed at my expense until Levi quieted them with a vigorous head shake. "Be serious, guys. That bear could never have reached the pedals with his paws."

I didn't normally mind the joshing, though the Bigfoot / black bear thing was annoying. No man who lived his whole life in these mountains could admit to being scared by a simple black bear, but I had to let them believe that story. I'd never told them what had really transpired when I saw the mythical beast staring at me through my bedroom window. Sometimes letting something be, even if it was embarrassing, was easier than telling the truth.

Picking on each other was part of the camaraderie, and everyone spent time as a target, even if we had heard the jokes a hundred times before. Right now, though, I needed their attention. I locked eyes with my best friend, Cody Joe Duncan, who sat with his arms crossed at the far end of the table, and hoped he'd come to my rescue.

Everyone respected C.J. Not only did he tell the most riveting tales that could keep us in stitches, but he was also the biggest man in the group by far. His muscles may have sagged over the years, and his overalls might strain to contain his girth, but he could still menace with his bulk. He nodded at me, placed his hands on the table, and waited for quiet to descend. Once he had everyone's attention, he turned back toward me and asked, "This isn't some setup for a yarn, is it?"

The tension flowed out of my body for the first time since I'd discovered my missing car. In response to my nod, C.J. patted the empty chair beside him. "Sit. Let's figure it out."

WITH C.J.'s intervention, the tone at the table shifted. The jokes faded into mutterings.

"What's this world coming to?"

"Kids today."

"Millerton ain't what it used to be."

Every morning, we agreed civilization was crumbling, though the debate raged whether Russia, China or the Middle East, music or video games, or Republicans or Democrats were more to blame.

"Did you hear anything? Your dog bark?"

"That poor ol' dog is deaf as a doornail. She snored through the night."

In truth, I only heard her rattling when I got up in the middle of the night to pee, but I didn't want to point that out. Someone might mention my car had been stolen from just outside my window, and I hadn't heard anything either.

Levi picked at the biscuit crumbs on the paper wrapper in front of him. "Maybe your grandson borrowed it?"

My jaw clenched. I resented the question, partially because the same thought had flashed through my mind. I did my best to protect him from others, though, which was why I let a black bear take the blame for his Bigfoot stunt.

During Wyatt's first fifteen years of life—time when neither of us had known the other existed—the boy gained many unsavory skills. He'd once picked the lock to my house when I'd left my keys inside and made it look so simple, I wondered why I bothered to lock it again. He'd hot-wired a tractor we needed to start and joked it was easier than doing it on a car, which implied he had personal experience with a car. So, yes, he had the talent to take my car, but in the five years since he'd moved to Millerton and lived under my roof, he'd lived a far more conventional life. After that first tumultuous year, at least.

"He has nothing to do with it."

Levi sipped his coffee and settled the cup down on the Formica top. "Maybe one of his buddies. He hangs with a rough crowd."

"Not anymore. After Jessica died…" I swallowed. Shelby had been better at talking about mother-daughter troubles and how she didn't know about her grandson's existence until he was fifteen. I didn't like to share, even among friends. Those were private family matters, but sometimes I couldn't avoid mentioning how Wyatt had been orphaned. "The people surrounding him before his mother died weren't good, but his friends now aren't like that."

Levi held up his hands in surrender.

Abe poked at his scrambled eggs with his fork. "Don't take this wrong, but why would someone steal your car? I mean, it's kind of old and leaks oil and…"

Ronnie settled his coffee cup on the table. Tall and lean, he wore blue work pants and Red Wing boots. As the plant manager at one of the few remaining factories operating in town, he was the only person sitting around the table with a full-time job. Tommy still coached football at the high school, but we kidded him that the way the team played, he might as well be retired like the rest of us.

Once Ronnie had our attention, he said, "Maybe kids stole it just for the fun of it. Some young buck teenagers probably took that treasured car out for a joyride."

A little hope rose in me as I traced a coffee ring on the table with my finger. "Yeah, maybe it's just some kids funning around."

"There's some good news in that."

"How so?"

Ronnie paused as all eyes turned toward him. A grin spread across his face. "Too embarrassing for their friends to see them in that old trap. They ditched the thing in the woods or some cornfield before sunup. Have to maintain their reps, after all."

The men roared with laughter as my face burned. "Hardy har har. Y'all are too funny for words. That car is a classic."

"A classic piece of..." Abe hesitated and glanced at Martha. She fired back a warning stare. Luke shook his head at the huddle of old men and pretended not to listen. Chastened, Abe lowered his voice. "Crap."

"THAT CAR IS A CLASSIC." Nathan Thomas wiped his hands with a greasy rag as he leaned against the deli counter. He was the only person working in Abe's Market who wasn't a family member, but he might as well be. He and Danny had grown up together and were best friends. As a kid, he'd learned from Abe how to fix cars. Now he ran the shop out back and was widely known as the best mechanic in Miller County. "Those old Novas can sell for a mint if they have a well-tuned engine and a sweet paint job."

Smirking, Levi wiped biscuit crumbs from his chin. "Too bad Purvis's car had neither."

The men laughed, of course. I even noticed young Luke smile as he stocked the shelves. My car wasn't going to win any beauty contests or road races, so it was a fair joke, even if it did sting a little. Fortunately, Nathan saved me from having to retort. "It has the bones, though." He offered a small smile of understanding and asked, "Never wrecked? Original parts?"

Grateful for his help, I nodded.

He turned to the others and said, "See, that's the foundational stuff a collector values. You take an old car like Purvis's and sand the exterior, prime, and paint. Then you go under the hood and install new gaskets to stop that oil leak. Replace the belts, sparks, points, filters. Check the transmission and make sure all the fluids are fresh. Some people like to modify the engine, of course, but others just want to restore it to original. That means finding original parts."

Harlow asked, "Where do you find them? Junk yards?"

"Sure, if you have the time, but there are better ways." Nathan grinned and said, "Have you guys ever heard of this newfangled thing younger people use called the Internet?"

They groaned at him. Tommy—still Coach Burleson to Nathan and Danny—said, "Always was a smart aleck back in football practice. I swear he and his buddies ran more punishment laps than any of my teams."

Nathan ignored him. "You can order vintage parts from lots of trustworthy stores online, so you don't have to go poking around scraps. Car show guys want the authentic stuff like vintage belts with all the correct markings for the day."

Ronnie leaned back in thought and rested the back of his head in his hands. "Where do they get the parts?"

"The legitimate way is from the manufacturer. Stocked inventories from old garages. Harvesting from junked cars."

Ronnie glanced over at me before continuing. "And the not-so-legitimate way?"

Nathan wrung the rag in his hand and stuffed it into the back pocket of his coveralls before answering. "There's a fairly strong black market in stolen parts. An honest mechanic, a guy like me, always ask where parts come from, but it's not hard to find garages that won't ask. And, of course, shade tree mechanics might do anything."

"You can tell a stolen part from a legitimate one? Are the parts traceable?"

Nathan grimaced and shook his head. "Any good mechanic can spot a counterfeit part, but stolen parts are much harder. Most don't have traceable serial numbers. The block and frame are stamped, of course, but not most parts. Mostly you look for the original packaging or junkyard receipts, something that tells you the person got them honest."

Ronnie leaned his elbows on the table. "So you're saying that, for a dishonest person, an old car like Purvis's, one with mostly original parts, might be worth more chopped up?"

Nathan's face drooped, and he avoided eye contact with me. "Yes."

"You think some collector stole it?"

"No. Not a collector." He accepted his bag of breakfast from Danny's outstretched hand to take back out to the garage. "I told you the car was a classic once fixed up, but it's not valuable now. As is, the parts may be worth more than the car, but that isn't saying much. No offense, Purvis, but the parts on your car aren't pristine, so they aren't crazy valuable. No collector is going to risk stealing a car out of a man's driveway just for parts. Why take the risk Purvis catches them and fills them up with buckshot just for trying?"

My belly fluttered in frustration. "Then why'd you bring it up?"

"It probably is kids who took it. If so, some farmer will find it in his field, or a ranger will find it parked on a fire road." Nathan looked right at me. "If someone stole it for parts, though, you aren't looking for a collector. You're looking for someone who'd take a lot of risk for only a little money. That makes it some meth head or someone like that stealing it and selling it to a chop shop."

I slumped in my chair and groaned.

6

T he bell over the front door interrupted our discussion.
We all turned to watch Sheriff David Newman enter the
store. My stomach clenched at the sight of his uniform, the
shiny badge glittering under the store lights.

Shortly after Wyatt had come to live with us, a social
worker arrived from the county with a guardian ad litem in
tow. As the judge who released him had ordered, they were to
monitor his behavior and report back on his transgressions.
They were a nuisance sometimes, but we grew to accept their
involvement. They seemed to have Wyatt's best interests at
heart even if we didn't always agree with them. And whatever
they put in their reports seemed to convince the judge that
Wyatt was where he needed to be.

The sheriff, however, was different. One of his deputies
had pulled Wyatt over in my car less than a week after he
arrived. It was two in the morning, and he was over the speed
limit. The deputy quickly figured out Wyatt didn't have a
license and wasn't old enough to be driving. We got called
down to the station. The police asked if I had given him
permission to use my car or if he had stolen it. "Sorry,

deputies," I said. "I told him to keep it on our gravel road out here. He's learning, and I didn't see any harm in that since we don't have traffic. It's the way my papa taught me to drive when I was a kid."

Wyatt's eyes grew wide in appreciation as I covered his misdeed. Without my help, the police couldn't charge him with a stolen car, so they wrote him tickets and released him into our custody.

The next day, the sheriff showed up at the house. He told me he called over to Knoxville and got all the details of Wyatt's crimes. He warned us he would be watching him like a hawk. If he crossed the line, the sheriff would see to it that the judge would know it. As the sheriff settled into his car to leave, his last words were that he didn't like trouble coming into his county uninvited.

Watch him, they did. Deputies would pull him over and search the car. They searched his book bag at school. They stopped him once when he was skateboarding in the park. Fortunately, they'd never found anything, but they sure tried. I've never forgiven the sheriff for that.

Now it was an election year, and Newman had a strong opponent, someone who might be able to beat him. Our good sheriff was making himself quite visible, and that included dropping by Abe's Market most mornings to greet people and shake hands. He was, after all, an elected official fighting to keep his job.

Once he made it back to the deli counter, he accepted the large to-go cup of steaming coffee from Danny's outstretched hand. "Can I get one of your sausage biscuits too?" He patted his stomach. "Just a small piece of cheese. Got to cut back a little, you know?"

Danny smiled his best salesman's grin. "Didn't you hear, Sheriff? All our food is calorie free."

"Your mom told me that about her apple pie for years."

"It's true." Danny leaned forward conspiratorially and pretended to whisper, "Don't tell Ma, but mine's better than hers. Come back at lunch, and I'll cut you a slice."

"Nothing wrong with my hearing, young man, or my baking. You certainly never griped about it growing up." Martha did her best to appear fierce as she stood among her plants, but the smile in her twinkling eyes belied the stern look on her face.

While wearing a sly grin, Danny spun his wheelchair and tossed a sausage patty onto the sizzling grill. I never would have thought to tell his mother, but as good a cook as she was, Danny had upped the quality of the food in the deli since he took over from her.

The sheriff blew the steam off his coffee and cautiously took a sip. He glanced at us as if he hadn't noticed we were there. He approached casually, as if he didn't do the same thing every day. "Good morning, gentlemen."

Levi looked around in mock surprise before bantering a response. "Ain't no gentlemen here, Sheriff. Just us old farts."

The sheriff tsked. "Well, you got me there. Maybe I should refer to you retired gents as men of leisure."

We laughed—well, they did. I mostly just sat there—despite having heard the line a dozen times before. No rule against retelling jokes, but none required me to laugh either.

C.J. slapped a meaty hand on the thigh of his blue denim overalls—the clean pair he wore for going to town. His ample belly jiggled under the denim as he guffawed, more than I thought was necessary. A mop of gray chest hair curled out of the top of his black T-shirt, a contrast with the closely cropped hair on his head. "Now, see, I like the sound of that. Sounds all sophisticated. Better than what Abe labels us." He gestured to the small engraved plaque screwed into the wall at the end of the table. The bronze had tarnished, but the lettering remained easy to read—*The Liars' Table*.

Abe installed it as a joke on a group of retired factory workers twenty years earlier. The first thing they did was typical—they argued whether it was Liar's or Liars'. The debate still spiked up now and then, mostly when some flatlander wandered in and made some comment about it. To me, it had always been clear. It wasn't just one liar sitting around the table then, and that still wasn't true now.

Back then, while we were still working our jobs, we saw them as a bunch of puttering old men with nothing better to do than passing the last years of their lives spreading town gossip and telling tall tales of their glory days, most of the stories too ridiculous to believe. Now we were the ones swapping tales. Not gossip, of course. Women gossiped, not us. We just shared news.

The sheriff tilted his head toward the handheld radio scanner propped up against the wall. If anyone asked, we kept it turned on in case the volunteer fire department put out an all-hands call, not that any of us had done more than direct a little traffic for the Christmas parade or sit around the station house talking about the big fires of years ago. Smoke eating was for the young men in town. On the rare occasions when the alarm sounded, we listened with interest to the response and speculated about the event.

The radio also broadcast the sheriff's department's dispatch. We could've turned that channel off, but no harm in listening. Like most days in Miller County, the little box was mostly quiet with only routine chatter.

Newman said, "Nothing much happening, is there?"

Abe's eyes twinkled. "Hasn't been broadcast yet, Sheriff, but we have us a major crime wave."

"Is that so?" Newman cocked his head. "I'll bite. What's up?"

"Purvis here had his car stolen."

A puzzled look crossed the sheriff's face. "Who would steal

that old…?" He waited until the chuckling around the table subsided and focused his attention on me.

I slumped down in my chair and waited on the inquisition, answering the same tired questions. Yes, my car was missing. No, I didn't know who took it. No, I didn't hear a thing.

And then he asked, "And Wyatt?"

My body tensed. I sat rigid in my chair. Here it came. The eyes of the law were targeting Wyatt again. "He had nothing to do with it."

The sheriff held up his hands. "I wasn't accusing him. I meant did he hear or see anything?"

I picked at some dirt under my fingernail and willed myself to calm down. "Nothing."

The sheriff nodded and straightened. "I'll put the word out. Deputies on patrol will keep an open eye. Want me to have a deputy swing by here and take a report? Or do you want to stop by the station this morning and handle it with the front desk?"

"What do you need a report for? Can't you just look for it?"

"We will, but that just covers Miller County. You'll want the Highway Patrol and the deputies in neighboring counties looking. We need to get it into the computer system to alert everybody."

C.J. piped up for me. "I'll bring him down right after breakfast. Rather have that deputy out looking than sitting here doing paperwork." We all understood the math. A big rural county with only a handful of deputies working at any moment meant long response times. No reason to compound that for something simple.

"Perfect." The sheriff turned back to me. "I know filling out a bunch of forms may not seem like much, but you'll need it for your insurance if we don't find it."

Levi chuckled. "With the insurance payment, maybe you'll be able to buy us breakfast one morning."

"Fat chance." I shrugged and flopped back in my chair. "All I got is liability insurance. The premiums were too expensive for the other stuff."

The sheriff took his to-go order from Danny. "Well, then, let's hope we find it, and it's not wrecked."

"Wrecked?" I slumped down in my seat. "I don't want to think about them wrecking it."

Ronnie grinned. "The good news is that as old and decrepit as that thing is, you won't be able to tell if they did."

7

I thought breakfast was never going to end.

After the sheriff left, the Liars' Table talk turned to politics, the decline of civilization, world peace, fishing, and hunting—the usual topics, and none more important than the other. We took turns telling jokes—the dirtier ones spoken quietly to avoid the wrath of Martha—and laughed no matter how many times we had heard the punchline. We teased each other as only good friends do, our way of showing affection.

Most days, I didn't care how long we sat and talked. Saturday sessions always lasted longer than any other day because Ronnie, the only person with an actual schedule, didn't have workers to supervise on the weekends. Without others in the building, he could drift to the plant at his leisure to catch up on paperwork. At least, he claimed the need for reporting to his corporate bosses required his weekend presence. We suspected it was because he didn't have anywhere else to be. Just like the rest of us.

On this particular day, however, I did have something to do. Yes, I had agreed to do a police report on my stolen car, but watching some deputy hunt and peck on a keyboard to fill in a bunch of useless information wasn't interesting. I wanted a more direct solution.

Without a way to get around on my own, though, I needed C.J.'s chauffeuring. I needed to convince him to give up his usual Saturday afternoon fishing trip.

Eager to get moving and nervous about his response, I couldn't sit still. Throughout breakfast, I glanced repeatedly at the clock over Danny's stove and twisted so much in my chair that C.J. elbowed me a couple of times to settle down.

It felt like an eternity, but finally, the talk dwindled, the coffee cups were drained, and the dishes scraped clean. Ronnie fished his wallet out of his pocket and tossed a wad of bills onto the center of the table for his portion of the meal. "Well, boys, it's been fun, but work awaits. I've got to head into the office."

Levi's face crinkled with puzzlement, although I suspected he was about to ask the same question he did at least twice a week. "I don't get it. You've paid off your house and car. You've got savings socked away from all your years at work. You could get your social security check. Why are you still working? When are you going to quit that place and retire?"

Ronnie snorted. "What would I do instead? Sit around this table all day with you guys doing nothing?"

"Pretty good life, if you ask me."

"Besides," Chip piped up, "we don't sit here all day."

"Oh, yeah. What major plan do you have?"

"I'm going to the fire station this morning."

Ronnie raised an eyebrow. "And what are you going to do there?"

"Sit around a table, drink coffee, and shoot the breeze." Chip tilted his head toward Martha and lowered his voice. "At least over there we can cuss when we want to."

With that final exchange, the morning magic of the Liars' Table was broken. We added our own money to the growing pile on the table. After everyone had contributed, Abe stuffed it into an envelope and slid it under the cash register drawer, uncounted and unreconciled against the bill as always. I've never seen anyone calculate a check for our breakfast.

At long last, C.J. and I were away from the others and outside. The parking lot shimmered in the sun. A cool breeze rolled off the mountains, but the summer heat was building. We walked past the collection of full-size pickup trucks to C.J.'s Ford Ranger. I've always kidded him about being the biggest man in town driving the smallest truck. Even with the bench seat adjusted as far back as possible, the fit behind the steering wheel was tight for him. Once he wedged himself into position and I was settled in the passenger seat, he slid his key into the ignition. Before he started the engine, he asked, "Ready to go do your report?"

I ran my fingers through my beard. "You know the sheriff won't really try to find it. The paperwork is just to make it look like they're doing something."

C.J. snorted. "I don't think they're going to form a major crimes task force to search for your car, but they still might stumble across it. You heard him about the report alerting other cops in the region."

"Maybe." I bit my lip. "But if it was kids and they hid it in the woods or a field or something, they might never spot it. I was thinking we could look for it."

I should've expected he wouldn't be surprised. We'd known each too long. He had probably been wondering when I was going to ask. His protest was half-hearted. "Instead of fishing?"

A harried dad drove a minivan full of kids into the city park across the street, soccer or baseball or skating in their future. Such innocents, heading for a day of summer fun.

"Yes."

He twisted the key, and the engine puttered to life. "Then

let's go appease the paperwork gods, so we can go car hunting."

THE STEADY BASS thump of a radio announced Wyatt's arrival before we saw him. His 4Runner barreled down Broad Street. When he spotted us, he braked hard, turned into the parking lot, and screeched to a stop, blocking us in before C.J. could back out of the space. I'd lectured him countless times about his reckless driving but to no avail.

He scrambled out of his SUV and stood beside my open window, bouncing with excitement on the balls of his feet. "Guess what?"

"If the sheriff sees you driving like that, you're going to get another ticket."

He dismissed my concern with a wave of his hand. "You're not going to believe this—"

"Aren't you supposed to be working?"

"I am. Finished up the Coleman project this morning and headed to Jenkins's place now to rough in the wiring. Now, would you hush?" He grabbed my arm. "I know where your car is."

My lecture was derailed, and my mouth clamped shut. I shook my head to clear it. A single word bubbled out. "What?"

"Losing your hearing, old man?" His grin stretched from ear to ear.

C.J. chuckled at his insolence.

I grumbled. "Don't call me old."

He ignored me. "A buddy of mine knows where it is."

My pulse quickened. "Really? Where?"

"Over in Knoxville."

The excitement of hearing my car had been spotted faded

quickly. A lump formed in my stomach. "Knoxville? As in Tennessee?"

Wyatt's face scrunched in thought. "Is there another one?"

"No. At least, I don't think so. Maybe." Knoxville was a fine enough town, but it carried bad memories for me. "What I mean is… what's one of your friends doing in Knoxville?"

Wyatt stepped back from the window and looked across the parking lot, an obvious attempt to avoid eye contact. "Noah lives there."

"So… he's an *old* friend from Knoxville?" I gripped his shirt and pulled him close to the truck. "I thought you didn't stay in touch with any of them."

He shook off my hands. "He's one of the few. Most of them"—he shook his head and looked away from me—"are lost causes. Noah is different. We were in school together."

The fact that Noah was a school friend didn't provide much comfort. Wyatt's school history, at least the parts the social workers had pieced together and shared with me, was checkered, to say the least. In many towns, Jessica had never even bothered to register him. For some reason, she had in Knox County, but that seemed to be the end of her parenting there. His records mostly detailed truancy, detention, and suspensions. His grades the last semester were straight Fs. Many teachers assumed he had dropped out and were probably happy he had. A note in his school file said only that he and Jessica didn't live at their address of record, suggesting they might have moved out of the county. In other words, the school personnel assumed he was no longer their issue.

"This friend…" I swallowed, always uncomfortable with the past and never wanting to know the details, but this was a time I had to ask. "Was he doing drugs before you met him?"

"Everybody I knew was."

"He's clean now?"

"I wish. I beg him to get clean. But…" Wyatt loosed a

mirthless chuckle, a haunting sound signifying sadness rather than humor. He shrugged in defeat. "What I want for him doesn't matter. You can't get straight until you're ready. I know that."

"I just worry—"

"You don't need to." Wyatt pushed up his sleeves. "I'm clean. I'll go take a piss test if you want. I never want to go back to that."

Will these doubts always plague me?

C.J. laid his hand on my shoulder. He didn't have to say anything because I knew what he would tell me. He had sat with me through many a long night as Wyatt struggled with his demons. C.J. had a brother who had suffered with opioid addiction for years, so his experiences were both a comfort and a worry. As much as I wanted to think of Miller County as an oasis from the troubles of the rest of the world, it wasn't true. You could get any illegal drug here just as easily as anywhere else. Knoxville wasn't special in that regard for any reason other than my own memories.

I changed the subject. "Is he sure it's my car?"

Wyatt snorted. "The Christmas car? Man, that thing's unique. A green driver's door, a red passenger door, and everything else primer gray. Not too many of those on the road."

C.J. clapped his hands together. "Perfect. Let's go tell the sheriff."

"Hang on." I turned back to Wyatt. "If we call the sheriff, we'll have to tell him how we know it's there. You still being in touch with your old friend may not look so good. If it turned out not be mine, then we open up a big old can of worms for nothing."

"How else could we know?" C.J. asked.

I chewed my lip. "How far is it? Two hours each way?"

Wyatt and C.J. exchanged glances. C.J. asked, "So?"

"I'll go look for myself. To be sure."

"And do what?" C.J. asked.

"Just be sure. If it's mine, I'll figure out a story about how I found it. That way, I can leave Wyatt out of it."

Wyatt said, "I can handle it, Grandpa. I haven't done anything wrong."

"I know. But what about Noah? Do you really want the cops looking for him?"

He rested his arm on my open window. I could see him thinking it over before he said, "We'll go on a couple of conditions."

"We?" I didn't like the sound of that. "The whole point is to leave you far from this mess."

"I don't care. I know where it is, and you don't. The only way I agree is if I'm with you."

"You can't leave. You're working."

"You're not going today anyway," Wyatt said.

"Why not?"

"The place where it is? Not good. And on a Saturday night, really not good."

"I'll be fine."

"No, you won't." He leaned back from the car. "Besides, you can't get over there and back before dinner with Grandma. You'd have to miss for the first time in forever."

I looked at my watch and saw he was right. "Fine, so I'll go tomorrow. Alone. I don't want you going."

"How? You don't have a car, remember?"

I pointed at C.J. "He can drive me."

C.J. retorted, "The hell I can."

I ignored my friend and grabbed Wyatt's arm. "I don't like you going over there. Being near those people."

"I'll be with you the whole time. What could go wrong? When we find it, we'll call the cops and let them handle it. If it's not there, we'll grab some chicken from Bojangles, eat some lunch, and come home. Call it a vacation."

"And Noah? I don't want you seeing him."

"I won't call him until we're safely back here. No way he'd have any clue we'll come tomorrow."

My stomach clenched. My promise to Shelby as she began to fade was that I would look after Wyatt. "I would feel better if C.J. was with us."

We turned and looked at the big man. He grunted and asked, "Bojangles?"

We nodded.

He loosed a long exhale and waved his hands. "Fine, but you're buying my lunch."

Wyatt rubbed his hands together. "A road trip. It'll be a blast."

8

W yatt's first year in Millerton had challenged us in ways we had never expected. The conflicts with the sheriff were bad enough, but we struggled at home as well. Before he came to live with us, he had never lived with the rules and expectations that we set for him. He responded by challenging us in every way he could conceive. All the problems seemed to end when Bigfoot made his first appearance.

The first sighting wasn't really a sighting at all. We found a footprint right after sunrise.

The afternoon before, Wyatt and I had tilled the small plot Shelby used to grow vegetables. I was trying to teach the boy about working with his hands. He had a natural talent that had never been nurtured. I figured learning some crafts would be good for him after years of idleness. School was hard because he was so far behind. He felt out of place with the other students. But he enjoyed building things in my small workshop and helping his grandmother with various chores.

He had carried his first cup of coffee of the morning out to the yard to enjoy the sunrise—also something he hadn't spent much time admiring in his misspent youth. Barely a minute passed before he came racing back in the kitchen, saying something had walked through the fresh furrows of the farm behind our house.

Just like the guys at Abe's when I told them later, I assumed a bear had wandered through, especially considering it was early spring.

Fancy-pants scientists have always loved arguing about silly things like whether black bears truly hibernate in the Great Smoky Mountains. The winters are too warm this far south, they claimed. They descended into these technical discussions about body temperature, heart rate, and respiratory systems. They pointed out that bears might wake up on some warm January day and go for a little leg stretcher. Without a fancy degree or more letters after my name than in it, I was not educated enough to have those debates. I had just always said bears go to sleep for the winter and wake up grumpy and hungry in the spring.

Mama Bear gives birth to cubs right around the first of the year. She grows tired of those youngsters squawking by April and starts venturing out for food. The cubs stay with her for a year and a half until she gets tired of their teenager attitude and wishes them good luck in their second summer. Then she goes looking for a papa bear to start things all over again.

Papa Bear, in the meantime, doesn't have squat to do with the cubs except the creation process. Once Mama is pregnant, he goes off for the winter, kind of like a bachelor who sleeps off a party. When he wakes up in the spring, he's tired, hungry, and horny to do it all over again. Whether bears hibernated or they didn't, they were certainly wandering about grumpy in the spring.

When Wyatt claimed to have seen a print in a freshly tilled garden, I guessed he had seen the track of some hungry, randy bear looking for fun.

I humored him by following him outside, but one glance at

the print in the mud told me that it wasn't made by a bear. It was a paw of some sort, not a hoof like an elk's, but it was more elongated. People have often confused a bear track for a human's—especially flatlanders with their summer homes tucked up on the ridges—but I've lived in these mountains all my life, so I grew up knowing what a bear paw looked like. That wasn't an ursine print in the fresh earth.

Nor was it a man's print. What man ran around barefoot at night? And had toenails long enough to look like claws coming out of their feet? And needed a size twenty or more shoe?

I had never seen a gorilla track and didn't even know what one looked like, but that's what I thought of. That was nonsense, and I knew it, but I couldn't think of anything else.

I told the guys over breakfast at Abe's Market about what I'd seen. They laughed and waited for more of the story. They wanted a punchline. But I didn't have one. I told them the simple truth, and that never quite worked at the Liars' Table. Levi was the one who suggested maybe I'd seen evidence of Bigfoot. I told Shelby and Wyatt that over dinner that night, and we all shook our heads.

A few days later, the jokes from the guys had died down, and we'd moved on to other topics. I walked outside my house after a night of spring thunderstorms. The driveway was muddy, and puddles were scattered about the yard. Something had walked a straight line past the house, leaving a clear set of footprints. With more than one track, it was obvious it walked upright on its hind legs. No animal I knew, other than human, could do that. A bear could for a few steps, but this was across the entire yard.

Wyatt showed me how to take pictures with my phone. I put my own boot right beside the thing and snapped a photo showing how much longer it was than my foot. I shared the images around the Liars' Table. They asked if I'd seen or heard anything, but I had to confess that I had no clue other than the tracks. They remained convinced it had to be a bear, even with those huge paws. I shared their theory at the dinner table that night. Wyatt thoughtfully suggested we might be able to gather more evidence.

A few nights later, I didn't need any more convincing because it peeked through my bedroom window. Freaked the crap out of Shelby. She screamed to high heavens, which scared it away before I could pick up my cell phone and figure out how Wyatt had shown me to take a picture.

I had seen it quite clearly, though, and I still thought of a gorilla—a dark face, shaggy hair all around, and wild, piercing eyes. The creature was vaguely familiar, yet totally alien.

I didn't sleep a wink that night, trying to figure out how to describe it to the guys. Despite my two prior embarrassments, I told them everything that happened and assured them Shelby had seen it as well.

Levi decided we might make a fortune if we could capture a photo of it. Tourists would come for miles to see it like they did the Lizard Man down in South Carolina.

We gathered at my house that evening. Each man found a hiding spot where we could get comfortable and wait, being as quiet as a bunch of old men could be. Nature began to stir around us. A couple of deer wandered across the field. Lots of squirrels scampered between the trees. Some bats came out in the dark and swooped as they devoured mosquitos. Just as my butt was growing numb, and I was questioning how long I planned to stay out there (a question Shelby had already asked me), something large rustled in the woods.

We waited as twigs snapped and leaves rustled. It snuffled and snorted, even grunted once. Its shape began to form in the shadows—large and hairy but difficult to make out because of its black fur. And then he emerged from the woods.

He was big. His black fur had some gray streaks of age. A few scars from past battles crossed his face. But he didn't stand upright. He shuffled along on all four paws. And he rooted through my trash.

Levi busted out laughing, and the other men joined in. Then that bear stood on its hind legs, glared at us, turned, and ran back into the woods.

"There's your Bigfoot," Levi said, doubled over with his hands on his knees, he was laughing so hard.

I tried to explain that the footprints I had seen weren't in the shape of a bear. I tried to describe that the face in my window didn't belong to a bear. I even argued he wasn't big enough to have made that track. But they wouldn't listen.

After they left, I told Shelby and Wyatt what had happened since they had waited inside. I figured Wyatt didn't want to join us in the watch because he didn't want to hang out with a bunch of old men, so he surprised me when he seemed very disappointed we had quit so early. Maybe, he suggested, we would have seen it if we waited longer.

He had a point, so I decided I would watch on my own. Besides, I was determined to prove them wrong.

I didn't tell Shelby because she wouldn't have approved. Instead, as we settled into bed, I told her I had left some stuff outside that I needed to put up for the night. In the excitement of the bear, I had forgotten. I guessed she believed me, or she would've said it was too dangerous to go out there alone if I really thought there was some wild animal on the loose.

Once I got outside, I realized I didn't have long until she would come asking what was taking so long. Fortunately, I didn't have to wait but a few minutes before a shadow emerged from near my workshop. I knew I had the creature in my sights because it walked upright, calmly and confidently like a human. I pulled my phone from my pocket and waited until it got close.

It didn't behave as I expected. It walked in a straight line to the driveway and then bent down. In the dark, I couldn't make out what it was doing, but it seemed to be fiddling with its feet. It stood and took a few long, exaggerated strides. Then it bent back down and handled its feet again.

My confusion grew when it walked in a more normal—less exaggerated—stride with something in its front paws, or hands, or claws, or whatever. It set the object down and then sneaked —it looked as if it tiptoed—to my bedroom window.

In the light coming through the window, I could see the creature clearly now. A head like a gorilla, a chest and back of black fur, blue jeans, and a pair of black sneakers. Keds, in fact. As the thing reached up to scratch on the window, I edged up behind it and tapped on its shoulder.

Wyatt spun around, his eyes wide under the gorilla mask. He was more frightened than I had been when I had seen him through the window days before. He sheepishly slipped the mask off his head and said, "It was just a joke."

We went into the kitchen, and he told me the whole story. I had to give him credit—what he had done was quite creative. He had whittled, sanded, and shaped a pair of elongated, claw-like structures out of a board. He attached a pair of leather straps and strapped them onto his shoes like skis. With that creation in place, he could leave the footprints for me to find.

The gorilla mask he had found in a Goodwill store, which was where he had gotten the original idea. Someone's old Halloween costume had been left in a bargain bin. The coat was a woman's fake fur discovered at the same store.

I was mad, sort of, but mainly because I had been fooled. Mostly, though, I was amused. His prank took a lot of time and effort.

Shelby and I lay awake that night, talking about his stunt. It was so different than the other things, like stealing my car or running off. It was, in fact, one of the most normal teenager things he'd done. I had never even suspected his involvement.

The next morning, before I left for the Liars' Table, I told Wyatt how creative I thought he had been. I wished him a good day. His eyes were wide, his face shocked. Maybe he had expected we would punish him. Instead, he seemed to realize he really had a home. His grandmother and I would stand by him.

I'd gone to Abe's Market that morning. I let them tell their jokes about me and a black bear. I didn't care. The best lie I had ever had with them was the one I didn't tell.

9

With Wyatt's discovery of my car's location and our planned Sunday road trip to Knoxville, my Saturday afternoon schedule cleared. C.J. attempted to persuade me to file the police report, but I resisted. The sheriff himself had said the main purpose was to notify neighboring agencies so they would know it was stolen if they stumbled across it. If my missing car was over in Knoxville, that wasn't needed. If Wyatt's friend was wrong, then I could file the report Monday morning.

C.J. relented when I suggested we go trout fishing instead, his favorite thing to do besides the Liars' Table. With the hot afternoon ahead, he readily agreed to standing in a cool mountain stream, casting our flies. We escaped the heat of summer many days this way.

Fishing was a tough sport to explain to those who didn't indulge. People would always ask, "How's the fishing?" They didn't really want the answer because they would follow up with the wrong questions. Were the fish biting? How many were caught? How big were they? Success wasn't defined by the size or number of your catch, but by the fun you had as the time passed.

With our hip waders pulled up high and our feet growing numb, we told stories and kidded each other. My best friend and I laughed and joked the afternoon away in Coogan's Cove. With that distraction, I didn't worry about my stolen car, Shelby's health, or Wyatt's past.

How was the fishing?

We didn't catch a thing.

The fishing was great.

As THE AFTERNOON APPROACHED EVENING, we packed up our poles and drove back into town. C.J. dropped me off at the front door of the Mountain View Nursing Home, a sprawling one-story redbrick facility on the edge of town.

Like the rest of the citizens in Miller County, the people who lived here were working class. They didn't have deep pockets of savings or private insurance to pay for their long-term care. Medicaid paid the bills. The meager government reimbursements barely covered the cost of medical care and food. The employees did everything they could to keep the buildings maintained on a limited budget. Paint peeling from the eaves and the splotchy roof testified to the challenge.

Groups in the community volunteered to make the place as pretty as possible. The local Rotary Club planted and maintained a rose garden at the entrance. An Eagle Scout project installed a pair of benches on either side of the flowers. Church groups gathered donated clothing for the residents. Drawings by local students decorated the hallways. The building looked better through those efforts, but, underneath, it was still old and decaying.

I waited until C.J. was out of sight to face the closed double front doors. No matter how many times I entered this building, I needed to brace against the coming assault on my senses. I rested my hand on the handle and paused to gather myself. With my nerves steeled and a deep breath of fresh outdoor air, I pulled it open and stepped into the dim hallway.

The floor shimmered with wax, testament to the efforts the workers made. The pine scent of cleaning supplies hung in the air but did little to mask the smells of sickness and impending death underneath. No matter how hard the employees strived to keep the place clean, they couldn't overcome the age of the building or the incontinence of many of the patients.

The young lady talking on the phone behind the glass of the reception area smiled and waved a hello. I was too frequent a guest to require further inquiries to my right to be in the building. I passed her station and came to a crossroads of sorts.

The hallway to the right housed younger patients rehabilitating from factory injuries or automobile accidents. They were down but not out. The chattering noise floating from the rooms testified that they would one day leave and rejoin society, perhaps with a limp or a wheelchair or missing limb, but alive.

A cluster of people waited outside a computer room to use one of the three computers that still worked. A sign on the wall beside the clock read Fifteen-minute Time Limit. They waited their turn to email their families or simply surf the Internet, something my Shelby could no longer do.

To the left was a wing filled with the healthiest of the seniors, the newest arrivals who needed assistance from time to time but largely lived on their own. They dressed each day and cared about their appearance. Some gathered in the brightly lit dayroom for games and activities. Others headed outside to enjoy sunshine and fresh air. They chatted with frequent visitors or other residents.

As evening approached, book readers filled the chairs. Dinner was served in a dining area at the end of the hall, a cheerful spot to enjoy a meal. The tables didn't have linen tablecloths or candles flickering in silver centerpieces, but none of us had those things at home either. What they did have was the camaraderie of others of the same age and situation.

While this part of the building was lively and hopeful, few of its residents would ever exit the building and go home. As their bodies and minds weakened, they would exchange their rooms for ones deeper in the building. The halls grew quieter the farther back you went, the sounds of nurses' shoes squeaking on the floor prominent. The residents were older, sicker, and declining. Those fortunate enough to still be mobile needed walkers or wheelchairs. The less fortunate were bedridden.

Rather than having meals in common areas, they ate food brought to their rooms and served on bed trays. The caring nurses and aides worked hard to make their stays positive and comfortable, but a hush blanketed the space. Visitors were less frequent and less bubbly. The reality permeating everyone was that the next step for the patients was slipping away to death.

I, unfortunately, headed even farther into the building. With a smile plastered on my face, I nodded to both staff and patients. As a daily visitor, I knew all their faces. I was surprised when I saw a new resident. I was dismayed when I could no longer locate a longtimer.

Without having to ask directions, I followed the maze of hallways to the rear of the building. A pair of locked doors blocked further movement. A sign read Restricted Access. A large red button was mounted to the wall.

The patients beyond suffered from severe dementia of one sort or another. While Alzheimer's was the most commonly known, the variety of names was astounding, an education I wish I had never received. Regardless of the specific cause, the result for the mind was quite similar.

The cases here were not mild where the person might

forget something—plenty of the patients in the front sections of the building had that. These advanced stages caused a person to wander and potentially hurt themselves or others. They could become combative or violent, or they could withdraw into a shell. Unlike the rest of the patients, who were generally free to wander the halls or the gardens outside, these patients left their wing only with a family member or medical escort.

I took another deep breath to steady my nerves. With a shaking finger, I depressed the button and looked directly into the security camera aimed at my face. Seconds later, I was rewarded with an electronic buzzing and the click of the locks releasing. I stepped through the door and waited until they clanged shut behind me. A loud snap indicated the lock had reengaged.

Shortly after Shelby had moved into the unit two years earlier, I learned the hard way the proper protocol of waiting for the locks to reset. I moved too quickly, and a man slipped past me and through the doors. Alarms sounded, and staff caught him before anything catastrophic happened, but I was left shaken by the possibilities I had created with my relaxed attitude. Now I knew better than to leave the exit unguarded.

The dayroom beyond was brightly lit with childlike artwork taped on the walls. Bedrooms circled the main room, their doors all visible to the central nursing station. At first glance, the room seemed a happy and cheerful place, but a careful look around told you about the patients.

In one corner, a man stood conversing with a smoke detector mounted securely on the wall. He seemed convinced the device had cheated him in a card game and demanded his money back. To his increasing consternation, the machine denied everything, though my ears were deaf to the inanimate object's argument. An orderly was doing her best to distract him before he became too agitated.

To my left, two men in old armchairs debated baseball, a quite normal thing. The topic, however, was whether the Milwaukee Braves should be allowed to move to Atlanta after they had already moved from Boston. I could have joined in the conversation since my friends had wrestled with the same topic when we were kids. We were as mesmerized in 1966 about the Southern city gaining such a storied team as these two men were now.

A pair of women in wheelchairs whispered conspiratorially, planning how to escape their house for a high school dance without their parents knowing. I doubted their parents used electronic security systems and monitoring bracelets, but pointing out such inconsistencies was a fruitless exercise. I had learned long ago to go with whatever the conversation might be.

Standing in the calm oasis of the nurses' station just inside the entrance, a heavyset woman smiled when she saw me. "I was worried you were going to miss dinner."

"Never."

"Good for you. Your nightly visits mean so much to her."

I wish I believed that. Most of the time, I doubted Shelby remembered my visit the night before. "How is she today?"

Teresa Peters shrugged her shoulders wearily but kept the bright look on her face. "Good days and bad. You know how it goes."

I understood what she wasn't saying. "Guessing this isn't a good one."

"She's had better." Teresa tilted her head toward the back of the dayroom.

Shelby sat on the couch, a blanket covering her lap, and stared at the blank TV screen mounted on the wall.

"I've tried to get her up and walking, but she won't get off the couch. I'm hoping you can entice her."

I knew from long experience how difficult that challenge

would be. I noted that the television was off. "Was she watching her soap operas? She used to love those things. I couldn't interrupt them except in the direst of emergencies."

Teresa snorted and shook her head. "Morning shift tried to turn it on, and a puff of smoke rolled out of the back. Maintenance messed with it for a while, but they think it's done for."

The plots of TV shows might be too complicated for most of the patients in this wing to follow, but the flickering lights of the screen and the sounds coming from the speakers could soothe them. Cartoons worked as well on them as they did on kids. The staff counted on the distraction to make their jobs easier. "When is a new one being installed?"

"I wish soon, but I doubt it. We sent the requisition in, but we don't have much hope. Rumor mill says it won't happen until the new budget year. The last of the contingency fund was used up when they had to patch the leaky roof on B wing."

I was incredulous. "They can't afford one TV?"

Teresa tsked. "It's not just one. There are at least a half-dozen busted TVs in front of this one on the list. Plus, they need to replace some of those ancient computers in the rehab dayroom. Maintenance is doing everything they can, but fixing broken wheelchairs and beds has to come first."

I wondered how Wyatt would feel if he came home and discovered I had taken our TV and brought it out here. "What about a donation?"

"They've asked, but no luck so far. The churches are pretty stretched and already help us with extra clothes and personal items for some of the patients. That's easier because they just convince people to pull their old clothes out of their closets, but most people around here don't have a spare TV sitting around."

I watched the patients milling about the large room, no TV noise to keep their attention. It wasn't fair. Wyatt might just have to read a book. "If I found an old one and brought it in, can I make sure it comes in here?"

"If you can do that, I'll hug your neck." Teresa smiled. "You already do too much. That picnic table and those benches you and C.J. built for the yard have been a huge hit."

I felt my face burn and tried to shrug it off. Good deeds were meant to fly below the radar, not to be trumpeted. "Just some old scrap lumber we found and slapped together. Not a big deal."

"It's a very big deal. The patients love getting outside into the fresh air when we have the time, but they need places to sit. Little stuff like that gives them freedom."

I sighed and watched my wife. "I wish she could enjoy that freedom more."

Teresa reached out and squeezed my arm. "On those good days, you get to take her out there. But on the bad ones… well, maybe not all who wander are lost, but Alzheimer patients who wander get lost."

I was conflicted. If she couldn't go outside, there was no danger Shelby would figure out our car was missing. On the other hand, I enjoyed the nights she was well enough for us to walk around and pretend things were normal. "So, dinner inside?"

"Sorry. You'll see for yourself, but no outdoor pass tonight."

I CROSSED THE LINOLEUM FLOOR, dread in my heart but a smile fixed on my face. I nodded and spoke to patients in wheelchairs and those perched on furniture as I passed. The faces here rarely changed, so I knew them all by name. Some I remembered as vibrant souls long before they'd come here, but even the ones I met in this building I took the time to speak to.

Sadly, visitors were even less frequent here than in the

previous sections. The patients' personalities were often quite different than they had been in their earlier lives. Long-kept secrets could be blurted out without warning. Well-known family history would be forgotten, ignored, or—worst of all—disputed. Social norms and decorum, which were expected in the outside world, were often forgotten since the mind no longer kept bad thoughts at bay. Some people couldn't handle the dissonance of a grandmotherly figure cursing like a sailor or a kindly grandfather firing off racial epithets.

Some of the patients never received any visitors at all. Their families had given up all hope and stopped coming, some with excuses and others without. It was just too much to see their loved ones disappear into themselves. For those patients, I was one of the few people they saw outside of staff, patients, and other patient families. I made it a point to be nice to them, to pause and speak if they wished, to participate in whatever fantasy world they found themselves. I could ignore the impure thoughts and improper statements. I couldn't ignore the people suffering the isolation of their dreaded diseases.

Once through the gauntlet, I approached the couch where Shelby sat. Some days, she never swam out of her fog enough to acknowledge me, but tonight her head turned toward me. She didn't draw away in fear. Maybe, I hoped after my rough day, my Shelby would appear for a while. Sometimes memory came back slowly. Other days, it was like a switch being flipped.

"Good evening, darling."

I held my breath for her response. She smiled warmly at me. She patted the cushion beside her and invited me to join her. "I do like a man who calls me darling."

No clear sign one way or the other of whether she knew who I was, but I hid my disappointment that she hadn't called me by name and hoped for more. I settled onto the couch but resisted taking her hand. Sometimes my touch was welcomed, but other times it frightened her. Once she screamed that I was hitting her when all I had done was brush her hand with my fingertips. It took two nurses to calm her down, and I had to leave before she ate. I had learned to move slowly until I knew her mood. "Have you had a good day?"

Her face scrunched in puzzlement. Short-term memory was always the hardest. Sometimes, she even forgot the question seconds after I asked it. She appeared to be processing her memories of the last several hours for an answer to my question. With a smile, she leaned toward me. "With a handsome man like you sitting beside me, how can it be anything but good?"

I held my breath as she looked around the room. I prayed this was going to be one of the good nights.

She returned her attention to me and scooted a bit closer across the couch. With her voice barely above a whisper, she said, "My name's Shelby. I thought I knew everyone, so you must be new in town. I haven't seen you here before. What's your name?"

My chest tightened in disappointment, but I had learned long ago to take whatever I could get. "My name is Purvis. It's great to meet you, Shelby."

10

If I were a romantic man, I'd tell you we fell in love at first sight.

That would be a lie.

The truth was we grew up together. We had some of the same classes, hung out with the same people, and when we were old enough for such things, went to the same parties in high school. I could say the same thing about almost everyone my age in Millerton. Small town. Small school. We were simply friends with a small f. We said hi to each other.

I liked fishing, hunting, and camping, like most of the guys, but I was never going to be a sports star. I was small for my age. Heck, I'm still a small guy. I don't know if it was because of that or just how I was, but I preferred reading anyway. I read Tolkien, Bradbury, Asimov, Salinger, and everything else I could get my hands on.

Shelby, however, was into the sporty type. Horace Pearson, to be exact. Played football, basketball, and baseball and was good at all of them. Always said "sir" and "ma'am" to adults but then was snarky behind their backs. He ended up being student body president our senior year and was now on the

County Commission. Still slick. I had never voted for him, not even back in high school. But Shelby thought he was the bee's knees.

She and I did go out once. It wasn't a disaster, but it wasn't magical either. She spent most of the time telling me about how bad Horace was since she had broken up with him a week earlier. This wasn't shocking news because they broke up and got back together more times than I could count. A week after our date, they were a couple again. As I said, ours was not a magical date that changed our destiny.

I wasn't broken up by their reunion. I was focused on my life goal then—getting out of Millerton. I didn't want to be a farmer, didn't want to work in a factory, didn't want to stay a day longer than I had to in Podunkville. Without money for college, I found my solution at Career Day.

All the military branches were there. I chatted with each of them to find the perfect fit. I ruled out the marines before they could reject me. The guys signing up with them were a little too gung ho. The navy was out. I wasn't a big fan of the water except for fishing. I'd only seen the ocean a few times in visits to Myrtle Beach. The army seemed okay, and I almost did that, but then the air force recruiter promised me the moon.

Promised might be a strong word. In fact, thinking about it, I might have mentioned the outer space stuff first, mesmerized by Arthur C. Clarke's writings. I thought all astronauts were from the air force. The recruiter didn't try to dissuade me. I signed up with literal stars in my eyes. Goodbye, small town. Hello, world.

Hello, Lackland Air Force Base was more like it. My assigned specialty was far removed from the glories of the heavens. I was assigned to materials management. Nowhere close to being in the CIA either, despite what I let the guys think back in Millerton. I did, however, rise to the exalted rank of airman first class, E-3, pencil-pushing specialist. Might have made E-4 if I had stuck around longer. And if I hadn't been involved in some unofficial forklift racing.

Mostly, though, I was homesick. I missed football Friday nights, hanging out with my friends at the Point, going to the drive-in. Every time I sat down in the mess hall for a meal, I missed my mother's cooking. I wanted the fresh air rolling off the mountains in the morning, the rain drizzling down my back on a hot summer day, and the icy water of a trout river. Put a mountain boy in Texas, and all he wants is to go home.

IN MY FREE TIME, I wrote letters, a funny thing for a guy who was more interested in reading a book than finishing a book report. I wrote everybody in Millerton I could think of. Some people responded. Some didn't. This was long before email and social media, so it took a while for the replies to come. When they did, I snuck off and read them, devoured every word.

They described the mundane parts of mountain life. Crops coming in. Layoffs at the factories. Who died. Who was dating whom. Who wrecked a car or flipped a tractor. Who got into a fight or got arrested. Who got married and was having kids. And even more scandalous, who was having kids without getting married, not a common thing back in the day.

As soon as I consumed someone's letter, I hurriedly scribbled out another missive. With each round, though, fewer people replied, and they took longer to do so. They weren't being mean, just busy with their own lives.

Shelby responded every time.

The guys in my barracks thought she was my girlfriend. I didn't tell them otherwise. I let them think the letters were steamy and romantic. They weren't at all. They were routine descriptions of errands and chores and friends.

We weren't in love. We were friends who became good friends. Maybe that was enough. I had certainly grown to love her over the years since. It was why I went to have dinner with her every night, even if she wasn't always inhabiting her own mind sometimes.

I had often wondered what would've happened if either of us had met someone else. If Horace hadn't broken up with her again and again. If she had simply stopped writing like all the others. If I hadn't gotten caught racing a forklift and written up by some NCO. If I had reenlisted. If I hadn't gone back to Millerton, would we have each found someone else to love?

The question was moot because I did go back.

After all my bragging in high school about leaving and never coming home, I worried what people might say. Rather than returning with my tail tucked between my legs, admitting the world had beaten me, I needed to strut. For a young man, that meant I needed a car. I bought a Chevy Nova. Slightly used. Yes, the same one.

That was a huge purchase on an airman's pay, but I wanted all my old friends, the ones who had written a few times before they stopped, to see me driving it. The best place to be seen, at least as a young adult in Miller County, was the old drive-in theater out on Hilltop Road.

It was sad to see that old field overgrown now, the screen little more than a frame of wood standing like a skeleton. Back then, teenagers crowded into their cars on Friday and Saturday nights, watched movies, and made out. When the wind shifted, the smell of cows from the neighboring Hickman farm cloaked the area. Sort of a scratch-and-sniff effect for the bad flicks on the screen.

Of course, I couldn't go to the drive-in without a date riding in my new car. I decided to ask Shelby. And, for some crazy reason I can't explain, I decided to do it face-to-face on my very first day back from the military. Unannounced.

I drove up in front of her house, my hands all sweaty and my body shaking, far more nervous than I expected to be. I didn't realize how much of a terrible idea this was until I shut off the engine. I went up and knocked on her door. Her dad answered and looked at me as if I was crazy. He called her downstairs despite how insane I must've appeared. Or maybe because of it.

I had everything rehearsed but stammered along until I finally just blurted it out and asked her on a date to the drive-in. She stood frozen like a statue. Her mouth opened, hesitated, and closed again. I was sure she was going to turn me down, but after several painful seconds that seemed like hours, she asked me what movie was showing. I didn't have a clue. I hadn't bothered to check. I hadn't even been home yet, though my parents were waiting for me. When I told her I just wanted to go with her, she smiled and said yes.

For the record, I still couldn't tell you what movie played. We didn't make out or anything like that, but we sat in that car, talking about our hopes and dreams, about what we liked and didn't. We discovered more in common than not. We both wanted to live in Millerton forever, even though it took me longer to figure that out. We wanted big families with a house filled with noise and chaos. We wanted someone to grow old with, to rely on, to trust. We wanted to be the grandparents that spoiled the grandkids rotten.

When we returned to her house, we parked at the curb out front. We talked some more. We laughed. We kissed. We sat out there so long, her father finally turned on the porch lights to make sure we knew he was sitting inside waiting on her. I walked her to the door, knowing I was going to marry her. And the next summer, I did.

With a steady paycheck from my office job in one of the factories—that air force materials management training turned out to be more valuable than I thought—we bought that big house. It had enough rooms for all the kids we wanted. We picked the one closest to our bedroom to be the nursery. Once a kid grew out of the nursery, or was forced out by another baby coming in, they would move upstairs to one of the other rooms. The children would spread in the house—the oldest farthest from our room and the youngest near. They would double up as needed.

With everything ready, we finally got busy with the fun part. Making babies. Lots of babies. Big family. And some day, we dreamed, we would rock in the chairs on that front porch as grandchildren played in the tree.

Only that never happened.

The only baby who lived in that nursery was Jessica. When she became a teen, she moved to the most distant room, the empty rooms between mocking us and our quiet house. It had stayed that way until that fateful day when it had grown even quieter.

What does this have to do with finding my car?

Nothing.

Everything.

11

C.J. had waited for me to finish at the nursing home and was taking me home, saving Wyatt an extra trip. He spent the time rattling on about what a bad idea going to Knoxville was.

I finally interrupted him by blurting out, "Did you know Shelby kept every letter I sent her when I was in the air force?"

Startled, and probably trying to figure out what this had to do with anything, C.J. slowed the truck to take the next turn. "She told you that?"

"After they diagnosed her with Alzheimer's and she went to live at Mountain View, I was organizing her stuff. It was hard to look at her clothes every day when I knew she wouldn't ever come home. In this one drawer, she had all her, you know, delicates. I guess she figured I would never look in there, and she's right, I didn't until she was gone. When I pulled the clothes out, I found all these envelopes bundled together with lace strings."

"Your letters."

I turned my head to look out the window and sniffled. I hadn't planned on telling him any of this, but it suddenly seemed important. "Every one of them. At least I think it's all of them. It's not as though I remember them all, but she had the letters she had sent to me too. I knew I had brought them home but just figured I'd lost them or something. She had organized everything in order—her letter to me, my reply, her reply, and so on. They were worn and faded as if she had pulled them out over the years and read them. I never knew she did that."

My friend nodded. "Women are so much more romantic than we are. When Wanda died, I found all sorts of things I didn't know she had kept. She even pressed flowers I had given her in her Bible."

I felt a tear slip down my face and kept my focus on the passing tobacco field. "When things went downhill, she remembered less and less about what she had for breakfast. The nurses suggested I read to her—a favorite book, journals, her old letters. After dinner now, I'll sit beside her bed and read them to her like it's a novel until she falls asleep. It's like reliving an old conversation just on paper."

"She must really like that."

"When she knows they are between us, yes." I sighed. "I must've read them a hundred times by now. Probably more. And I figured something out."

"What?"

"I love her like crazy. I don't know if she knows it."

He startled, his eyes growing wide in disbelief. "Of course she knows it. You two have had a long, happy marriage."

"We had our rough times."

"Everyone does."

I didn't want to dig into all that. I told C.J. almost everything about my life. Almost. "Sometimes she doesn't realize they're our letters. She doesn't remember my name or who I am. She thinks I'm just an employee or a volunteer reading her a Nicholas Sparks novel or something, just letters back and forth."

"That must hurt."

More than I could explain. "But I go for the nights she remembers some. Sometimes, she can say the words of the letters along with me, her eyes closed and conjuring up the memory somewhere from that fog. And I don't just mean *her* letters. She quotes *my* letters too. That means she read and reread them all these years until she memorized them."

"Those must be the best nights."

"They're good but not the best."

C.J., bless him, waited on me to explain rather than asking. It gave me the time I needed to choke back the emotions. "There are nights when I go inside, and she recognizes me but not the now me. She'll be back in the days Wyatt first came to us, or maybe before Jessica left, or just some random day in between that was good. But the one that happens a lot is she thinks it's the day I came back from the service, knocked on her door, and asked her for a date. I've pulled up in front of her house in the new-to-me Nova, my discharge papers still wet with ink, and asked her dad to let me take her to the movies."

"And you play along, like that's what's happening?"

I nodded. "I get permission from the nurses to take her onto the grounds, outside the security doors. We wander around the parking lot, hand in hand like it's our first date. She asks to see my new car. Asks if it has a radio as if she's never seen the inside of it. I guess, in her mind, she hasn't. I take her over to that old clunker, but she thinks it's smelling clean and new. I open the passenger door and hold her hand as she sits down. I cross around the front, watching her watching me, and then get in behind the steering wheel. I don't even start the car because it's like halfway between being real for her and being a dream. We pretend the car is new, and we're watching the movie. At some point, just like on that first date, she'll slide across the front seat and rest her head on my shoulder." My voice failed me. I studied my gnarled fingers in the silence.

C.J. pulled a red handkerchief out of his overalls' pocket and blew his nose with a loud honk. "Damn allergies," he muttered as he gazed out the windows at the mountains rising like hulking shadows against the evening sky.

"I know I'm lucky she's still alive. It's not fair because you don't have Wanda around anymore, but I get to relive the best night of my life over and over because of that car, only it took me a lifetime to figure out it was my best night." I turned to my friend. "What if tonight had been one of those nights? What if she was ready to go on our date, and I had to tell her I'd lost the car?"

C.J. wiped the back of his hand across his eyes. "That can't happen. We'll get that car back."

SUNDAY

12

S unday morning dawned in typical August fashion. Large,
fluffy clouds floated through the hazy sky. Mist rose over
the fields. The sticky air hinted of the thunderstorms to come
rolling across the ridges later in the day. The smell of tilled dirt
from the surrounding farms filled my lungs.

Once upon a time, I had loved summer. A boy free from
the confines of school could run through rows of corn taller
than himself and roam the acres of trees growing on the hill-
sides. Farmers still raised the old staple crops—corn, apple
trees, beans, and tobacco—in the lower fields of the valley, but
the best cash crop for the steep slopes were the Christmas trees
that took years to grow. The vastness of the tree farms created
perfect playgrounds for kids, at least until someone spotted us
and shooed us away.

After I returned to Millerton as a young man from the military and worked full time, the long hours of daylight gave me
time for leisure after a day of labor. Shelby and I could go for
an evening walk through the fields or sit on the porch and
watch the sunset.

Now that I was retired—and with Shelby living at the

nursing home—leisure time was all I had. Mornings started early—long before sunrise—because my body no longer let me sleep through the night. I bustled around the house in the dark, doing my best not to wake Wyatt, until it was time to venture to Abe's Market and hang out with my friends. Once breakfast ended, dangerously close to lunchtime most days, I headed back to the house, did a few chores, and napped in the hammock with Belle by my side until it was time to leave for dinner with Shelby.

When I returned home in the evening, I ate my own dinner and waited for the sun to set so I could go to bed and sleep until it was time to do it all over again. What good were the extra hours of the day if I did the same thing no matter what? I had grown to prefer the shorter days of spring and fall. It was dark when I awoke, no matter what the month, but at least those seasons brought an earlier start to the evening.

My complaint with summer wasn't limited to hours of light. The summer heat was tough on an old man. I scratched Belle's ears as she snoozed in the shade of the sprawling maple tree and thought about how the hot weather was tough on old dogs too. This was probably her last summer. I had no idea how I would handle next summer without her. I had resigned myself to the fact that Shelby and I would never sit under this tree again. It seemed unfair that I would lose Belle too.

The old dog snorted in her sleep, her nostrils flaring and her back legs kicking on the ground as she dreamed. She shifted her head in my lap and resumed snoring contentedly. I leaned back against the bark of that broad trunk of the old tree, a protruding root poking me in the butt, but I wouldn't move until I had to. Belle deserved her cuddle time.

A plume of dust rose to meet the rising sun, the first hint of C.J.'s approaching truck. The sound of the tires crunching through the gravel road brought Wyatt from inside the old clapboard house, mercifully dressed and not still in boxers like yesterday. The screen door banged shut, a rifle shot across the yard. Belle opened one eye and scanned the horizon. She must have decided nothing needing chasing, sniffing, or barking because the eye drooped closed, and her steady breathing resumed. I ran my hand down her side, stroking her warm fur.

C.J. stopped the truck in front of the house and waited for the dust cloud to settle before creaking open the door. He stood, placed his hands on his back, and stretched as if he had been driving all day. We mumbled our "good mornings" to each other, a quiet familiarity of old friends between the three of us. The breeze rustled the tree's branches, and birds called in the distance as we chatted about nothing.

Once the sun rose fully above the mountain range, I disturbed Belle's morning nap long enough to usher her for a pee in the yard and into the cool interior of the house. She curled up on a tattered rug in front of the dark fireplace and resumed her slumber, no protest that we were leaving her for a few hours. I pulled the front door closed quietly so as not to disturb her.

The choice of which car to take was easy. I didn't have one. C.J.'s pickup truck would have required us to sit shoulder to shoulder on the bench seat. We piled into Wyatt's SUV, the most comfortable option by default. C.J. sprawled across the back seat and sipped his coffee. I settled into the front passenger seat. Wyatt started the engine and did his best to get the meager air-conditioning blowing before driving down the gravel road that bisected the sprawling cornfield.

Nothing had changed in this part of the county for years, but I rarely had a chance to just sit back and watch the scenery flow by the car windows. An old barn sagged in the middle of a field. Houses and trailers were scattered along the road, old properties like mine that farmers had carved out from their land and sold to raise cash in one of the common bust years of agriculture.

The biggest building was the white clapboard church that loomed at the intersection with the paved road. Its steeple rose high into the air, a landmark for everyone who lived in this cove. A sign by the front entrance cited the biblical scripture of the week—Proverbs 12:22: *The Lord detests lying lips, but he delights in people who are trustworthy*—and touted a fundraiser for the church's annual mission trip to El Salvador.

This early in the morning, only a few cars congregated in the asphalt parking lot. As the sun rose higher, the lot would fill and overflow along the edge of the gravel road as families gathered for the services.

I couldn't help myself as we drove by—I turned and looked the other way, so I wouldn't be spotted. My reaction was silly because a lone car on a dirt road always received attention. The Good Reverend Brawley, if he happened to be looking out his window, sure knew Wyatt's car.

For years, Shelby and I had sat in the same pew week after week near an open window, fanning church bulletins to stir the humid air as the minister cautioned sinners to mend their ways. C.J. sat with us. Wanda sang in the choir.

After the service each week, we returned to our house, cooked a big Sunday afternoon meal, and ate under the maple tree as my dog—I have always had dogs—frolicked in the yard. As the afternoon drifted into evening, we tossed horseshoes, and sometimes, on the hottest days and under the scorn of the women, sipped a cold beer or two.

C.J. stopped attending services first, shortly after Wanda died. He still came to the house Sunday afternoons for dinner, at first making excuses that some chore took longer than expected and made him miss the service, but later admitting he couldn't listen to the singing voices of the choir without hurting too much. The sympathy he received when people noticed his eyes tearing up was too embarrassing to him.

I told him that was silly, even admonished him it was okay

for a man to cry every now and then. I stuck with that opinion even after we received the news of Jessica's death and Wyatt's existence, but after Shelby began her slow decline, I understood his reaction. When she could no longer go to the services, I stopped attending. I told people I needed to stay with her in case she hurt herself. When she'd moved to the nursing home, I had never returned to the church.

With Abe's Market closed on Sundays, no Liars' Table to sit around, and no desire to enter the church, C.J. and I were as apt to spend the morning fishing as anything. Our friendship was all the churching either one of us needed.

FEW CARS TRAVELED the country roads on a Sunday morning, so Wyatt made quick time through Millerton to the interstate. Broad Street was even less busy than normal. With all the empty streets and sidewalks and darkened storefronts, I realized how much it resembled an abandoned town in the scary movies Wyatt liked to watch. I imagined zombies hiding in the shadows of the factories in the industrial park. Even Ronnie didn't venture there on Sundays, but attended the small black church out on the west side. Maybe vampires slept in the storeroom of Abe's Market, closed for the day as the Morgan family gathered at their downtown church before going out to the house for the Sunday dinner Martha would prepare. Visions of werewolves scampering unmolested through the three blocks of the vacant business district flashed through my head. Even Sammy's Pub, a place targeted by many of the ministers during their sermons, respected the Sabbath and locked its doors.

I shook the thoughts from my head as we approached the entrance to Interstate 40. The quiet of town was shattered with the sprawling truck stop, the Walmart, and the smattering of fast-food restaurants all open and bustling. Sunday was just another day out here, except for the Chick-fil-A, of course, whose drive-through lanes sat empty.

We ignored C.J.'s request to grab a biscuit from Bojangle's and merged onto the interstate for the drive through the Pigeon River Gorge and into Tennessee. Slow-moving semis clogged the right lane, the hills and turns making it impossible for them to go faster. Tourists, impatient with the pace, raced in the left lane much too close to each other's bumpers.

Neither truckers nor tourists seemed aware of nature's beauty sprawling around them, but it always awed me. The tumbling water of the river had carved the ancient gorge deep into the mountains, stone walls towering over the road on either side. Beyond those walls lay hundreds of thousands of acres of undeveloped land—the Pisgah and Cherokee National Forests and the Great Smoky Mountains National Park. This wild land sheltered us and served as a barrier to keep the rest of the world out. Until the interstate opened during my childhood, getting through these hills was a challenging task. Even with it, travel could be daunting. Only a few exits were scattered for the many miles and were irrelevant to most people since the roads didn't go anywhere except into the wilderness. People like C.J. and I, though, ventured out to Fines Creek or Coogan's Cove for trout fishing among the many creeks or in the Pigeon River itself.

As we approached the Tennessee state line, we passed the old hydroelectric plant. I'd always marveled that it was built not only before the interstate but before roads of any sort came through the gorge. The construction workers who built it—and their families who lived in the company town created to house them—traveled by the river itself.

Within a few miles, we exited from the gorge, the road straightened, and the pace of traffic quickened. The town of Newport flashed by shortly before a third lane of concrete was added in each direction as Interstate 81 merged with its traffic from Virginia, the nation's capital, and beyond. Even on a Sunday morning, the road was thick with cars headed into Knoxville. We were leaving the serenity of our mountains behind and entering the wider—and wilder—world.

I was mesmerized by the waves of humanity around us. C.J. must have been thinking the same thing as he broke the silence. "Makes you appreciate Miller County, doesn't it?"

A small red car whipped past at eighty miles per hour and abruptly changed lanes in front of us, missing another vehicle with only inches to spare. My seat vibrated from the bass thumps emanating from the cranked-loud stereo. I shook my head in disbelief. "I seriously doubt he's late for church."

"I don't know," C.J. replied. "The way he's driving, he better be praying."

I gripped my hands together and thought how happy I was we had decided Wyatt should drive. His younger reflexes and experience with traffic kept us safer. When we got some space around us, Wyatt glanced into the mirror at his rear seat passenger and asked C.J., "When were you last over here?"

No reason for Wyatt to know that answer, because it was before he came to us, but I knew the question hurt C.J. My friend turned his head to watch the traffic and probably hide a tear. "Eight years ago, right after Wanda got her diagnosis. We knew it was probably going to be her last Christmas. I asked her to name any present. She wanted to see the Christmas lights at Dollywood one last time. I didn't think it was much of a present because we did it every year. Besides, I had thought it would be too tiring for her, but it was a great trip. She loved how festive it made her feel, despite the chemo."

Wyatt licked his lips as he scanned the traffic around him. His voice shook as he asked, "You never came back?"

C.J. looked down at the floor of the car. His voice was so

quiet I barely heard him over the noise around us. "Once she was gone, I had no reason to come back."

Wyatt twisted his hands on the steering wheel. "I bet the lights were amazing."

C.J. could only nod.

"I heard Dollywood was fun. I've never been, though." Wyatt shrugged, and the inside of the car grew quiet. I thought, as I often had, of how abnormal Wyatt's childhood had been. I figured most of the kids in his school had traveled the few miles out of town to the sprawling park. No wonder he hadn't gone to class often. Their lives were so foreign to his, he couldn't have been able to find much in common with them.

To break the awkward silence, I said, "When Shelby started having her episodes, we both knew things were going to end sooner or later. I asked her if there was anywhere she wanted to go before it was too late. She said she wanted to see a show at the Ryman Auditorium in Nashville. I got us tickets—I didn't care what it was, just that it was there—and booked a couple of nights at a hotel. Spent more money than we could afford, but I'm glad we did it."

Wyatt said, "First time you left me home alone since I had moved in."

Shelby and I had quietly debated whether to invite Wyatt to join us for the trip, but we both wanted some alone time. His first few months had been rough and challenging, though the Bigfoot incident was the beginning of his settling down. Now, though, thinking of all he had missed as a kid, I wondered what he would have thought of such a trip. "We should have taken you with us."

Wyatt shook his head. "That was for you and Grandma. Besides, it meant a lot to me you trusted me enough to leave."

"You were ready."

Wyatt grinned. "I was, but Belle wasn't. That dog paced

the house for days. I was a poor substitute for you in her mind."

I didn't want to tell Wyatt I'd probably spent more time on that trip fretting about Belle than I did him. Instead, I focused on a passing billboard advertising moonshine for sale in Gatlinburg. Legal moonshine made no sense. Moonshine was what it was, not because of the distilling process, but because it was untaxed liquor. Revenuers chased moonshiners because they wanted the tax money, not the recipe. To tax liquor and sell it in a store meant it was not moonshine anymore, which was just proof tourists will buy anything.

Wyatt, however, was still focused on our out-of-county travels. "Sounds like you two only left Miller County for your wives."

Traffic slowed as we approached the bridge over the Holston River, the entrance to Knoxville. As I watched the water flow under the bridge, I thought of how it would soon merge with the French Broad to form the Tennessee River. From there, it dumped into the Ohio River then the Mississippi, the Gulf of Mexico, and beyond. Just the day before, I had stood knee-deep in the Pigeon River, fishing. Had the water that had swirled around my legs already made it to Knoxville?

The traffic came to an abrupt stop, startling me out of my thoughts. I finally answered Wyatt. "I came over here to get you after your mom died."

We stared at the mass of taillights in front of us. Wyatt softly said, "You did that for Grandma too."

Of course, he was right. Fortunately, C.J. saved me from answering. "Your grandpa spent all his time in school talking about leaving Miller County and never coming back, but not me. I couldn't imagine waking up every morning without seeing those mountains."

Wyatt looked at C.J. through the rearview mirror. "Your wife was the same way?"

"After we got married, Wanda and I would take off once every year or so for vacation at Myrtle Beach or Pigeon Forge —even drove to Washington D.C. one time—but we never even talked about living somewhere else. I've never been in an airplane and never wanted to."

Thankful to have avoided Wyatt's earlier comment, I said, "It didn't take me long in the air force to figure out I had already lived in the best place in the world. I couldn't wait to get back."

Traffic began to inch forward. We could see a mass of flashing lights, the apparent cause of our slowdown. Wyatt said, "I grew up thinking Millerton was an awful place, and I had never even seen it. All Mom talked about was how little it was and how everyone was always in your business. She used to say no one could ever get ahead there."

Wyatt's reaction when we'd first seen him had made that clear. "You sure didn't want to go home with us when we came for you."

"No, I didn't."

We drove past two crumpled cars in the breakdown lane. Firefighters were stowing their gear. A wrecker was hooking up the first vehicle. A teenage girl sobbed into her cell phone. A middle-aged man gestured while speaking to a police officer.

Wyatt said softly, "But I'm glad I did."

13

A fter we passed the accident, traffic opened up and flowed. Within a few minutes, the downtown skyline came into view, small by big city standards but overwhelming compared to Millerton.

Wyatt guided the car off the highway onto the surface streets below. He expertly twisted and turned through the roads. I was soon quite disoriented. I could find my way along winding rural roads without a single signpost but would get quickly lost in any city within just a few blocks.

The first neighborhoods appeared to be in renaissance, older homes in various stages of renovation situated on small but well-kept lawns. Young, well-dressed people strolled on the sidewalks or sat at cafe tables in front of coffee shops. I imagined couples debating decorating choices and then searching through the antique shops for that perfect find. In the evening, those lattes and mochas they sipped would be replaced with long-stemmed glasses of white wine or frosty mugs of craft beer. Their conversations would be political debates or thoughtful discussions of the latest serious novel they pretended to read.

A few blocks later, the situation transitioned. The houses weren't as well-kept. A loose gutter here or there. Some paint faded from years of sun. A rusting bicycle laid in overgrown grass. No one strolled about the uneven and cracked sidewalks because there was nowhere to go on a Sunday morning. No sidewalk cafes. No quaint stores.

The farther we drove, the more things declined. A very tall, leggy woman—or maybe man—in fishnet stockings and high-heeled shoes waved at us as we drove by. She looked disappointed we didn't stop to buy what she was selling and adjusted her tight faux-leather mini skirt. Her halter top was tied in a knot, revealing a flabby stomach.

As we slowed at the next intersection, two young men leaned against a telephone pole. They stopped their conversation and glared at us, a clear sign we were unwelcome intruders. I was thankful Wyatt had insisted on our not coming over on a Saturday night.

After hesitantly looking right and left despite the lack of traffic, Wyatt committed to a direction. We worked our way down an even narrower road with cars parked on either side. The small houses were packed close together. Fences enclosed the front yards, postage-stamp-size areas choked with weeds. A man lay sprawled on the front steps of one house—sleeping, I presumed. Or hoped. I didn't want to find out.

At the next turn, we saw a long building, which was nothing but a string of cheap apartments. In a cracked parking lot in front of the first apartment sat a familiar Chevy Nova. Wyatt nodded toward it and said, "Just as Noah told me. There it is."

We inched past, our heads turning to watch it, and then circled a vacant lot to an older cinder block convenience store with iron bars on the windows. We pulled beyond the gasoline pumps to the rear of the building. Wyatt shifted into park but left the engine idling. We had a clear view of the quiet apartments and my car.

Wyatt smiled and said, "Look on the bright side. Not often is your car the best looking one around."

Weeds battled for supremacy in the cracks of the pavement. A smattering of cars parked between faded lines. Leaked oil blotted the ground. Pushed by a light summer breeze, a fast-food cup skittered across the lot and under the Nova.

A gold Chevy Impala rested on cinder blocks, its hood raised to expose an empty engine compartment. The shattered front windshield hung loosely in its frame. In the street out front, a Ford Fiesta with faded blue paint leaned like a drunken sailor, its right front tire flat. The remaining dozen cars in view appeared in better shape, at least operable if at the end of their lives, though most featured crumpled fenders, plastic-covered shattered glass, or duct-taped trunks. The least scarred carried only scratches, dings, or rust.

The parking lot of sad cars framed the front of the nondescript two-story apartment building, little more than a rectangular box with peeling paint. No gutters lined the faded and stained roof. Dried mud splattered the wood siding. A graffiti-tagged plywood board covered the lower window of the third apartment, burn marks streaking the wood siding above.

Each of the eight entry doors opened onto small square concrete porches. Two steps led off each stoop to the hard-baked ground barren of grass or bushes. Cigarette butts, plastic bottles, and crumpled cans littered the ground. I suspected I could find hypodermic needles scattered among the debris.

C.J. leaned across the seat and jabbed a meaty finger toward the Nova. "You're positive that's yours?"

I grunted in disbelief, but Wyatt was the one who pointed out the obvious. "Green driver's door. Red passenger door. Primer gray paint. What are the odds? Of course it's his."

"What about the Tennessee license plate?"

Wyatt squinted against the bright sun. "Common tactic. Steal the license plates off another car and slap it on there. Keeps things from being too easy for the cops." He turned to me and asked, "Now what?"

"Call the cops." C.J. shifted his weight in the back seat, the springs squeaking in protest. When we didn't respond, he grunted. "That's what we said we were going to do."

I replied, "I never reported the car stolen. When we say we found my car, they'll ask what stolen car because they can't find a report. Then what do they do?"

C.J.'s mouth fell open. "What do you think they do? Don't you watch those detective TV shows? They run the VIN on their little computer and find it's registered to you. They check the glove compartment for registration and insurance—which will be in your name. Maybe they make you go back to Millerton and do the paperwork—I don't know how that works —but they sure don't just leave a car that belongs to you—one you can easily prove you own—sitting here in the middle of this neighborhood, do they? They impound it and hold it until you get the paperwork straight."

"I understand that." I turned in my seat so I could see both of them. "I meant we still have the problem of explaining how we found it without getting Wyatt's friend in trouble. It's not like we can claim we were just driving through here."

C.J. shrugged. "We're going to have to come up with something sooner or later if we're going to call the cops."

I swallowed hard. I hadn't told them what I was planning to do because I knew what their reaction would be. "Not if I just take it back."

"You'll what?" C.J.'s face reddened. "Are you nuts?"

"If it's my car, why not? What were we going to do yesterday if we found it? Were we going to call the sheriff? Or were we going to take it home?"

"Just going to take it, but that was Miller County. People

know us there and know your car. No one would have thought anything about us getting into it and driving off." C.J. leaned forward and rested his arms on the front seat. "In case you haven't noticed, we aren't home here. If someone in those apartments sees us, they might think we're stealing it and call the police."

I gestured toward the graffiti spray painted on the walls, the boards over the windows, the litter in the grass. "Does this look like the type of place where people call the police? I bet people who live here mind their own business. The last thing they want are cops poking around." When I didn't get an answer, I turned back to lock eyes with C.J. "It's one of those places where no one ever sees a thing. Or don't you watch those TV shows?"

C.J. nodded in resignation and shrugged, his shoulders nearly touching his ears. "You're probably right, but what are you going to do? Walk over there in broad daylight, look inside, and then hot-wire that car?"

"I don't have to." I dug into my pocket and extracted a key ring. Holding it high in the air, I said, "They stole my car, not my keys."

C.J. slumped into his seat. A quiet "oh" was all I heard.

"No one over there is going to question a guy getting into a car with keys in his hand, cranking it up, and driving away. If the cops do show up, I'll say everything you said earlier." I pushed open the passenger door and asked, "Are we done arguing and ready for action?"

I swung my legs out of the car, but Wyatt's hand gripped my arm to stop me. He was holding me back, his eyes wide. I tried to shake off the hand. "Now what?"

Wyatt pointed toward the apartments. "Him."

The lot was no longer empty.

14

A shirtless man emerged from the dark interior of the first apartment. He yawned, revealing gaps in his brown teeth, and stretched. His bony arms and skinny chest were covered in tattoos. His greasy hair was thinning on top but hung long over his shoulders. Several days of patchy, unshaven facial hair spread over his gaunt cheeks and chin. Baggy, camouflaged shorts hung low enough on his hips to reveal a lack of underwear, a detail I really wished I hadn't noticed. He wore unlaced high-top tennis shoes and carried a stained T-shirt wadded in his hand.

He plopped down on the top concrete step and tapped a cigarette out of a crinkled pack. With a flick of a lighter, he inhaled deeply, held it for several seconds, and blew a thin cloud of smoke in a stream over his head. He draped his arm across his knees and leaned his head forward onto the makeshift cradle.

Probably nursing a hangover, I thought as I slipped my foot back into the car. As quietly as I could, I pulled the passenger door shut. "Maybe I should wait. He looks like a pretty rough character."

Wyatt answered with a quiet and rattled voice, his eyes never leaving the man. "He does."

The nervousness in his voice was obvious. His face drained of color. His hands trembled on the steering wheel.

"Do you know him?"

"No. I've never seen him." A slow shake of the head, though his eyes never veered from their target. "But I know the type."

Wyatt had developed his bravado growing up in such an unstable environment. He had to bluff his way through many dicey situations, so he was usually confident, rarely frightened as he appeared now. I didn't think he had lied about knowing the man but sensed something bothered him more than he was letting on. "What about him then? Something has you freaked out."

Wyatt looked down at his feet, his mouth opening and closing as he struggled to answer. I waited patiently until he finally replied. "The ink."

"You mean the tattoos?" I studied the artwork crisscrossing the man's body. "He does have a lot of them."

"It's more than the number." Wyatt ran his hand along his lower arm, his fingers tracing the colorful rose tattoo done on his eighteenth birthday in memory of his mother. "It's the look of them. That's the homemade crap guys who've done time have. Mom dated a guy for a while with a bunch of those. Nasty dude."

I had been so focused on how much of the man's body was covered, I never noticed the lack of quality in the work. The lines of the images were shaky and unprofessional. The ink was mostly blue with only an occasional splash of color. Tattoo artists, like the one who had done Wyatt's arm, prided themselves on their craftsmanship, the beauty of their work. The designs on this man's body looked more hurriedly done without the tools a professional would use.

I didn't have any tattoos myself but knew plenty of guys who got them, particularly back in my military days. Most of the artwork hadn't aged well. As the skin sagged and muscle morphed into fat, the images became stretched and bloated. I tried to explain that to Wyatt when he expressed his plans to get one, but the boy was determined. He wanted to have a visible memory of his mother. I respected that sentiment, even if I didn't agree with the tactic. After the work was done, though, I admitted it was beautiful in its own way.

This man's tattoos appeared to have been made with anger instead of love. They added to his menace. "So, we know he's been in jail. Does that make it a decent bet he's the car thief?"

C.J. grunted in interest and leaned forward. "Looks to me like he wouldn't be too bothered taking another man's property."

"That's not really the question." I chewed my lip. The whole situation continued to bother me. "Why my car? Why would a man like that—or any man—drive all the way over to Millerton just to steal an old car? Why not steal one from around here?"

Silence reigned in the back seat as C.J. puzzled over the question. Finally, he hesitantly answered. "I don't know. Maybe he figured if he stole one from farther away, the odds were better he gets away with it."

"I'll buy that. But maybe he goes to Sevierville or Pigeon Forge a half hour down the road and steals a car from a motel parking lot. Or maybe he goes up to Morristown or over to Newport. But Miller County? Almost two hours away and all the way across the mountains."

C.J. shrugged. "The farther, the better?"

I turned to face my friend. "Think about that. You're saying to avoid arrest, he's going to steal a car not just ten or twenty miles away, but in the next state. And not just that, but he's going to go way off the interstate out into the sticks on some back roads until he runs out of pavement. Then he just happens to pick my house and steals an old car that doesn't have much value. Does that make sense?"

"Well, not when you put it like that." C.J. slumped back into the seat and crossed his arms. "How else do you explain it? I mean, unless I'm crazy, that is your car. And it is here. Do you really care why?"

The pit in my stomach continued to twist and grow. I started to ask Wyatt his opinion, but the apartment door swung open again. A little girl, maybe three or four, came running out the door. The man's face brightened as he tossed his cigarette into the dirt. She plopped herself into his lap, and he draped an arm around her. We couldn't hear what she was saying, but she was animatedly telling him a story. He smiled and laughed with her.

I heard C.J.'s seat squeak as he leaned forward again. "He doesn't look quite so menacing anymore, does he?"

They sat like that, talking and laughing with each other, until the door opened again, and a woman emerged, squinting against the bright sun. With her left arm, she held a squalling infant propped against her hip. A third child, a toddler in a saggy diaper, clutched her leg. She waved her right hand, smoke trailing from the cigarette it clutched, and yelled at the man. The words carried across the vacant lot, too muffled to make out, but her anger was clear from the distance.

The man kissed the little girl on her head and then helped her up from his lap. He stood and faced the woman, nodding as she talked. He retreated down the walk, his hands held up, palms open and fingers spread. His lips moved, the words too quiet to hear, though they appeared to be an attempt to mollify her.

She marched forward, driving him into the parking lot. With an extended finger in her cigarette-clutching hand, she jabbed his shoulder to emphasize her words. The cigarette glowed red, and ashes floated to the ground as she hurled her words.

A blind parted in one of the other apartment windows but quickly snapped shut again. No one was coming to the man's defense. He continued his backward walk, shrugging and talking as she continued to match him step for step. When his butt tapped against the side of the Nova, he reached into his pocket, extracted a set of keys, and opened the car's driver door. Seconds later, the engine roared to life, and he backed hurriedly out of the space. He shifted gears, revved the engine, and spun the tires as he escaped down the street.

"So much for any doubt he's the one who took the car." C.J. clucked his tongue as they watched the woman standing in the empty space, yelling invectives after the disappearing car. "Hey, how did he start the car so easy?"

"With my keys."

"I thought you had the keys."

"I have mine, but I leave the spare above the visor."

"The spare? Above the visor?" C.J. groaned. "That doesn't sound too smart."

I shot him a look. "You're saying I won't find a spare set of your keys above the visor in your truck?"

"No."

"In the glove box?"

"No."

"In a little box attached by a magnet under the wheel well?"

C.J.'s face reddened. He looked away and sputtered, "That's better than the visor."

I snorted and turned my attention back across the vacant lot. The woman retreated to the top step and sucked deep on her cigarette before flicking it out toward the road. With her now-empty hand, she peeled the toddler off her leg and shooed him inside the apartment with a swat of her open hand on his diapered butt. He ran squalling into the shadows, and she followed with the infant. The little girl was the last to disappear into the darkness of the apartment, and the door slammed shut behind her.

C.J. muttered, "Poor guy would probably have more peace in jail. We'd do him a favor getting him arrested."

"Well, we can't lose him now." I slapped Wyatt on the shoulder and pointed at the fading cloud of smoke. "Follow that car."

C.J. groaned and settled back into the seat. "I've seen that TV show too."

15

We drove for several blocks, well behind my Nova but with it in view. My mind raced, trying to understand the theft of my car and how this man was involved. The more I thought about it, the less it made sense that he was the one who stole it. He clearly had it, but that didn't mean he'd taken it. And if he hadn't, then who had? My suspicions grew about what had really happened. I needed to confront Wyatt about it. I had no choice but to ask. Apparently, Wyatt was going through the same debate because we spoke at the same time.

"I need to ask you something—"

"I have a confession to make—"

We exchanged glances, and I said, "I'm thinking the tattooed man didn't steal my car."

C.J. mumbled from the back seat, "Tattooed man. I like that. Very secret agent."

Wyatt ignored him and shook his head. "A friend of Noah's did."

My throat tightened, and I clenched my fist. "You mean Noah did."

The car was silent for a few seconds. "Noah was with him, so... yeah."

I rubbed my jaw. "If he... they... took it, how does this guy have it?"

"I'm guessing this is the dude Noah owed."

"And how do you know that?"

Wyatt looked out the window and chewed on the inside of his cheek. His answer came quietly. "Noah came to Millerton and asked me for money."

I studied my fingernails, and I counted to ten before answering, "So, you have seen him?"

The reply was barely above a whisper. "Just this once."

C.J. leaned forward, clasped a hand on each of our shoulders and squeezed. He spoke in a steady, calm tone. "Wyatt, why don't you start from the beginning and tell us what you know?"

Wyatt's face reddened as he gritted his teeth. He looked up into the rearview mirror at C.J. and hesitated. I nodded to him to let him know it was okay. We needed to stop with the secrets. With a loud sigh, he explained, "To understand, you have to know he was the only true friend I had back then. He was a runaway from some little farming town in Arkansas. He had a drunk old man who knocked him around and a mother who didn't stop it. He told me they probably never bothered to look for him when he left. He lived on the streets, earned his money doing whatever he had to do—and you really don't want to know those details."

I heard C.J. gulp. No one liked hearing these things. I asked quietly, more because I really wanted to know than to ferret out another lie. "So, he really wasn't a school friend?"

"I caught him rooting through the dumpsters behind the school, but I think that was as close as he ever got." A sly grin crossed Wyatt's face but then faded away. "He was scrounging for food. He was starving, and I felt sorry for him, so I split my sandwich with him. I got free lunches at school, so it wasn't that big of a deal, you know?"

Honestly, it sounded like a big deal to me, but I wasn't going to interrupt again.

Wyatt continued, "We were squatting in some vacant house at the time, so I let Noah tag along and crash there. Mom didn't always come home—sometimes for days—and she didn't mind that I had someone I could trust with us."

He licked his lips and looked away from us. "One day, we had broken into a house, and a cop car pulled up. I guess they had one of those silent alarms or something, but we hadn't noticed. Or maybe a neighbor called. Whatever, the cops were there, and we scrambled out a window and split up. The cop had to choose which of us to chase and picked Noah. I figured he would narc me out when he got busted. Anyone else would have. I mean, honestly, I probably would have ratted him out if I had been the one caught and it would get me off the hook. But he didn't. He never said a word. From then on, we were tight. If we stumbled on food, we split it. If one of us got money, the other got half. And, yeah, when we scored drugs, we shared them."

He looked over at me and said quietly, "I know you don't like hearing all the things I used to do, but you don't know what it was like. Both of us starving but sharing a piece of moldy bread. Craving drugs so bad you think your body is going to rip itself apart, but you split it with someone else. Being able to go to sleep and wake up and your stuff isn't stolen, and you aren't stabbed because your friend was watching over you. Yeah. He was my friend."

I caught Wyatt's eyes and tilted my head back toward C.J. "I won't pretend to understand everything, but I do respect friendship."

Wyatt nodded, his eyes filling with tears. His voice was unsteady when he resumed. "The last day I saw him was the day we came home and found her. It was obvious the second I saw her she was dead. I can't chase the image out of my head. Her lips were blue. Her eyes rolled back into her head. Vomit dribbled out of her mouth."

He sniffled. "I didn't want to believe it. I couldn't think straight. I shook her. Shouted at her. And when that didn't work, I held her head in my lap and begged her to wake up." He ran the back of his hand across his nose and sniffled. "Noah heard the cops coming. He tried to get me moving. I couldn't. Or maybe I could, but I didn't care. He jumped out a window and ran."

I leaned back in the seat. "That was the night they called us and told us about you. So when you threatened to run, you were going to go find him?"

"I knew where he'd be. In that house. He had nowhere else to go. I was worried about him. I really struggled with what to do. I had abandoned my friend."

"But you stayed in touch?"

"Not exactly. One of the guys in my last rehab had a friend-of-a-friend kind of thing. I was able to pass my cell phone number over. He would call when he could, which wasn't often. Last week was one of those times. He said he was getting his life back on track. Had gotten clean. Worked some real jobs. Then he told me another friend who had gotten out of the life had called him and said there was a job in Raleigh if he wanted it. Even would let him crash in his apartment until he got enough money saved up to get his own place. Noah said he was leaving everything behind—not that it was much—and driving from Knoxville to Raleigh, just passing through Miller-ton, and wanted to see me."

I asked, "You believed him?"

Wyatt shook his head firmly. "First rule of drugs—an addict will lie about anything. I hoped it was true, but no, I didn't just believe him. I agreed to meet but not at the house. I said we'd get a cup of coffee out at the truck stop by the inter-state. For the first time since Mom died, I saw him."

"Did the job not work out or something?"

He sighed and tapped the steering wheel with his fingers. "The second I saw him, I knew everything he said was made up. First, he had some guy riding with him. Claimed it was his friend in Raleigh, but that made no sense if he was driving there to meet him. I didn't even have to ask because one look at them told me neither one of them was clean. Their eyes were wild, clothes were filthy, and they both stank as if they hadn't had a bath in weeks." He grunted in disgust. "I can't believe I used to be like that."

"What did he want if he wasn't going to Raleigh for a job?"

"What every addict wants—money. He told me he owed some guy big. Claimed the guy would kill him if he didn't come up with the green."

"They thought you would just give them money?"

Wyatt laughed. "I think their real plan was to rob me. At least that was his friend's plan. Maybe Noah thought of it. Maybe he was just along for the ride. I don't know, but I was glad I had picked the truck stop with lots of people around."

I had witnessed how hard Wyatt had struggled to get off drugs, but I still couldn't fully grasp how much of a grip they had on people. "You said *claimed*. You don't believe someone was going to kill him?"

He shook his head. "The street dealer, the guy who actually sells to junkies, is just some guy trying to make a few bucks, probably pay for his own habit. He isn't going to kill a customer over a few hundred dollars. He'll beat the crap out of them, make an example out of them, but he doesn't want to go to jail for life. They just say that to make the junkie desperate enough to steal something or break into a house or whatever they need to do to cover what they owe."

C.J. harrumphed. "Man, the movies lie."

Wyatt turned to him. "People do get killed, but it's over insults, or because someone gets high and does something stupid, or because they steal from the wrong person. The big guys, they'll kill you without a thought, but those guys don't deal with a junkie like Noah. So, unless he crossed someone, I don't see him owing money to anyone but another addict or his dealer."

I asked, "What did you do?"

"I paid for their coffees and told them I was going home. Said if he was ever really ready to get clean, I would help him go to NA meetings, but I was never going to give him money. And I left. I saw them in my rearview mirror yelling at each other as I drove away. Vowed to never see him again until he got clean."

A warmth spread through me. A few years ago, Wyatt had been just as addicted and had had to claw his way to get clean. He had come so far in those years that he could even sit with a junkie and not be tempted. I realized, a little to my shock, that I was proud of him. "Good for you."

"I should've been more suspicious. When your car was stolen, it didn't take me long to think of them. Noah told me they followed me home from the truck stop. I guess I was too into my music or something and didn't even notice them. They were going to steal my 4Runner, but they got scared and took yours instead because it was farther from the house. He gave it to his dealer to pay off the debt."

I pointed at the guy driving my car in front of us. "So that's his dealer?"

Wyatt studied it for a long time before shaking his head. "Maybe. I don't know. Maybe it's just some guy who bought it from the dealer, or maybe the dealer owed him money and paid him with the car. Who knows?"

"What will happen to Noah if the cops arrest the tattooed man with my stolen car?"

Wyatt shuddered. "If he suspects Noah turned him in to the cops, a beating for sure. Maybe more. It could be bad."

I thought for a minute. "So another reason not to involve the police. I've got to try to steal it back. We have to keep your friend's name out of any police report."

16

"Are you nuts?" C.J.'s face flamed a bright red. His cheeks puffed out, and spittle flew from his lips.

"Probably."

"You're going to risk your life to keep this Noah character's name out of a police report? Why would you protect the guy who stole your car?"

Wyatt spun around and glared at him. I reached over and put my hand on Wyatt's neck and spoke calmly. "Because he's Wyatt's friend."

C.J.'s eyes darted between our faces. He looked down at the floor and nodded. He spoke quietly. "Think this through. You're trying to protect Noah because you think this... tattooed man... is dangerous. If you're so scared of him, what are you going to do when he shows up at your house?"

That thought had crossed my mind only about a hundred times, but I kept shouting it down. Time to get it out of my head and see if it made as much sense out loud. "Why in the world would he think some old man would steal his own car back? Wouldn't his first suspicion be one of his neighbors or some junkie or"—I flicked my hand at the decaying neighborhood around us—"both?"

"But—"

"Even if he thinks I might have done it, it's two hours to Millerton. A four-hour round trip. Would he really spend that much time to check on some car that isn't worth much, especially if he wasn't sure who took it?"

"But—"

"Even if he wants to go to Millerton, the tattooed man doesn't know where we live. Noah stole it, not him. Noah probably couldn't find the place again if he wanted to. It's not exactly easy to find when you're sober, much less spaced out of your gourd."

C.J. crossed his arms. "Are you finished?"

No, it really didn't sound any better out loud, but I didn't have any argument left. "I think so."

"I still think you're nuts."

WYATT KEPT our target in sight, but with enough distance between us that we didn't draw attention. I hoped. We were staying back as far as we could without losing him.

Whenever his brake lights flared, I assumed he had spotted us. Any minute, he would jump out of the car, yell at us, flip us the bird, or worse. Grab a baseball bat out of the back of his car—no, *my* car—and smash it into our windshield. Drag us into the street and demand to know what we were doing. Or maybe just pull out a gun and shoot us.

But he never did any of those things.

After weaving through the neighborhoods, we came to a stop at an intersection with a main road, wider and with more traffic. He shot out in front of someone who had to brake hard. They blew their horn, but he ignored them. I urged Wyatt to catch him before we lost him, but we had to wait on a clear spot. We were a dozen cars back by the time we started moving.

Because we were back so far, we almost missed seeing him turn. We would have if he hadn't driven so aggressively. He cut off a car trying to come out of the parking lot and bounced over the edge of a curb. I cringed at the thought of my poor car being so abused, but at least we knew where he went.

The store turned out to be a Dollar General, one of those discount places that have popped up like pimples. Even on a Sunday morning, the parking lot was crowded. By the time we pulled in, he had already nabbed a space right in front of their glass doors. He obviously didn't care about the handicapped parking sign. An elderly couple glared at him as he jumped out of the car, but he ignored them and entered the store through the automatic doors.

Wyatt asked, "Are you really going to do this?"

A lady with a screaming baby loaded bags into her car two spaces from him but didn't appear to be in a hurry to leave. Two men leaned on an old Pontiac a half-dozen spots later, laughing and talking. A pair of preteens rode their bicycles in circles at the end of the lot, dodging between cars. Worse than all the people, though, was his parking choice. With the plate glass storefront and compact floor layout, he could see the Nova from almost anywhere inside the store. If I attempted to take it, he would see me.

I replied, "Not here."

Wyatt asked, "So, what do we do?"

"Wait for a better chance." I directed him to park in an empty space at the far end of the lot. "What he's doing in there?"

With a sarcastic tone, C.J.'s voice floated from the back seat. "Just a guess, but I think he's shopping."

The same plate glass window that gave the man a clear

view of the stolen car gave us a way to spy on him. He beelined for one aisle and grabbed a large package, though we couldn't make out what it was. He joined the line at the cash register and fidgeted as he waited. Once at the front of the line, he pointed to a shelf behind the gum-chewing cashier. She turned, extracted a carton of cigarettes, and laid it on top of his package. He pulled a wad of crumpled bills from his pocket and paid for his purchases. After getting his change, he smiled at her and tried to chat, but she dismissed him with a nod to the next customer. He picked up his purchases, said something else to her, and came back out into the sunshine. When we could see what he carried, C.J. laughed. "Diapers and cigarettes. Some dangerous criminal."

The commonness of the excursion shocked me. Too many movies, I guessed, but I expected him to meet another shady character, glance furtively over his shoulder, and hand over an envelope of cash for a briefcase of drugs. I had never seen a crook buying diapers on the big screen. My stunned mind felt numb trying to reconcile it. "He's running errands. His wife—or girlfriend, or whatever she is—gave him a honey-do list. He doesn't even care he's driving a stolen car."

C.J. muttered, "Well, it's not like you've reported it stolen yet."

"He doesn't know that."

He tossed his packages onto the passenger seat, lit up another cigarette, and jumped into my car. The engine roared to life. A puff of blue smoke fired out of the back, chasing the two bicycle kids away. He reversed out of the space, scattering pedestrians. Wyatt shifted his car into gear and followed him back out to the street.

We were again several cars behind him in the heavy traffic. I fretted that a traffic light would turn red after he passed, and he would disappear into the crowd. Wyatt reminded me we knew where he lived, but I didn't want to risk him doing something with the car.

He turned into the entrance of a sprawling strip shopping center, one of those nearly abandoned places where most of the stores were dark and vacant. The big box stores that had anchored it had left long ago for newer or better-located facilities. The small retailers that stayed behind struggled to attract traffic on their own. The biggest sign out front was a For Lease or Sale sign. I wondered aloud, "Now what?"

Chuckling, C.J. pointed at a storefront covered in banners. "Lunch." He patted his stomach and made a smacking noise with his lips. "Wish we had time for pizza."

The tattooed man didn't bother with a handicap space this time. They were too far away and the lot devoid of cars. He stopped right in front of the restaurant at the curb marked "Fire Zone—Violators Will Be Towed." When he got out of the car, he left the door open and engine running, an easy mark if I had time. Unlike at the Dollar General, people weren't milling about, but the tattooed man hadn't gone far. He stood at the counter not ten feet inside the glass door. I didn't see how I could casually walk up to the car without him noticing. It didn't matter because only minutes passed before he came out with a large pizza box and tossed it onto the back seat.

As he moved toward the exit, we were faced with a tough choice. The few scattered businesses attracted so little traffic that no other car was moving in the lot. If we waited for him to leave before we started moving, we risked losing him. If we followed, we risked him noticing us. Hoping he would think nothing of us, I motioned Wyatt to drive. He came to a stop with a full length between us and the Nova, but it wasn't far enough. The tattooed man looked into his rearview mirror, and our eyes met. I did my best to look through him, like I was staring at the McDonald's across the street, but he seemed to have his eyes locked on mine. I muttered under my breath, "Act natural." Wyatt fiddled with the radio. C.J. actually whistled. It would have been funny if sweat hadn't been rolling down the side of my body.

Had he recognized us? Was he suspicious about why we were behind him? Maybe he was just irritated at having to wait in traffic.

When the light turned green, the tattooed man hesitated for a second but then dropped his gaze and drove down the road. Wyatt followed slowly, keeping a healthy distance between us. We debated what to do, but we were safe out here in the middle of people. Nothing unusual about a couple of cars going in the same direction on a busy road.

Time was running out for us, though. What would happen when we hit the neighborhood streets? Without the camouflage of surrounding traffic, he would recognize us for sure, so we couldn't follow him off the main drag. Even though we knew where he lived, we'd have to be careful even just parking near his apartment. We were running out of options. We needed a break.

He passed through an intersection as the light turned red. Wyatt was going to run it, but I grabbed his arm and pointed ahead. He was turning into a business just two driveways up from the intersection. We wouldn't lose him.

The business he visited was a stand-alone, one-story, concrete-block structure. The glass front showed the rows of auto supplies inside. The parking spaces out front were occupied, cars with their hoods up as their owners replaced parts bought from inside. He maneuvered around the people to the side of the building and parked in an open spot. He turned off the car and looked around at the others in the lot. If we had been following closely behind him, he would've seen us, but from our vantage point at the light, we were hidden. He seemed satisfied with the surroundings and walked to the front of the building and inside.

C.J. leaned forward. "Good news. Maybe he's a mechanic. He might be able to fix that oil leak."

"I was going to fix it but haven't had a chance."

"It's been leaking for three years. What's been keeping you busy?"

I could only grunt in reply since no answer came to me.

C.J. leaned back in his seat with a grin plastered on his face. "Maybe you should leave the car with him for a few weeks and then report it stolen. Looks like drug dealers have more time on their hands than you do. You might be able to get that thing back as good as new."

I ignored him. When our light turned green, I pointed to the gas station next door on the corner of the intersection. Wyatt pulled in beside the far gasoline pump, as close as we could get to my car. We were hidden from view from inside the auto parts store. My car sat twenty-five feet away. No one was watching us.

I made my decision. "Now."

C.J. asked, "You're actually going to do this?"

"Sure, why not?"

"Maybe he's got a gun?"

"Really? Where's he hiding it? He's barely wearing clothes." When I got no reply, I pointed to the rear of the building at a connecting drive between the auto parts store and the gas station. "We even have a back way out. We can go behind the gas station to the street and get away before he's aware we're here. This is as good as it's going to get."

Wyatt protested, "He hasn't stayed anywhere long. What if you're halfway across the lot when he comes back out?"

I tried to sound more confident than I felt. "I'll walk right past him into the store. Why would he notice me?"

"What if he recognizes you from the pizza place?"

"What if he does? It isn't a crime to visit the same stores."

C.J. muttered, "I don't think he's all that worried about what a crime is."

"If we sit here and keep jabbering, he's going to get done in there and come out. Then we'll be forced to take it from his apartment. Either one of you want to try that?"

They looked at each other and shook their heads. I pushed open the door and stepped into the parking lot.

Wyatt's voice quaked from behind me. "Grandpa?" I turned to look at him. His face was drawn tight with worry as he said, "Be careful. Please."

I leaned back into the car and squeezed his arm. "You just head over to that exit and wait on me. When I come behind you, lead me back out to the interstate as fast as you can."

When I saw his reluctant nod, I stood and closed the door behind me. I brushed the front of my shirt as though removing wrinkles mattered at the moment. I pulled my car keys from my pants pocket. With them tight in my hands, I glanced to the front corner of the store. The good news was he couldn't see me from inside. The bad news was I couldn't see him either. Was he chatting with someone? Waiting on a clerk to pull a part from the stockroom? Or was he paying and walking out the door right now?

I took a deep breath, locked my eyes on my car, and put one foot in front of the other. I tried my best to appear casual, as if I was just shopping for car parts, but I didn't think I succeeded.

Halfway across the open space, movement flashed across the corner of my eye. Two men speaking Spanish came around the corner and climbed into a pickup truck. When the truck cranked, music blared out of their radio. They pulled out of their space without even looking at me.

I reminded myself to breathe and restarted my walk. Twenty feet to go. Fifteen.

"Hey!" I turned to see a heavyset man jump out of the way of a pair of skateboarders. "Watch where you're going, you brats!" They flipped him the bird, cackled, and kept going.

My imagination was getting the best of me. Maybe he had recognized we were following him out of the pizza place. He had pulled in to this store because he had friends in there. They were waiting and watching, popping crowbars or baseball bats in their hands. Why did we think a bunch of amateurs like us could tail a professional criminal undetected? He was circling behind me right now, ready to pounce and take my wallet. He would steal Wyatt's car, too, and drive away laughing.

I squeezed my eyes shut. My heart pounded in my chest. Sweat trickled down my back under my shirt. I tried to swallow, but my spit had dried up. I had to get moving, or my worst fears would come true.

Trying to crowd out my thoughts, I opened my eyes and scanned the lot. No one seemed to be watching, so I closed the distance to the car and reached out for the door handle. With my sweaty hand wrapped around the bar, I pressed my thumb against the button. The door clacked open, a thunderous noise echoing across the parking lot. My body tensed, waiting for a hand to fall on my shoulder.

Nothing happened, of course. The sound had been loud only in my head. As I scoped out the parking lot to the front of the store, I saw no one watching. With the realization that I might get away with this, I pulled open the door with a yank and slid inside. The keys jangled in my quaking hand as I tried to slide them into the ignition. I fumbled them, and they clattered to the floor. With a deep breath, I leaned down and scooped them up. With one final look to confirm no one was coming, I begged myself to calm down and got the key into the ignition slot. As I prepared to turn the switch, the passenger door was yanked open.

My heart skipped a beat. Bile rose in my throat. The air grew thick. I leaned against the driver's door as far away as possible and raised my hands to protect my face. Through my fingers, I saw a figure lean into the car and look at me. C.J.'s voice came to me as he asked, "What are you doing?"

"I thought you were…" I tried unsuccessfully to swallow again. "You scared the crap out of me."

"Good thing we have diapers here. Want one?" He pointed at the recent purchase on the front seat.

My body relaxed as I shook my head. All I wanted was my car back. I didn't want to steal from the guy, no matter the bad things he did. He had a kid at home—and an angry wife—so he needed the diapers. I had never smoked, not unless you count that time I was thirteen, took a puff, and about vomited. I waved my hand at the pile of goods. "Take them out and put them in the parking space."

C.J. did as instructed and settled into the passenger seat. As he closed his door, he chuckled. "Can you imagine his face when he comes back and finds the car gone and diapers waiting?"

I laughed, more nervousness than hilarity, though I could see the humor. The poor guy was going to find his car gone and only diapers marking the spot. I almost felt sorry for him. Not enough to get caught, though.

I pushed the gas pedal to the floor and turned the key. The car sputtered and complained, but it started. Glancing repeatedly into the rearview mirror, I reversed out of the space and headed for the back exit. My mind continued to race with images of him coming around the corner, guns blazing as he chased us down, but he never appeared. We were soon following Wyatt as we twisted and turned through the neighborhood streets. Red-and-blue marker signs indicated Interstate 40 was just ahead.

Finally able to relax, I turned to C.J. beside me. "What are you doing in here? You thought I was crazy for taking my car instead of calling the cops."

"I do think you're crazy. Certifiable. Off the insanity charts. Totally, completely, cuckoo-for-Cocoa-Puffs insane."

"Why get in the car with me?"

C.J. shrugged. "As nutty as you are, I've still got your back. Always have and always will."

It made sense. I would've done the same for him. As we turned onto the interstate on-ramp, C.J. said, "Maybe we're like those lady movie characters. You know, Thelma and Louise, off on an adventure."

I looked at him out of the corner of my eye. "You remember how that movie ended, right?"

17

My hands were still shaking as I guided my reclaimed car down the interstate on-ramp behind Wyatt. My sweat-soaked shirt clung to my body. With a last glance into the rearview mirror to confirm we weren't being followed—not that I knew what I would've done if we had been—I merged into the flow of traffic heading east on the interstate. With the relative anonymity of the crowd of cars—though my car didn't hide very well among them—I took a deep breath to calm my nerves.

Instead of the surrounding scent of car exhaust I expected, I smelled melted cheese. My mouth watered as the aroma expanded to include pepperoni. "Mmmmm—something smells good."

C.J. stopped mopping his brow with a handkerchief, sniffed the air, and twisted his body to peer behind us. The worry fell from his red face and was replaced by a giant grin. He reached into the back seat and retrieved a large flat box with a cartoonish drawing showing a man spinning pizza dough. He settled the box in his lap and lifted the lid. The smells assaulted us, and my stomach rumbled in response. C.J. turned to me and clucked his tongue. "We forgot to give him back his pizza."

Between the stress of the morning and the absurdity of a purloined lunch, I couldn't help but chuckle at the tattooed man's misfortune. C.J. smiled at me, and soon we both roared with laughter, releasing the tension of stealing my own car back. I pounded the steering wheel, sucking in gasps of air between cackles. C.J. held his sides as he howled. Out of the corner of my eye, I spied a woman dressed in church clothes staring at us as though we'd escaped from a mental institution. We made quite the sight—two old country men driving a clunker of a car while chortling uncontrollably.

"Poor guy. Bet he has fun explaining all this to his wife."

"Can you imagine? Walking home with diapers in one hand, cigarettes in the other. No car. No lunch. I almost feel sorry for him." C.J. picked up a slice and bit into it. "Ooooh. It's a meat lover's special too. My favorite."

"Your doctor will not approve. For your own health, you better let me take care of it."

C.J.'s muffled reply came through his full mouth. "I take my cholesterol meds."

"Oh, yeah? What's your last count say? When did you last take your blood pressure?"

"No comment." C.J. tore the lid in half to create a plate for me and handed over a slice. "Besides, you promised to buy me lunch. I think you got off cheap."

Hungry from our adventure and the late hour for lunch, we made quick work of the large pizza. By the time we passed the town of Newport—Knoxville far behind us and mountains rising into view—the food was devoured. C.J. belched, sending us into another fit of relieved laughter. He cleaned up the debris and tossed the empty box onto the back seat.

"If only he had been kind enough to leave us some dessert," he said as he twisted his girth in his seat so he could peer into the back. He unbuckled his seat belt and swept his long arms along the floorboards. When he hit something, he stopped with a puzzled look on his face. He grunted as he contorted his body and brought forward from the rear a shoebox that had been tucked under the driver's seat. "What do we have here?"

With a glance, I dismissed it quickly. "Never seen it, so it must be his. Hope it's more food because I'm still hungry."

C.J. flipped the lid off and peeled open the foil inside the box. With a grunt of satisfaction, he announced, "Some kind of chocolate dessert. Maybe a sheet cake or brownies."

He selected one and handed it to me. While he was taking a second one for himself, I bit into it and started chewing. Shelby's baked goods were always moist and creamy, melting in your mouth so you barely had to chew. My mother's cakes and treats were the same. A church potluck offered oodles of delicious sweets.

This was nothing like that. The chocolate square was far too dry, crumbling in my mouth. There was a hint of sweetness in the chocolate, but a strange spice had been used that gave the whole thing a weird bitterness.

I chewed it up and swallowed. I ran my tongue across my teeth and wished I had a bottle of water. "No wonder he went to get pizza. Someone can't cook. They taste funny."

C.J. didn't seem impressed either. He was staring at the food in his hands as his jaws worked to break it up. He sniffed the treat, shrugged, and took a second bite. Through a full mouth, he said, "They smell weird too."

I inhaled deeply, bring the spicy scent into my nose. He was right. "Maybe they're old and went bad sitting in the car."

"He's only had the car for a day. Why would he put old brownies under the seat?" C.J. held the treat up in the air. "Maybe they're yours and have been here for ages?"

"When have you ever seen me bake? I don't think that oven

has been on since Shelby lived at home." I couldn't help myself and took another bite.

With a flourish, C.J. popped the last of the morsel in his mouth. "Not great, but at least it's something sweet."

"Barely." I finished off the last of my dessert even though I didn't care for it that much. C.J. was right about it being a little sweet, and that tasted good after the pizza.

"Want another?"

"Pass."

C.J. shrugged and wolfed down a second and then a third before wrapping the foil closed and slipping on the lid. He turned and placed the box on the back seat.

Curious what else the tattooed man might have put in my car, I asked, "Anything else back there?"

C.J. swept his hand under both seats before turning his attention back to the road in front of us. "Nope. That's it."

"Too bad. I was hoping he had a couple of ice-cold Mountain Dews or some beer in an ice chest to get this taste out of my mouth. Those things were awful."

"Pretty inconsiderate of him not to leave drinks for us." C.J. snickered.

I didn't really think it was that funny, but I giggled anyway. The morning had been stressful, and everything seemed funny.

The farther we drove into the mountains, the more eager I was to return home. Poor Belle had been closed up in the house for a long time. As a younger dog, she would never make a mess in the house, but that had become more challenging for her as she aged. I understood because I had to get up in the middle of the night to pee more often than not.

An image of Belle and me peeing together made me giggle again, but an uneasy feeling grew in my gut. My stomach tightened, and my bowels protested. Sweat broke out across my forehead. I felt light-headed and a touch dizzy. I craved something to drink. My mouth had dried up, and I couldn't produce enough saliva to swallow.

Out of the corner of my eye, I watched C.J. mop his brow over and over. His cheeks were flushed, and he adjusted the air-conditioning vents to blow directly into his face. His pupils were even dilated despite the bright, sunny day.

Despite how ill I was feeling, I developed a weird hankering for a snack. Visions of potato chips danced in my head. I tried to shoo the thoughts away and realized my fingers and toes tingled. Even my nose had grown numb. My voice sounded far away as I said, "Those brownies must've been bad. I'm not feeling so great."

C.J. grunted agreement but then chuckled. His voice reverberated in my ears. "I feel like I'm floating. Everything is blurry and weird."

We rounded a sharp curve and passed the Welcome to North Carolina sign. "I think I'm going to stop at the visitor center. We can get a drink out of the vending machines to settle our stomachs."

"And a snack. I can't believe I'm hungry again." C.J. stared out the window at the passing trees and the deepening river gorge running beside the highway. "Bet that guy didn't stop at the rest area after stealing your car."

"Why do you say that?"

"You know, no rest area for the wicked."

I groaned at C.J.'s bad joke but couldn't resist his infectious snickering. It wasn't that funny, but I couldn't stop myself. I giggled. The high-pitched sound startled me and made me giggle again. Between bursts, I managed to say, "No drinks for the thirsty either. Our car thief was not a great host."

C.J. roared with laughter, and the sound boomed in the car. "That wife of his probably already had the drinks in their fridge." He held up both hands as if he was holding soda bottles and spoke in a falsetto voice. "I have our drinks. Where's the pizza, Bubba?"

It wasn't funny, but I couldn't stop. I loosed a hearty laugh. A tear rolled down my face. "Bubba? You think he's a Bubba?"

C.J. slapped his hands against his own jiggling sides as though he was trying to contain himself, but his mirth only grew. His voice was high-pitched as he wheezed. "Only to hide his real name from his thieving buddies. It's probably something proper like Maurice or Clarence."

"Clarence!" I screamed and slapped the dashboard with my hand. "Where's the pizza, Clarence? At least you remembered the cigarettes, Clarence."

"And the diapers, Clarence." C.J. wiped a hand across his face, sweeping away the streams of water rolling from his eyes.

"Stop it." I squirmed in my seat. "You're going to make me pee myself."

That sent us both into hysterics. The more we tried to stop, the harder we laughed. Tears filled my eyes, and I could barely see the twisting interstate in front of me.

When the rest area sign finally loomed into view, I flashed my headlights to get Wyatt's attention and pointed to the exit ramp. As we neared it, I said, "No wickeds allowed." We doubled over with more laughter, though I didn't have a clue why it was so funny. We followed Wyatt's car into the lot, both of us laughing and poking each other on the shoulders.

Wyatt parked at the far end of the lot, well away from the crowds of tourists. He got out of his car, looked at us, and approached slowly. He stood beside the driver's door, waiting, and then rapped on the driver's window. Somehow, I had forgotten to open it for him. They sent us into another fit of giggles. Struggling to concentrate, I cranked down the window. "Sorry, sir, but we're all out of pizza. Drive-through is closed."

Confusion spread on Wyatt's face. C.J. guffawed. I leaned my head on the steering wheel, my body convulsing in merriment. I finally heard Wyatt's voice asking over and over, "Pizza? When did you get pizza?"

C.J. caught his breath first and sputtered, "The valet left it for us as a tip."

I hooted and managed to say, "Valets get tips. They don't give them."

"Well, this one even leaves little chocolates on the pillows." C.J. grabbed the shoebox from the back seat and held it up in the air.

Wyatt snatched the box from C.J.'s hands, opened the lid, and sniffed. His eyes widened, and his mouth dropped open. "Oh my God. You two are high as kites."

We spasmed with hilarity, but the way he said it got through to me. I had heard him use that phrase too many times. I took a deep breath, tried to calm myself, and managed to spit out a question. "What are you talking about?"

"These aren't regular brownies, you idiots. They're laced with marijuana."

That stunned us into silence. We looked at Wyatt's serious face as he held the box out in front of him. I turned to face C.J. and saw his wide eyes. I felt the grin spreading on my face and couldn't stop it. C.J.'s eyes twinkled with merriment, and his smile joined mine. We began chanting in singsong voices. "We're in trouble. We're in trouble. We're in trouble."

Wyatt closed the lid of the box, marched to a distant trash can, and buried it in the trash. He came back, leaned in the window, and told us to stay put. He said he was going to find some coffee or sodas or anything with caffeine. Then he warned us not to move one inch until he came back.

We both sat up straight and froze our bodies. That lasted for about five seconds until we started giggling again.

Wyatt walked toward the vending area, glancing over his shoulder at us and shaking his head.

18

Summer vacationers streamed through the rest area. Some stopped only briefly, long enough to run into the restrooms and grab snacks from the vending area. Others came out of the building clutching brightly colored brochures touting tourist attractions. A few walked their dogs through the grass and wandered to the fence at the edge of the field, a breathtaking view of the Pigeon River crashing through the gorge far below. None, however, paid more than passing attention to us.

If they did notice us, they probably laughed at the role reversal. C.J. and I sat on the top of a picnic table in the shade of a shelter. A pair of cold soft drink bottles rested between us, glistening with condensation. We sipped the liquid, hoping the caffeine would bring us down from our high. Wyatt stood in front of us, his arms crossed and a stern look on his face. I could sense his foot tapping as he tried to decide what to do with us, like a parent with a pair of misbehaving boys.

"You two feeling normal yet?"

We exchanged glances and shrugged. I still felt light-headed and foggy, but I attempted to show my steadiness by staring confidently at Wyatt. The bright sun, though, hurt my eyes and I had to squint. Behind him, the air above the asphalt shimmered in the summer heat. Or, at least, I hoped it was caused by the heat and not some drug-induced illusion. "We're as normal as ever."

C.J. chuckled and mumbled under his breath, "Not that that's particularly normal."

I fought off the threat of giggles at his insolence. He'd had three brownies to my one, but he was also twice as big as me. I wasn't sure which of us was more affected.

Wyatt said, "I'm trying to figure out if you're sober enough to drive."

I pointed at the parking stripes on the pavement. "Want me to walk that line, occifer?"

C.J. turned away to focus on a distant tree and bit his lip. I could feel his sides quivering as his arm brushed against mine. Wyatt glared at me and said, "Your eyes are still bloodshot."

I tried to be serious and inventoried my body. The sweating had stopped, the dizziness had faded, and my hunger had abated after a couple bags of potato chips and a pack of crackers, but I couldn't deny I was still feeling off. We needed to give it more time for the effects to fade.

Wyatt glanced at his watch again and nervously shifted his feet, his impatience obvious. His sense of duty wouldn't let him leave, but neither of us were accustomed to this much time together. In a single day, we had shared more than we had in the last month. We were able to live together precisely because we had separate schedules and a big house for space.

I asked, "You have plans tonight, don't you?"

He avoided my eyes. "Nothing important. It can wait."

I guessed, "A date?"

He shrugged.

"Someone special?"

He hesitated. "I don't know yet. First date."

He couldn't miss that, and certainly not because of my foolishness. "Go. We'll be fine."

He stood his ground and crossed his arms. I needed to give him more of a reason to leave. "If you go, you can do me a favor."

He cocked his head and looked at me. "What?" His tone still held his exasperation.

"C.J. and I need to sit here longer, I agree, but poor Belle is still locked up in that house. You can let her into the yard and then make your date."

Wyatt turned his head to the interstate crowded with summer vacationers. "It would be better if I stayed. The road through here is challenging, and with the traffic and your condition…"

"The worst is over. We'll sit right here until we feel one hundred percent. That should give it enough time to get out of our system." I gripped his forearm. "I really don't want poor Belle to suffer because of me." He looked doubtful but receptive, so I pushed a little more. "Then go have your date. After I sit with your grandmother, I'm going to want to go to bed early anyway. It'll be easier if you're out of the house."

He pursed his lips in thought.

"I promise we won't drive until we're ready."

Wyatt shifted on his feet, the discomfort obvious on his face. He needed more assurance, so I added, "We'll stay out of trouble. No more brownies for me… ever."

"I don't know…"

"Go on. Do your own thing. We don't need a babysitter."

Wyatt glanced back over at his car. "If you're sure…"

"I'm sure."

With obvious reluctance, he left. Within a few minutes, his car disappeared around the curve of the interstate. As soon as he was out of sight, I lay back on the top of the picnic table and covered my face with my arm. I had one final giggling fit.

C.J. NUDGED ME. A half hour had passed since Wyatt had left, and normalcy seemed to be reclaiming my body, though my stomach was still queasy. I reluctantly sat up and followed his pointing finger. A North Carolina Highway Patrol car cruised slowly through the parking lot of the rest area. The trooper scanned the crowds and the parked cars.

C.J. asked, "What do you think he's looking for?"

I watched him slow for pedestrians. "Probably just a routine patrol."

"But what does that mean? Looking for suspicious people. Drugs. Stolen cars."

"Yeah, so? That's my car. Wyatt got the drugs out."

"Oh, yeah?" C.J.'s voice shook. "What license plate is on your car?"

I had forgotten that the tattooed man, or Noah, or someone had placed a Tennessee license plate on my car in an attempt to make it appear less suspicious in Knoxville. Great idea for there, but now we were back in North Carolina. What if the trooper ran the license plate? Did they have those automatic license plate scanners on their cars? I had read they could alert the officer to anything in the computer database. I thought fast. "If he asks, we just play dumb. No clue where it came from. I just show him the registration to prove it's my car."

"Where's the registration?"

"Glove compartment."

"Are you sure? Did you check?"

Of course I hadn't checked. C.J. was right. I knew it would be missing. Why would the guy keep paperwork that proved the car wasn't his? How would I explain missing paperwork and a false license plate? The trooper drew closer, his head turning back and forth as he scanned for anything amiss.

C.J. asked, "What if he finds the brownies?"

"I doubt he's going to search trash cans."

"What if he finds something else in the car?"

"You said nothing else was in there."

"I didn't search the trunk."

I looked at him and said, "You're a ray of sunshine."

He shrugged, and we returned our attention to the patrolman. He crept closer, a steady, relentless pace. As he drew even with my car, he looked right at the two of us. I held my breath.

He nodded a hello. I raised my hand in a wave. He drove on. I exhaled.

C.J. said, "Let's get out of here."

I watched the taillights of the trooper's car as he merged back onto the interstate. "We're searching the car first. He didn't pick up on the license plate, but what if we got pulled over for speeding or something?"

"You? Speeding? In that car?"

Just what I needed—more jokes about my car. "Maybe it's Chevy Nova day in the highway patrol pool, and whoever writes the most tickets to Novas wins the prize."

"Do they really do that? I thought that was a myth."

"You're killing me." I cradled my head in my hands. "For whatever reason, say they stop us. The trooper naturally looks in the back seat and then asks us to open the trunk. What if there are more brownies and the second he sees them, he knows what they are. Wyatt did. Just like that." I snapped my fingers. "Don't you think a trooper figures it out just as fast?"

C.J. scrunched his face in thought. "I think you've moved from the *everything's funny* stage to *paranoid pothead*. We would just explain everything to him."

I looked up into the sun and smiled. "Yes, officer, this is my car. No, that's not my license plate. No, I don't have the registration. No, I don't know anything about those drugs you found in the trunk. You see my car was stolen. A report? No, sir, I never quite got around to reporting it. How did I know where to find it? The funny thing is Wyatt's old druggie friend stole it and then told us where to find it. No, we didn't get it back from him because he had sold it or given it to someone else. Why would the guy who stole the car tell us where it was? I can't really explain that. But, anyway, the guy who had the car must have been a drug dealer, so he must've left his drugs in it. No, we never saw him selling drugs, but he looked like a real hardened criminal. How did we steal it back from a criminal? You see, we followed him while he picked up diapers, cigarettes, and a pizza, but then he stopped at an auto parts store, and we drove off before he noticed."

C.J. chuckled but without the unbridled merriment of the earlier drug-affected humor. "The officer would probably say it was an original story."

"Then he would slap the cuffs on us and haul us off to the pokey."

He rubbed his wrist and snickered. "Pokey. You say that, and he might really believe we're just a couple of hicks dumb enough to steal your car back."

I gestured toward my car. "All I'm saying is we don't know if anything else is in there. Drugs under the seat or in the trunk or something like that."

"Ooooh, a kilo of cocaine in the trunk. We'd be like those Hollywood movie stars." C.J. rubbed his hands together in excitement, "No, a body. A body in the trunk! He was driving around looking for a place to dump a body."

I stared at my friend in horror. "Now you're really freaking me out."

After glancing around to ensure no one was paying attention to us, I sauntered over to the car as casually as I could and opened the driver's door. I bent over with a grunt and peered under the seat. Nothing loomed in the shadows except a little dirt from my boots and a couple of fast-food wrappers. I repeated the process on the passenger side.

C.J. stood and swayed. He balanced himself with a hand on the edge of the picnic table and announced loudly, "I'll search the trunk."

"Shhhhh," I hissed and looked around to see if anyone had overheard. "Can we do this without drawing attention?"

C.J. looked around at the crowded rest area parking lot and shook his head. He held up his hand, so I tossed him the keys. C.J. grabbed for them but missed, and the keys bounced off the table and into the grass. He bent over, swayed, and then fished them off the ground. He stood, steadied himself, and staggered to the rear of the car.

I hoped I wasn't stumbling around as badly as he was but returned to my own search. I rifled the glove compartment—my registration had been removed—and then opened the back doors and continued scanning under the seats. Satisfied the interior of the car was clean of any contraband, I joined C.J. at the now-open trunk.

My fishing rods lay jumbled across the floor. We opened and searched the tackle boxes, but they held only lures, flies, and hooks. We unfolded my waders and shook the boots to ensure nothing was hidden. I stood and sighed in relief, satisfied no illegal substances were tucked away. I reached up to close the lid, but C.J. stopped me and pointed. "What's in that bag?"

Following his pointed finger, I spotted a black plastic trash bag tucked in the shadows behind the spare tire. Maybe I had left it there the last time I went to the dump, but I sure didn't remember it. I leaned over and snagged the bag in my hands. It was heavier than I expected as I pulled it into the sunlight.

Visions from movies flashed through my mind of wrapped bricks of cocaine powder. What if C.J. had been right and the guy really had left kilos of drugs in my car? Could I just drop that into the trash can and leave? And how much powder is in a kilogram anyway? Why didn't we measure drugs in pounds since this was the USA?

I focused my thoughts and untied the top of the bag, surprised to see my hands shake. With the knot loosened, I opened the bag and looked inside.

The first thing I saw panicked me. I looked around again to make sure no one was close before removing a pistol.

C.J. asked, "It is loaded?"

As an answer, I removed the full magazine, cycled the slide, ejecting a round, and cycled twice more to ensure it was now empty. A glance inside the empty chamber confirmed the weapon was safe. I laid it gently on the floor of the trunk. I picked up the ejected cartridge and reloaded it in the magazine. "Not anymore."

I looked inside the bag and held my breath. C.J. leaned over my shoulder and gasped. We stood in awed silence until he asked in a whisper, "How much do you think it is?"

I reached into the bag and extracted one bundle. I fanned the twenty-dollar bills with my thumb. "The band says two thousand dollars."

"Just in that one bundle?"

Speechless, I nodded.

"How many bundles are there?"

I dropped the bundle back into the bag and ran my hand through the other stacks, flipping the bound bills over in my wake. "I have no idea. Twenty or thirty at least."

"All two thousand?"

"Nope. I see one bundle of hundreds."

"Hundreds?" C.J. whistled. "How much is a bundle of hundreds?"

"It says ten thousand."

"Holy…" He leaned against the car. "Is it yours?"

"You think I've ever had this much cash in my hands? Would've taken me years in the factory to save this much."

We stood in silence and studied the bundle until C.J. asked the obvious. "So it's his?"

"I guess."

We dumped the bundles of cash into the trunk and stacked them by denomination. My hands shook as we counted. "Ten, twenty, thirty, thirty-two, thirty-four..." Once the count was complete, we looked at each other and whispered in unison, "One hundred twenty-three thousand five hundred dollars."

Voices broke our shock. A young couple walked toward us, their children scampering through the parking lot. I realized they would easily see the money as they passed. I tossed the bundles back into the bag and shoved it behind the spare tire.

With horror, I realized I had left the pistol in full view. I jammed the magazine into the gun and tucked the thing behind the bag. I slammed the trunk closed and leaned against the car just as the couple neared.

The man looked at me strangely and reached over to touch his wife's arm. He guided her in a wide berth around us as she gripped their kids' hands. They climbed into a minivan parked a half-dozen spaces away, gave us one last glance, and then backed out.

I wiped the sweat from my brow and surveyed the parking lot. The tourists and truck drivers ignored us and went about their business. No one knew what we had. "What do I do now?"

C.J. slapped me on the back. "Keep it. If that was his money, he got it selling drugs or stole it from somebody or something like that. And you certainly can't give it back because then he'll know we're the ones who stole his car... your car... whatever it is."

"I can't keep it. That ain't right." Visions of the tattooed man filled my head. "Besides, he might come for it. It's dangerous."

"Trash?"

The overflowing can already held our brownies. If I put it in there, maybe it disappeared. But what if a custodian found it, and it became news? The tattooed man might hear about it and realize which direction the car went. Wouldn't be hard then to guess I'd taken it back. My bright idea didn't seem so bright anymore.

C.J. broke through my thoughts. "What do you want to do?"

"I don't know." I looked at my watch, shocked at how late it had become. "I'll figure it out. Right now, though, I'm going to be late for my dinner date with my wife."

19

The electronic lock clacked shut behind me as I entered the dementia unit. Shelby sat on the couch at the far end of the dayroom, facing the window and the view of the courtyard beyond. Her head tilted to one side. I couldn't tell with her back toward me whether she was sleeping, daydreaming, or staring into space with her mind in neutral.

Busy entering notes into the computer on the desk, Teresa didn't look up until I approached the nurses' station for my daily report on how Shelby fared. The information helped me understand what role I needed to play each night.

Teresa greeted me warmly, a smile replacing her studious look of concentration. The kindness in her face, though, was offset by a gentle shaking of her head letting me know the news wasn't good. "A good morning through breakfast, but then things went south. She accused Jolene of stealing her jewelry. Things got heated."

Throughout our marriage, Shelby had never made a big deal about wanting expensive jewelry. With money always tight, we were too busy buying groceries and keeping a roof over our heads to splurge. She contented herself with inexpensive earrings and necklaces for going to church or wearing on special occasions with only a couple of exceptions.

Her wedding ring was a simple band with a small diamond, not particularly fancy though it still cost a small fortune on my wages at the time. She treasured it, taking it off only for gardening in the yard, when she used harsh cleaning chemicals, or for any other activity that might damage it.

As our twenty-fifth wedding anniversary approached, she was despondent over Jessica's departure. I suffered from my own guilt. I wanted to do something special to take her mind off the troubles, so I splurged on a beautiful silver pendant. It wasn't excessively expensive, but she cried when she opened the felt box. She wore it to the restaurant that night, touching it repeatedly as if it was filled with priceless jewels.

When my mother passed, I had her old pearl necklace cleaned and restrung. I knew I could never afford to buy something like that and worried about Shelby's reaction. I should have known better. She cherished the gift because of the memories of my mother and their relationship.

That was it. She owned nothing else of considerable monetary value. We both worked hard and watched every penny of our paychecks. Finally owning our house free and clear meant more to both of us.

Residents in a memory unit traded belongings. They swapped clothes routinely. I was careful to always compliment Shelby's new blouse as I inquired where she bought it. She told me elaborate shopping stories while I watched her own clothes float around the room on someone else. The jewelry, even the inexpensive items, remained safely stored at home for that very reason.

I said, "She doesn't have anything here to steal."

Teresa snorted, an endearing trait that always made me smile. What made her such a good nurse with these patients was her appreciation for their creativity. "I know that. You know that. Unfortunately, Jolene enjoyed the battle. She confessed to the crime and swore we would never find the treasure she had hidden so well."

Jolene was a retired schoolteacher, admired in the community for her compassionate care of so many students over the years. In the nursing home, she'd developed a colorful use of all the profanity she had learned—and forbidden—from her students over the years. She also had a fascinating ability to weave stories from her years of reading crime novels. Many evenings, she entertained me with expletive-filled tales of mischief. "Did Jolene say how she pulled off the heist?"

"A master jewel thief wanted by Interpol would never reveal the details to a copper like me." Teresa rolled her eyes. "A person of her highly polished skills slipped past the elaborate alarm system protecting Shelby's vault, eliminated the security guards with a secret chemical gas, and cracked the code to the safe. The biggest danger came when she had to smuggle the loot past unsuspecting customs officers to get it out of the country."

"I assume she's hiding out in a nursing home to avoid arrest?"

Teresa scratched her chin as she pondered the question. "We're a Caribbean island today, I think, but I can't keep my geography straight."

The patients regularly wove elaborate tales. Teresa had taught me long ago to let the stories flow over me. Shelby once claimed she helped dig tunnels at night to escape from prison. I asked her what she and her fellow prisoners did with the dirt, and she said they spread it in the prison yard. She pointed at the linoleum floor. I complimented her on the beautiful flower garden she claimed grew there.

"Is she still upset by her 'stolen' jewelry?" I did air quotes with my hands.

"Forgotten by lunch, when we attempted to poison her

with lime Jell-O. She warned everyone—quite loudly—not to eat it. Fortunately, I had cherry in the cart, and a trade solved the problem. Then this afternoon, she became upset about *Dallas*."

As strange as the stories get, that one had me puzzled. "We've never been there."

The nurse's eyes twinkled with merriment. "Not the city. The TV show."

"Ah! She used to love that show. I never much cared for it." At least, I pretended not to care because it was a nighttime soap opera, but I didn't resist too hard when she made me sit down and watch every episode. About killed me the months we had to wait to find out who shot J.R.

With Shelby gone, though, I wouldn't have a TV in the house if Wyatt weren't living there. The only reason I ever watched anything was to do something with her.

I said, "I didn't know anyone was showing the reruns."

"I don't think anyone is, but even if they did, we wouldn't have it on. All that conflict agitates the patients." She tilted her head toward where my wife sat. "For some reason, though, she thinks she's missing the show. She's been yelling for us to turn it on."

Fixations weren't uncommon in dementia patients. Checking and rechecking to ensure lights were turned off to save electricity costs. Fear that retirement savings had dried up. Paranoia that government agents were going to show up with arrest warrants. I had learned not to try to convince Shelby they weren't true but rather to participate enough to tell a white lie and resolve the issue. "I'll find one of her favorite shows on another channel."

Teresa tsked. "I wish we could, but the TV's broken, remember?"

Nothing quite like being reminded of something you forgot while visiting a dementia unit. I was paranoid of winding up in a place like this just like my wife, so every forgotten detail freaked me out.

But the reminder about the TV not working did suggest that part of Shelby's restlessness could be attributed to a lack of entertainment. Any parent of a small child knew the hypnotic power of the flickering lights and sound from the television. Without it here, more than the usual number of patients milled about the room. Sitting night after night with Shelby, I knew how hard the nurses worked and how much easier their jobs were if at least some of the patients were distracted with something. The TV wasn't a luxury but a necessity. Budgets were tight, but why was something simple like this not solved? "No word yet on a new one?"

Teresa's laugh sounded less like amusement and more like exasperation. "Unless someone plants a money tree soon, I don't think it's happening. Let us know if you win the lottery or find some buried treasure."

In a way, I had found buried treasure, not in a hole but behind my spare tire. Whether from selling poison or stealing from people, that money had come from evil. Would it be wrong to use a little of it to give some sick people a little comfort? To offer some help to overworked nurses handling difficult tasks? Not to help just my wife but the rest of the staff and patients here. I had the ability to help, didn't I? Maybe I was meant to find that money. I'd just take a little, a couple bundles of bills.

When I turned the rest of it in to the police, they wouldn't know any was missing. Only C.J. and I knew how much was in that bag.

And the tattooed man, of course. Maybe. Maybe he didn't know exactly how much was there. If he came to claim his money before I gave it to the police, I'd just give him the bag. Maybe even act like I didn't know it was in the trunk, so he couldn't suspect me.

Standing there in the midst of that chaos, I made my decision. It was worth the risk.

"I left my phone in my car. I'll be right back."

Teresa looked startled and glanced across the room at Shelby's back. "I don't think she knows you're here yet, so you're good. Dinner will be served in thirty minutes."

MY DECISION MIGHT HAVE BEEN MADE, but that didn't mean doubts didn't plague me. I hurried out of the building, debating with myself the whole way. Was it theft to steal stolen money? Could I get away with it without raising suspicions? Could I convince a friend to go along with my crazy idea?

That last one was the biggest wild card, but first I had to retrieve the money from the trunk of my car. Hours remained before sunset, so the parking lot offered no camouflage. No shadows cast by overhead lights would hide my deed. And, being dinnertime, visitors walked to and from their cars. I nodded at the ones I knew, which was most of them in the usual curse of a small town. Fortunately, no one came over to chat, so I got to my car without anyone nearby. With a final, furtive glance, I opened the trunk and reached for the bag. I yanked it from its hiding place without thinking of what else was hidden. I dislodged the pistol, and it bounced noisily across the metal floor.

With my head under the lid, the clattering sounded uncannily like a gunshot. I jumped, almost banging my head. My pulse raced, and my muscles tensed. I was sure it was so loud that someone would come over to see what I was up to. In this age of mass shootings, people might easily reach the wrong conclusion about an exposed weapon.

If someone asked why I had a loose gun, what was my

defense? Saying "I wasn't going for the gun, just the stolen drug money" wouldn't cast my actions in a better light. Fortunately, I didn't have to find out. No one seemed to notice. I covered the gun with the plastic bag. After making sure no one was racing over to tackle me, I grabbed two random bundles of cash without looking and shoved them in my pocket. Checking one last time that nobody was watching, I slid the gun back into the bag so I wouldn't make that mistake again. I tied the bag closed, placed it behind the spare, and closed the trunk. I leaned against the car and breathed a sigh of relief. People continued to come in and out of the building, but no one seemed to be concerned about me.

Wiping my palms on my jeans, I reentered the nursing home and moved quickly down the corridors, but this time beyond the dementia unit. I had been through the door marked with a small Staff Only sign several times, but always with an employee. Staff members had used a badge to swipe the security lock. Without an accomplice, I didn't have any way through. I thought about calling the friend I intended to visit, but what if he came to the hall to talk rather than letting me in? I didn't want to hand him the money in the open where anyone could see.

As I debated with myself, the door burst open. A young woman pushed a rolling food cart taller than herself through the opening. I instinctively grabbed the door and held it. She smiled and thanked me. As she pushed her goods toward the resident wings, she never looked back. I slipped into the employee section unauthorized.

Getting in was one thing, but I needed to work my way through the entire section. The glass-enclosed administrative offices came first. I had been a frequent visitor because there was always a bill to settle or paperwork requiring i's to be dotted and t's crossed. Would anyone stop me? I inched down the hallway until I had a clear view. The lights were already off. The office staff had left for the day.

Bright light flooded out of the next open door, the entrance to the staff lounge. I knew from previous visits that the room held all the usual accoutrements of an employee break room— vending machines, microwave, refrigerator, sink, tables, and chairs. Normally, several people sat around eating, drinking, or just chatting, so passing by the door unnoticed was unlikely. I tried my best to walk confidently, to look as though I belonged, and hoped no one challenged me as I passed. To my surprise, the room was empty. Mealtime in the residential areas was one of the busiest times in the facility, so no one was on break.

The remainder of the hallway consisted of a few more doors, all closed, until I finally arrived at my destination—the maintenance area. The door was shut, but I guessed Bobby Jenkins would be working. He was one of the few guys my age still putting in a regular workday, and I had seen his truck in the parking lot. I stuck my head through the door and spied my target in the back corner of the room. He was soldering a broken joint in a wheelchair.

Before I could speak, he must've sensed my presence. He flipped open his welder's helmet and smiled. "Purvis. Haven't seen you in a dog's age. What brings you to my dungeon? Pull up a chair."

"I can't stay. Have to get back to have dinner with Shelby, but I've got a favor to ask."

"Anything for you, and anything for Shelby. You know that."

"Hear me out before you agree." I pushed the hallway door shut and leaned against the workbench. "I understand from Teresa Peters that money's real tight. No way to get a new TV for the dementia unit."

Bobby nodded, his eyes downcast. "I work all the miracles I can keeping things humming around here, but I couldn't get that thing working again. Amazing it lasted as long as it has. Been telling the suits for three years we better start replacing TVs before they go, but you know how bean counters are. They tell you they have to wait until they absolutely have to replace something, and then when it breaks, they act surprised."

"Yeah, I understand." I tried not to watch the door, but I wondered how long I had until someone else came in. "If someone gave you a cash donation, you could replace it then, right?"

"Depends." Bobby took off his helmet and placed it gently on the workbench. "Let's say a relative, like you, brought in an old TV and left it in that ward. Odds are pretty good it would stay there. But cash donations go to the office. You'd have to ask them if you could be specific about what they spent it on. I'd worry they'd tell you it would go into the general fund. Around here, that means it generally won't go where you need it."

"Not quite the question I'm asking." I wrapped my hand around the two bundles in my pocket. I hadn't even looked to see what bills I had grabbed. What if it was two bundles of hundreds—twenty thousand dollars? How would I explain that? "What if *you* were handed the cash. Could you get the things needed without the suits getting involved?"

Bobby's chair squeaked in protest as he leaned back. He stared at the ceiling for a moment and asked, "Hypothetically?"

After I nodded, he kept his eyes fixed on the fluorescent light. He let an uncomfortable silence settle before speaking. "My experience here says that the suits only care about money going out the door. They don't ask a lot of questions about things that come in. We get things donated all the time, and no one asks a thing. So, yeah, I could probably figure out a way for a TV to work its way into Shelby's unit."

I looked down at my hand resting on the workbench and was surprised to see it trembling. I had expected getting a single TV into a single unit wouldn't be a big deal. As he said, if I brought in an old TV and placed it in the dementia unit, no one would think a thing about it. Giving him the cash to buy a TV wasn't much different.

But that felt selfish. I would be using the money to solve my problem but not helping anyone outside that unit. What if I could do more? "What about the other TVs? And the computers?"

He hesitated. "That'd take a lot of money."

"But they wouldn't ask?"

He studied that overhead light more. "I don't think so."

I shoved my shaking hands into my pockets as I edged the conversation to the point of no return. "And you?"

"Some people, I would have to ask where the money came from."

"And me?"

His eyes finally dropped from the ceiling and focused on me. "I would figure a guy like you probably just had it stuffed in a Mason jar or something. If you—er, a guy like you— trusted me to handle things the right way, then I would owe him the trust that he came by it honestly."

I closed my eyes and took a deep breath. Too late to back out now. I had crossed the line. My hands shook as I pulled the two bundles out of my pocket and placed the cash on the workbench in front of us. To my relief, they were both twenty-dollar bills, but I cringed at the sight of the bright-purple band loudly announcing that each bundle held two thousand dollars. Why hadn't I thought to remove that?

Bobby's eyes grew wide. He loosed a low whistle. "That's some Mason jar."

Now that I was committed, I might as well go all the way. I

could retrieve more cash from the car if needed. "Is it a big enough jar?"

I held my breath as the clock on the wall ticked through a dozen seconds. Finally, Bobby slowly nodded. "Here's what I'm thinking. If I went down to the Walmart and bought a bunch of new televisions, that would set all the tongues wagging around here. Somebody would end up getting suspicious and start asking questions I couldn't answer."

My chest tightened as I lowered my head. I had pushed too far and asked too much. I reached for the money. "Sorry for asking. I don't want to put you in a bad place."

Bobby raised his hand. "Hear me out. New stuff would be like sparkly baubles for crows. But old stuff scuffed up with some scratch marks but still working? Pawn shops, consignment stores, places like that—I could probably find what you're talking about without raising too many eyebrows. The suits would think we got the broken stuff unbroken."

A glimmer of hope. "No one would notice?"

"The nurses will know because nurses know everything, but they'd never say anything." Bobby pursed his lips in thought but then nodded as he reached out and slid the money into a drawer like a Las Vegas dealer clearing a table. He extracted a key from the ring dangling from his belt and locked it up. "I'll make sure it's taken care of."

I stood and had my hand on the doorknob when Bobby stopped me. "The dementia unit's TV will be the first one I 'fix.'" He made quotes in the air with his fingers.

20

I made it back to the secured dementia unit before the food trays arrived. Teresa looked at me oddly, a deserved reaction because of my earlier behavior. I waved my cell phone in reply as if I had simply retrieved it from the car and returned. I could only hope she didn't notice how much time had passed. With a plan in motion, I didn't need to attract any unwanted attention.

Shelby sat in the same position as she had when I left. I made a wide berth as I crossed the room, hoping to attraction her attention without startling her. Her eyes were open but not focused on me or, as best I could tell, anything else. I approached slowly, praying my old Shelby might be in there somewhere, but she didn't give me any indication she even knew I was there. I used my softest voice to ask, "Have you had a good day?"

She shifted her head to look at me with her foggy eyes. Her hand shook as she rubbed the side of her face. She blinked twice and focused on me, but no light sparkled. "Same as the others, I guess."

No recognition was in her voice, so I had to fish to determine where I stood. What year was she living in? Did she recognize me? Did she think I was a friend or foe? Or were we off in some far galaxy that I would never comprehend? I had to keep my questions general until I figured things out. "Looking forward to dinner?"

Ever so slowly, the corners of her mouth turned up into the first smile of the night. Her eyes began to twinkle. "Oh, yes."

That reaction gave me some hope. I didn't know if the improvement was caused by my presence, the hint of coming food, or some thought I couldn't see. I was happy to have recovered my car for the next time she was well enough to go outside, but tonight wasn't the night. My goal became simple— a quiet meal together as strangers, friends, or spouses. Anything else was a bonus. "May I have the pleasure of dining with you?"

She clasped her hands together and giggled like a school- girl. "So formal. Such a gentleman. Such manners you have." We had both shared a love of reading in our early days of dating, delighted to discover we were closet bookworms in high school. In my case, I was too small to excel in the popular sports of football and basketball, but I could escape into a story while my friends banged into each other on fields and courts. She was a popular cheerleader and student, which for some long-forgotten reason known only to teenagers meant she couldn't expose too much of her love of literature. Those uncovered secrets led to many of our conversations being in stilted, formal English. It was one of our private jokes.

"It would be my pleasure."

She blushed and fanned herself with her hand. With a polite and proper voice, she rejected me. "Some other night, perhaps, but not tonight."

My heart skipped a beat. These things happened. If only I could figure out what role I was playing, I had a chance for a pleasant evening. I pushed a little more. "Of course, a beautiful woman like you has plans for the evening."

"Oh, I do." She smiled. "*He's* going to join me tonight."

My heart pounded. The "he" could mean me. Sometimes she didn't recognize that I was me. She'd once even told me she had a husband who looked and sounded just like me. Another punch from dementia I just had to absorb.

Of course, "he" could also mean someone else entirely. Because I came every night at dinnertime, I knew no one else ever joined her for the meal in a real sense. But in the fog that was her mind, many others could be here. The only thing I could do was play the role of a gentleman, something I hoped I was, and wait until I understood the situation better. "I'm certainly disappointed, but I would never get in the way of a gentleman caller."

She leaned forward and wrapped her hand around mine. I tingled at the touch as she dropped her voice to a whisper, barely audible over the background noise in the cavernous room. "You are such a nice man, but so is he. So handsome. Treats me like a lady. He makes me feel so special."

Caring for someone with dementia was like walking across a minefield. You knew there were things hidden in your path, waiting to hurt you if you stumbled across them. Your only option was to keep moving forward, hoping to make it across the space safely. Then you got to do it all over again the next day. And the day after. I could only play along. If it turned out to be me she was waiting on, I would excuse myself, walk around the room, and hope she recognized me when I approached again. And if it wasn't me... Well, that was pain I just had to accept.

"He sounds wonderful."

"Oh, he is. In more ways than one." She fanned herself again, an exaggerated gesture accompanied by a look of delight. "That man is something else in bed too."

I gulped, struggling to keep calm. "How…" I licked my lips, focusing on my words. "Nice."

"Nice?" She cackled. "My husband is nice."

Dread filled the pit of my stomach. "Yes, he is."

"But we mustn't let my husband know about Horace. Horace rocks my world."

THE AFFAIR HAD BROKEN my heart. Even though it had been over for many years, its memory had a way of surfacing again and again. I didn't blame her for reminding me of it. I blamed that blasted disease.

Back when it happened, I didn't blame her either. I blamed myself.

21

W e didn't worry when Shelby failed to get pregnant right after our wedding. We were having too much fun. With plans to fill that big old house with the laughter of as many children as we could, we made love in every single room. Most of them multiple times. We even did it on the porch at night a few times, which makes my chastising Wyatt for walking around in his boxers a bit amusing. If I had had the hammock back then, we would probably have done it there.

We didn't tire of the lovemaking, but as month turned to month, as the seasons rotated through the year, we began to wonder what wasn't working. Other couples our age already had children or were, at least, pregnant. We didn't talk much about it for fear of jinxing ourselves, but doubts crept into our minds. Each month we held our breath, wondering if we had finally been successful. When her period came, regular as clockwork, we would shrug it off and laugh and say we had to try harder. But the laughter became less and less. Something wasn't right.

On her doctor's advice, she visited a fertility expert down in Asheville. To modern couples, this probably sounds weird, but she didn't tell me before the appointment. She went through all those tests and never said a word. It was our first real secret as a couple, and I guess our first lie. She'd told me she was shopping with friends at the fancy mall down there. I never wondered why she didn't bring home any purchases.

One night, she prepared my favorite dinner and topped it off with my favorite dessert. When I had taken my last bite, she started talking. She told me about all the procedures they had performed. She went over test results in excruciating detail. I kept waiting for the big reveal, for the reason, but she said they had determined nothing was physically preventing her from becoming pregnant.

I remember the pause to this day. The silence of the house as she hesitated, waiting to see if I understood what she was saying. Finally, she gently told me the doctors suggested I might need to be tested.

We men are funny creatures. Our egos are wrapped up in being men, or at least, what we perceive it to mean to be men. Any suggestion we are something less insults us to the core. We can't handle it. I was no exception.

Nothing could be wrong with me, I protested. Everything worked. We knew that. We'd certainly proven it over and over. She patiently explained to me the possibilities her doctor described. Instead of listening to what she said, all I could think of was that she had discussed such intimate details with her doctor. I'd never discussed any of those things with anyone. I imagined running into him in town and seeing the look in his eyes, the look that said I wasn't a complete man.

Shelby, bless her, ignored all that and persisted. I resisted for weeks but finally agreed. For her, I would see the doctor.

In the privacy of his office, he explained that he needed a sample for testing. In my naivety, I asked how they obtained those. Then I sat there in horror while he explained what every man already knew how to do.

I complied, which wasn't nearly as pleasurable as it might imply. When the lab results came back, the doctor gave me the news. I had failed. My delivery system worked just fine, but production was a problem. Putting it bluntly, I was shooting blanks. My count was so low, the odds of me getting Shelby pregnant were nil.

As my head buzzed in disgrace, the doctor described options to consider, things we could do to improve the situation, medical alternatives we could explore. We even talked about my choice of underwear, much to my horror.

Shelby eagerly listened to every possibility. She pulled out a pad of paper and took notes. She gathered brochures and took them home to read. The next day, she went to our local library and researched, bringing home books to study. Meanwhile, I wondered what the librarian thought.

She attacked the problem. I—pardon the unintentional pun—withdrew.

Of all the mistakes I've made in my life, my reaction was one of the worst. If only I had approached things with the same maturity, the same eagerness that Shelby did, then things would have turned out differently. Instead, I acted like a spoiled child throwing a temper tantrum.

Our frequent lovemaking sessions became infrequent. She scribbled notes on charts and took her temperature and arranged pillows and studied positions, all in an effort to help my weak, pathetic little soldiers do what every man should be able to do. When the time came for me to perform my masculine duties, I did everything imaginable to avoid it. I watched TV. I tinkered on my car. I weeded the yard. I made sure I was assigned to overtime projects at work.

I regretted it all.

If only I'd talked to Shelby, worked things through, she never would've gone to Horace. The affair never would've happened. But when our problems flared up and I pulled away, she needed a friend. Someone to listen to her. Someone to understand. I wasn't doing my job as a husband and a partner, so she turned to someone else. To the only person who knew her as well as I did.

Horace Pearson. The old high school flame.

He listened. He understood. He cared.

I didn't think he had ill intent at first. I knew Shelby didn't. But they crossed the line.

If only it had been a one-time thing. That they never did it again. That it was simply a bit too much to drink, a little too much closeness, a hormonal mistake.

But that would be yet another lie. The affair went on for weeks. Weeks became months.

Then she found out she was pregnant.

HORACE DID what he had always done when things got tough —tucked tail and ran. He stopped answering Shelby's calls, avoided her in town, skipped events when he knew she would be there. She was crushed. Embarrassed to be seen in the same places as Horace, she dropped off several volunteer committees. For the first time in a long time, we found ourselves together again.

We couldn't pretend the affair hadn't happened. Her pregnancy and my infertility shouted that to us every day. To everyone else in town, though, it signaled the start of our family. We received congratulations and baby showers. Our parents were thrilled. We did our best to fake our enthusiasm.

I didn't know what to do. I was angry. Hurt. Embarrassed.

Mostly, though, I was guilty. Shelby never blamed her affair on me, but I did. If I hadn't acted like such a fool, she would never have been looking for comfort in the first place.

We talked for the first time in months. Haltingly at first, but more and more openly. Did we love each other? Did we want a divorce? What were we going to do about a child?

We recognized how broken we were. Best of all, we recognized we needed help. We considered going to a counselor down in Asheville, far away from the rumor mills and prying eyes of a small town. Instead, we found a closer answer. So close, it was in sight of the house.

We had always been on-again-off-again churchgoers. A little better than the Easter & Christmas crowd, but not by much. The church just down the road had brought in a new minister. The Reverend Jacob Brawley was a young man, a shade younger than us and fairly new to the area. We barely knew him, but he seemed from the pulpit like someone we could trust. We made an appointment with him and confessed everything. We told him every sordid detail. It seemed easier to talk to him because he was a stranger.

I expected him to be shocked at my infertility and the affair. I imagined him kicking us out of the church and then writing a sermon with us as his parable. He turned out to be far more understanding than we had ever thought possible. Importantly, our trust was rewarded because not a whisper of what we talked about ever circled around town. He kept our secrets.

He listened. We talked. He never judged us but let us judge ourselves. Slowly, Shelby and I rebuilt a trust between us. There was never that one moment when we decided to stay together. No aha moment. It was more a matter of little decisions. We had enough foundation to rebuild our marriage. We liked being with each other. We had a baby coming to think of. It wasn't fair for a child to be raised in this world suffering the consequences of our actions. We resolved to renew our vows and raise our family. We were happy.

If only that was where the story had ended, we could say we'd lived happily ever after.

That would be a lie. I'd known it when Jessica was born.

22

My half-eaten sandwich waited on the small table between the rocking chairs as I watched the sunset. Belle and I had the house to ourselves, thanks to Wyatt's date. That was good because I wouldn't have been good company. Between a long travel day, the excitement of recovering my car, an accidental ingestion of marijuana, and Shelby's reliving of the affair, I was irritable and exhausted. Even my dog opted to snooze on the far end of the porch, well away from me.

Despite how tired I was, I couldn't sleep. Just a few feet from me, tucked in the shadows of the trunk of my car, sat that bag of ill-gotten funds. What was I supposed to do with it?

Giving the money to Bobby had been a spur-of-the-moment decision. I saw a need, I had the ability to help, and I did it without thought. At the time, it didn't feel any different than C.J. and me building that picnic table.

But I knew in my heart it was different. I could pretend all night that I did it to make the nurses' jobs easier and to make the residents' lives better, but the truth was I did it with a selfish motive at heart—to help Shelby cope with her disease.

No, that wasn't even true. I did it because I desperately

wanted my Shelby, the one who remembered who I was, to be waiting when I walked in each night.

The guilt weighed on me as I wrestled with my conscience. What was I to do with all that money?

After seeing Bobby's suspicion and discomfort, I couldn't go back to him with more money to spend on the nursing home. Even if he were willing, sooner or later, someone would notice new supplies appearing in the building.

Despite C.J.'s suggestion, I wasn't going to keep it. Not because of some crazy belief that I had enough money—I had plenty of ways I could use it—but because of where it came from. Drugs had killed Jessica. They damned near killed Wyatt. I didn't want anything to do with something that came from such evil.

For the same reason, I didn't want to return it.

That left giving it away. There certainly wasn't a lack of need in Miller County. Plenty of people here could use the help—clothing, food, utility bills, rent, medical costs. If only I could figure out how to get it in the right hands, that money could do a tremendous amount of good, but I didn't know other people like Bobby who could get things done and keep it quiet. What I needed to do was find such people.

Or, better yet, such a person. A single person who could be trusted to do the right thing with that much cash.

I picked at the crust of my bread as the sun dropped behind the ridge. The valley fell into a peaceful darkness. Out here in the country, we didn't have streetlights. The glow from the stars and the rising moon provided enough illumination to see all we needed. Lightning bugs danced above the fields as they flitted about finding mates. A distant light from the farmer's house twinkled on the horizon. The church steeple rose in the distance, the illuminated cross at its peak sparkling against the night sky.

I sat up with a start. Belle raised her head to see if it was bedtime. Realizing she was early, she flopped her head back onto the wooden porch with a thunk and resumed her snoring.

I had thought of one person I could trust. He had helped me before and kept my confidence. He wouldn't keep a penny of it for himself. He would ensure every red cent went only to the deserving. I believed in him because he was the man who helped save our marriage. The Good Reverend Jacob Brawley.

There was just one problem.

Brawley was so honest, he wouldn't be willing to just go along with the Mason jar story. If I handed him a bag of money, a trash bag no less, filled with bundles of cash carefully wrapped in currency bands, he would want to know the details. Once he had them, no telling what he would do. Honest men weren't very trustworthy in those regards.

How did I get him to take the money from me?

The answer was simple. He couldn't know where it came from. The donation would have to be anonymous. He would have no one to ask.

I rocked the chair back, troubled by that last thought. If that bag showed up with no explanation, the reverend would hesitate. So I needed to explain, but without him knowing who I was.

I jumped out of my chair, startling Belle again. We tossed the mail each day into a basket on a small table just inside the front door. Most of it was junk mail I rarely opened and threw into the trash on the day I hauled garbage to the dump.

Thumbing through the stack, I found what I was looking for—the bill from the local electric co-op. I pulled the invoice out of the envelope and returned it to the pile. The envelope itself would prove it came from a local—a member of the co-op. I flipped it over and scrawled the beginning of a note on the back:

Dear Reverend Brawley:

I chewed on the end of the pen. How could I explain where the money came from? I decided to do what I did best— start with a nugget of truth and then lie like crazy.

I am an old man near the end of my life. I've always set aside money from every check I've ever earned but never trusted those banks. Now I find myself with more than I need. I have no heirs to give this to, but I want to see it put to good use.

You helped me once, long ago, and so I trust you. I also know you've helped many people, so you won't guess who I am. That's good because I want this to be anonymous.

Please take this money and see that it goes to those who need it most.

Would it work? I didn't know, but I was running out of time. I needed to get this done before Wyatt came home. I didn't want that money sitting near me all night. I clomped back out onto the porch. Exasperated, Belle looked at me again to see why I was messing up her routine.

"Want to go for a ride, girl?"

She looked around as if to tell me it was dark and entirely too late for such shenanigans. But when I walked down the steps to my car, she stood, stretched, and followed. I retrieved the bag of cash out of the trunk and opened the door. Belle dutifully jumped into the passenger seat, and I placed the bag on the floorboard below her. I opened it to slide the envelope with the note on top. The gun flashed in the moonlight.

If he saw the weapon, the preacher would know the money was tainted. Besides, the pistol would be traceable in a way the cash never would be. I extracted it from the bag and slipped it under the seat. I then laid the envelope on top of the cash and retied the bag.

We headed down the gravel road to the church. I kept my headlights off so I didn't draw attention. The night sky provided all the illumination I needed.

The lights were on inside the parsonage, but the church itself was dark. The outside floodlights bathed the building. Fearful that Brawley's curiosity would be aroused if I pulled into the parking lot, I drove to the paved intersection, did a U-turn, and then parked on the gravel road. I would hear any car long before it came upon me, so I wasn't worried about someone coming along. I lifted the bag and said to Belle, "I'll be right back, girl. Wait here."

Doing my best to avoid the brightness of the floodlights, I snuck across the grass to a large bin set up near the double-door entrance to the church. Donations of clothing and toys could be slipped through doors that pulled down on the sides, but once they slammed shut, the design prevented people from stealing the goods inside.

The contents were emptied each morning and evening, so nothing sat too long. Volunteers helped in the afternoon, but Brawley handled the task himself in the morning. He claimed it was because he walked over so early, but teenagers had been known to drop off empty beer cans in the dark of night in typical juvenile behavior. He didn't want his volunteers messing with that.

I pulled open the drawer, placed the bag inside, and closed it. I heard a satisfying thunk as it slid down the chute and fell to the bottom of the bin, secure until morning. I was rid of it, and trusted Brawley would do the right thing.

I skulked back across the yard, drove Belle home, and slept peacefully.

MONDAY

23

"We wouldn't have found it without the bear."

"This ought to be good." A smirk crossed the sheriff's face. He set down his coffee on the corner of the table and folded his arms across his chest. "What does a bear have to do with finding Purvis's car?"

I slumped in my chair as the rest of the men around the Liars' Table leaned forward, eager for a fresh story. C.J. hadn't warned me he was going to launch into this tale, but when Harlow had pointed at my car parked in front of Abe's Market and asked how I recovered it, I didn't have a good answer. C.J. saved me from answering, but I sweated since I had no idea where the story was going. The fact that the sheriff, waiting while Danny cooked his daily breakfast, stood and listened with interest made hearing the story for the first time even more stressful.

Once all eyes focused on C.J., the large man leaned forward, lowered his voice, and launched into his story. "It was Boris for sure, the biggest, baddest black bear in these mountains."

Levi snorted. "No way. No one's seen Boris since I did on that fishing trip."

"It was him. Must be a tough summer because he was thinner than I remember. Maybe only nine hundred pounds. Maybe a half ton."

I cringed. Anyone who lived in the mountains saw black bears because they were so numerous, but they were far smaller than C.J. described. In my own life, truth be told—not that I would have done that at this table—the biggest bear I had ever seen was half the size of the legendary Boris. Of course, when I told and retold that particular story, I added a few pounds. No one around the table would scoff because they each had their own story of Boris. Tommy even rolled his eyes and muttered, "He has lost some weight since I ran into him up past Soco Gap."

"I wondered the same," C.J. agreed. "I thought it was one of Boris's sons or something, but then I saw the gray hair around the muzzle and the jagged scar on the side of his face. His huge claws covered the center line on the road. He turned his big head and stared at me with those eyes. His message was clear. Ain't no human going to tell ol' Boris to move."

Chip nodded. "That's for sure. When I ran into him—"

C.J. cut him off before a fresh story could interrupt. "I knew I couldn't hit him 'cause he would've totaled my ride. Damn bear—sorry, Martha—is almost as big as my little truck. I stood hard on the brake and turned the steering wheel as fast as I could. Threw ol' Purvis here bouncing around inside the cab like a rag doll. He almost went out the window."

I could feel my face burn as all eyes shifted toward me. I didn't want to sound so helpless, but I didn't want to contradict anything either. Before I could think of a retort, C.J. continued.

"The left front bumper clipped the beast—even found hairs on it last night when I got home—but it didn't hurt him at all.

He howled in anger and took a swipe at us, but I was already off the side of the road and sliding down a hill. He came crashing through the trees right on our tails. I was sure he was going to tear us limb from limb."

Abe's eyes twinkled in merriment as he leaned forward. "Did he leave claw marks on your car door like he did mine that time?"

"I saw those claw marks, and I've had hound dogs with bigger paws," C.J. said. The men erupted with laughter as Abe's face reddened, but C.J. didn't give him time to retort. "He never got to our car 'cause I yelled out my open window to back off. Told him I had had enough of a bad day and didn't want to tangle with him. I said I was sorry I had clipped him. He stood like three or four feet away, stamping those mighty paws on the ground hard enough we could feel it shake. His nostrils flared as he snorted with such force he fogged up the window."

Chip cocked his head. "I thought your window was open."

"The front window." C.J. waved his hand in dismissal. "He stood up on his back legs and roared. He was so big, he eclipsed the sun and cast this huge shadow over us. The saliva dripped off those sharp teeth as he growled and bared his fangs. I turned to Purvis here and said it was good knowing him and all 'cause I was sure we were about to meet our Maker."

The sheriff leaned forward. "What happened?"

"We came to an understanding. I mean with those scars, it's clear Mr. Boris has had a few bad days himself. He dropped down on all fours and looked both of us right in the eyes. He was breathing real heavy as he studied us." He turned to me. "That ol' guy had some foul breath, didn't he?"

What could I do? The story mesmerized me as much as everyone else. I nodded ever so slightly.

"And then a miracle happened. It was like he flipped a switch because he just decided to leave. Turned and walked away."

The sheriff rolled his eyes. "Just decided, huh?"

"Just like that." C.J. snapped his fingers. "He sauntered off to the woods, tree branches cracking as he went through."

Abe snorted. "Sauntered. I like that word."

"Well, he sure didn't run. He wasn't scared of us—that would be silly. We just came to an understanding."

The sheriff took a bite of the biscuit Danny had handed him and chewed thoughtfully. He swallowed and asked, "What does that have to do with finding Purvis's car?"

"Because when that bear went crashing through the woods—"

Abe snickered. "Sauntering."

"He pulled the branches back, and we saw this glint of metal. Once we were sure he was gone, we got out of the car, followed those bear tracks, pushed those branches back, and there it sat just as good as new."

Levi hooted. "That car ain't been as good as new in about thirty years."

I leaned forward to protest, but Harlow interrupted with a question. "Do you think the bear was the thief?"

Once the laughter died down, C.J. shook his head. "Of course not. I wouldn't make up something silly like that."

Tommy rolled his eyes. "No, of course you wouldn't."

"The sheriff was right. It was probably just some kids out funning, and they didn't really do no harm to the car. They made a mess of things rifling through the glove compartment —lost his registration and everything—but Purvis didn't think they stole nothing except his license plate. They didn't mess the engine up because it started right away. We just had to get it and my truck back up on the road. That took a while and some really expert mountain driving, but soon enough, we were good to go. Ain't that right, Purv?"

I searched the faces around the table, trying to decide who believed the tale and who didn't. If I had been a listener, I would've guessed the bear wasn't real or was just a normal-size bear, but I would've believed the part about finding the car on the side of the road. After all, it was parked out front, so they wouldn't suspect that part of the story. I decided to go with C.J.'s lead. "That's about it, though I think next time I'll toss ol' Boris some breath mints."

Everyone laughed, a sign of appreciation for a well-told story. Even the sheriff was smiling with them. "Well, I guess it's a good thing you never did that report, Purvis. Now I don't have any paperwork to close out."

The sheriff sipped his coffee and waited for the men to quiet down. "I think Preacher Brawley is going to have a good story to tell too."

My heart skipped a beat at the mention of the reverend. When I had arrived for breakfast, C.J. was already seated at the table and wolfing down his food, so I hadn't had a chance to tell him what I had done the night before. He leaned back in his chair, folded his hands across his belly, and asked the sheriff, "Now, how can a preacher man top a story about a bear finding a stolen car?"

The sheriff grinned with confidence. "He called me early this morning with quite a find. He checked that donation box they have out front for their mission work, and someone had stuck one of those plastic garbage bags in there filled with cash."

My stomach burned with acid, and I lost my appetite. Of all the things I had thought the reverend might do, calling the sheriff hadn't even popped into my mind. Maybe that was because it was the last thing I would have done.

Harlow grunted. "So someone did a bake sale or something and dropped off the cash all anonymous like. What's such a big deal about that?"

The sheriff leveled a stare at him. "I've never heard of a bake sale raising over a hundred thousand dollars."

I felt C.J.'s eyes burning into the side of my head. I shrank down in the seat and did my best to ignore him.

Levi whistled low. "A hundred grand? Who around here has that kind of money?"

The sheriff grew serious. "That was why Preacher Brawley called me. He worried it might be dirty money, maybe a bank robbery, or drug money, or something else like that, so he wanted to make sure it was okay to keep."

Frustration bubbled up. I had taken the time to write that note, and it hadn't worked at all. I meant to just think it, but instead the words came out of my mouth. "It's just cash. What does it matter where it came from?"

The sheriff turned his gaze toward me. "If it's stolen, it's got to go back to the victim. If it's drug money, then that might be different. We certainly wouldn't give it back to drug dealers. But we'll hold it and see if we can figure out where it came from."

"You mean you confiscated it?"

"No, not exactly. We do have it, locked up down in the evidence lockers to keep it safe, but Preacher Brawley gave it to us voluntarily. He said he couldn't do God's work with it if it belonged to someone else, so we promised to investigate and let him know. If we can't find the rightful owner, we'll probably give it back to him."

I couldn't help asking, "How long will that take?"

The sheriff shrugged. "Weeks, at least. Don't worry, though, it's nice and safe. No one can get to it there without going through a bunch of hoops. I can't even just go get it."

"WHY DID you give Reverend Brawley the money?"

We stood in the parking lot in front of Abe's Market. After a few more stories had been traded and breakfast consumed, the men of the Liars' Table scattered about town for the rest of the day—Ronnie to his job and the rest to the important tasks they claimed to have or the errands they said they needed to run. The real plan, though, could well be to head home to a hammock under some shade trees, a rocking chair on a porch, or a recliner in an air-conditioned den. Once the others had driven off, C.J.'s smile slipped off his face.

I leaned back against my car, without a single bear claw mark or scratch from brush, and crossed my arms. "Because I trust him. He comes out regularly to the nursing home to visit Shelby. Teresa tells me. It doesn't matter that I don't go to Sunday service or tithe like I'm supposed to—he still visits her. That's how I know he's an honorable man because he does the right thing even though there is nothing in it for him."

C.J. chewed on the side of his cheek and looked up at the sun. After a few minutes of thought, he said, "Yeah, he is, but maybe too honest."

That stung, but he was right. "I didn't think he would call the sheriff."

"We could have done it. You and me." He adjusted the straps of his overalls. "We know everybody around here who needs some help. We could've slipped little envelopes with cash in people's mailboxes. We could've paid some doctor bills so people got treatment they needed or covered some heating bills this winter so some kid doesn't shiver. Maybe we could've put some teenager down at the high school in a drug treatment program like the one Wyatt did. Small amounts so no one would get suspicious like Brawley did."

"You don't think word would've gotten around about that?"

"Sure, but it would've been like the stories we tell at breakfast. Rumors would fly around about who got the money. We'd know if some people didn't mention it. Others would claim to have gotten something when we didn't give them any. It could've been fun."

"But all those stories would have caught the sheriff's attention too."

"I don't think so. No one would've known what to believe, so why would the sheriff get suspicious? And even if he did, about what? No crime in giving people a little money."

C.J. was right, of course; we could have done it. We probably could have gotten away with it. Dealing with that money, though, for all the time it would have taken, was too much to bear. "I just couldn't have it near me. Knowing where it came from."

He finally turned and looked at me. "Because of Jessica and Wyatt?"

I nodded.

"I get that." C.J. looked up at the mountain ridges, buying himself time to think, and heaved a heavy sigh. "But you should've told me before you did it."

"Yeah, I should have." Eager to extract myself from the conversation, I fumbled my car keys out of my pocket. I opened the driver's door, but paused before getting in. "You should've told me you were going to make up that cockamamie story. Who's going to believe that crazy thing?"

C.J. smiled and shrugged. "That's the point. Everyone thinks we just stumbled across the car on the side of the road somewhere just like the sheriff figured, and we embellished the story of finding it a little bit. The sheriff isn't going to waste time looking for some high school kids joyriding. No one is going to wonder how you got your car back. No harm done, no questions asked."

Made sense. I settled into his driver's seat. "You're probably right."

"Of course I am." C.J.'s face beamed with pride. "You gotta admit, it was a good story. Those guys are going to remember it for a long time."

24

The steeple loomed as I approached my turn toward the house. I had never been a particularly religious person— an on-again off-again churchgoer who had been in the off phase since Shelby got sick. Even if I didn't go in the building as often as I should, though, the familiar sight of that cross high up in the air normally comforted me.

Now it mocked me. The decision I had made the night before had been hasty. Like so many things in my life, I hadn't thought through all the possible consequences. C.J. had long joked with me that I might be book smart, but I lacked common sense. I could tell you about every book that Jack London ever wrote—could quote long passages in most of them—but I wouldn't survive a day in the wilds of Alaska. Nor, much more realistically, the wilds of the Appalachian Mountains.

I hadn't connected in my mind that an honest man like Reverend Brawley was exactly too honest to accept the money without question. I needed to slow down, to think, to figure out what was around the bend.

Start with the sheriff. What would he do next? Wouldn't

deputies spread out and knock on doors of the houses near the church? We were an isolated community in an isolated town. Only a dozen or so families lived out our road. What could my neighbors tell them? There had been nothing to see or hear.

Except for a blacked-out car stopping in front of the church.

My pulse accelerated as I thought about the stupidity of driving down our gravel road with the headlights out. My very act of trying to be inconspicuous could have attracted attention instead. Maybe they would have thought it was just a teenager sneaking out for the night, forgotten about it, and moved on, but if a deputy asked if they saw anything suspicious, alarm bells might have gone off.

"Come to think of it, Deputy, I did see something odd. A car sneaking down the road, lights off like he didn't want to be seen."

"Did he do anything else unusual, ma'am?"

"Why, yes, now that you mention it, that car reached the main road, turned around, and stopped right in front of that church."

Stupid, stupid, stupid.

So what? Maybe someone had seen a car, but no way they'd been close enough to identify me. No houses were close except the parsonage, and the preacher would have told the sheriff if he saw me. He probably would have just come down and asked me himself what I thought I was doing. All they had was a car. Unless...

"Then, deputy, that car came back down our road and turned in to Purvis Webb's house."

I wiped the sweat off my palms and thought about that for a moment. If my neighbors had seen a car pull into my driveway without its lights on, they would've called. Asked if everything was okay. We might not all be best friends, but we did look out for each other. We didn't take kindly to burglars out here. So they had absolutely no way to connect me to the money.

I sat up straight and looked at the white clapboard building. I could be identified if that place had cameras.

Did churches have surveillance cameras? In the old days, no one would have thought such a thing, but the world had become a sinister place. Churches weren't immune from crime and violence.

Down in Charleston, that crazy racist kid sat with a bible study group before shooting nine people to death. I'd heard plenty of stories of brazen thieves sneaking in and stealing from purses or offering plates. Some churches had even hired armed security guards.

Not in Miller County, though. Those things didn't happen here.

But Brawley was a smart guy. He would think of the possibility. Since I hadn't been active in the church, I wouldn't have known if such things had been talked about. Maybe the police already had grainy footage of me slinking up to the door and sliding that trash bag into the contribution box.

With shaking hands, I turned the car onto the gravel road and eyed the church. No deputies searched the grounds. A couple of cars sat in the parking lot, but I didn't know whose they were. The minister's car was parked at the parsonage, but that didn't mean he was there. He walked to the church most days since it was so close. None of the vehicles looked like law enforcement.

I scanned the walls for signs of cameras. Nothing was noticeable, not even in the shadows under the eaves overhanging the doors. Those things were so small that maybe I couldn't see them from the road, but I didn't think the church had any.

Get a grip. Relax.

Neither the reverend nor the sheriff had any reason to

suspect I was involved. The only other person who knew anything about the money was C.J.

And Bobby.

The police would have no reason to ask him anything, but what if Bobby heard rumors? How long would it take him to connect the dots between a surprise donation to the church and my contribution to the nursing home? Would he call the sheriff or ask me?

And even if signs pointed to me, would the police suspect me or Wyatt? Would Wyatt get into trouble for something he knew nothing about?

Stop it.

I brought the car to a halt in the middle of the dirt road and leaned my forehead against the steering wheel. Thinking things through to the possible conclusions seemed more exhausting than it was worth.

What if the police figured things out and came to me? What would happen if I just told them the truth? C.J. could confirm my story. Maybe it would be embarrassing to admit what I had done. Maybe it was even wrong to have given the money to the nursing home. But it really wasn't that big a deal. I just needed to let things flow and see where they went.

With that resolved in my head, my body relaxed, and my breathing slowed. I aimed the car down the dirt road and started moving again. The sun felt warm on my skin with my arm hanging out the window of the car. The afternoon would be August hot, but under the shade trees, my yard would be comfortable for stretching out in the hammock. Belle would sprawl in the grass and snore. We could enjoy the afternoon breeze rolling off the nearby mountains and forget this craziness. I would go have dinner with Shelby. Maybe the TV would be working in the dayroom.

A glint of chrome flashed in the sunlight ahead of me. I

lifted my foot off the accelerator and squinted. A car was parked in my driveway.

Wyatt should be at work and shouldn't be home for hours. He would only be here if something had happened to Shelby, but the nursing home would have called me first. As much as I hated lugging around a cell phone, I did it just in case something happened to her.

Preacher Brawley? The sheriff? Fine. Let's get this over with.

With shaking hands, I turned into my driveway. A beat-up Ford Explorer was parked in my spot under the shade tree. It wasn't the sheriff. Or the reverend.

Confused, I pulled in beside the Explorer and got out of my car. Belle came up to me, her tail wagging slowly. I reached down to scratch behind the dog's ears. She sniffed my pants legs and then walked over to a grass patch, squatted, and peed.

Wait. What is she doing out?

I turned to call her when the license plate on the Explorer registered in my brain. A Tennessee plate.

A voice from behind me called out, "Not much of a watch dog, is she, old man?"

The tattooed man stood inside my house in the shadows of my kitchen.

25

The screen door squeaked open, and the tattooed man stepped out onto the porch. Behind him, my door frame was splintered where the lock used to be. A boot print was clearly visible beside the doorknob. I debated running, but I wouldn't get far. Besides, my feet were frozen to the ground. I expected yelling, but he spoke in a quiet, measured tone that scared me even more. "Nice car."

As he came down the steps, he extracted a crumpled pack from his pants pocket and tapped out a cigarette. He flicked his thumb on a plastic lighter, touched the flame to the tobacco, and inhaled deeply. He held his breath for several seconds and then blew a stream of smoke high into the air, his actions much like they had been the day before. As the smoke dissipated, he pointed at the car with the two fingers holding the cigarette. "Is it yours?"

The question threw me off-balance. Why wasn't the first question about the money? Did the man really care about an old car? I decided to work the conversation like I did with Shelby—stay noncommittal until I knew what he knew and

182 | D. K. WALL

what he wanted. I opened my mouth to answer but discovered my throat was dry. My answer came out strained. "Yeah."

"You the one who took it from me yesterday?"

I didn't trust my voice, so I nodded and shrugged, an admission and an expression of innocence wrapped in one.

He studied me through the cigarette smoke curling in front of him. "Who was with you?"

I didn't want to involve anyone else. Whatever was coming wasn't going to change for me because I gave up others. I swallowed to clear my throat and tried to sound more confident. "Just me."

The man studied the cigarette as though the secrets of the world were contained within. His voice shifted deep, the tone resonating with menace. "That's lie number one, old man."

I tried to protest, but he shushed me. "If you were alone, how did you get over there? You didn't walk from here. And you didn't just happen to be in that parking lot and snatch it like some punk looking for a joyride. Got it?"

I nodded.

"Don't lie to me again. I don't have the patience for it. Do you feel me?"

Feel him? What a weird phrase. I hesitated.

"Out with it. Who was with you?"

"A friend."

"Here I thought it was just some stranger who gave you a ride." He took a deep draw on his cigarette as the sarcasm settled over me. "Give me a name."

I was too scared to lie, but I didn't want to tell the truth either. I decided to use C.J.'s real name, but that answer wouldn't do the tattooed man any good since nobody called him that. "C-c-c-cody."

"Is C-c-c-cody around?"

I shook my head.

The man glared at me intently, probing to see if I lied.

He must have been satisfied because his eyes finally dropped to the car. He admired it like we were standing on a used car lot, and he was considering a purchase. "How did you find it?"

"Just saw it."

He sucked so hard on the cigarette, his cheeks collapsed. The tip grew bright red, and the crackling sound of burning tobacco was loud in the summer morning. When he lowered the cigarette to his side, ashes fell to the dirt. He looked up toward the mountain ridges and exhaled slowly. His voice was quiet and even, the tension clear. "That makes the second lie, old man. Don't go for three. If you lie again, this conversation will get much less pleasant. Do you feel me?"

He really didn't seem like the touchy-feely type.

"You didn't drive all the way over to Knoxville for a day trip and accidentally stumble across your car. Somehow, someway, you knew exactly where to go." His eyes shifted back to me in a laser focus that drilled into my skull. "So let's try this once last time. How did you find it?"

I tried to think of a plausible explanation, but nothing came to me but the truth. No harm for me in the truth, and frankly, I didn't know Noah. I didn't owe him anything. If I had to blame it on him, I would, but I'd try not to give up his name if possible. I could do that much for Wyatt. "We were told where it was."

"By who?"

"A friend of my grandson's, but I don't remember his name. They were friends when my grandson lived there, but he's been living here for five years now. They don't hang out anymore, and I've never met him." Mostly the truth, except for the not remembering his name.

He squinted. "So, this friend of your grandson's, who you've never met, sees *your* car, recognizes it, thinks to call your grandson, and tell him where it is. Quite the coincidence."

It didn't sound convincing the way he said it, but I was committed to the story now. "Just luck."

"Luck?" The tattooed man picked a fleck of tobacco off his tongue and flipped it through the air. "I want to make sure I never sit at the same poker table as you."

I shrugged.

The tattooed man locked his gaze on me. "That friend of your grandson's wouldn't happen to be Noah, would it?"

So much for not giving up the name. He already knew it. What else did he already know? "Maybe. Like I said, I've never met him."

The man extinguished the cigarette under his foot and closed the distance between us faster than I expected. He reached out his hand, and I stepped back, flinching before the punch landed. But it didn't come. Instead, he smiled and ran his hand along the hood of the Nova. "Fixed up the right way, this car could rock."

Standing so close to me, his smells assaulted me. The cloak of old cigarette smoke rose from his clothes. His body smelled of sweat. His breath matched his browned teeth. I did my best not to react and waited in silence. He leaned back against the car and crossed his arms. "When I came out of that store, I was stunned. What's the possibility a car gets stolen twice in a couple of days? A fancy, expensive car maybe, but an old piece of junk? And how was I going to find it? Because I really needed to find it. Call junkyards? Chop shops?"

He let a silence settle over us as he tapped out a new cigarette. I hoped he'd smoke enough to drop dead from a heart attack. "Then I saw the diapers and cigarettes right where the car should've been. That really confused me. A thief or a couple of kids taking a joyride wouldn't have done that. Even if they'd thrown them out the window to make some room, they would never have left them in a nice, neat little pile. I mean, what kind of person does that?"

He stepped toward me, and I shrank back as far as I could. I tried to keep my voice steady as I replied, "A nice guy. Someone who wasn't trying to hurt you."

"Exactly. Only an honest person would do something like that. What kind of honest person steals a man's car? The only answer I could come up with was the guy who owned the car."

"So you thought of me?"

"No, because I had no idea who you were. I didn't steal your car. I bought it off a guy."

"Noah?"

He laughed. "Nope. Like you claim, not that I'm sure I believe you, I'd never met Noah in my life. But it turns out he owed money to the guy I bought it from. He'd given it to him to pay off his debt. My guy didn't want to be on my bad side, so he told me everything he knew about the car. Then I asked to meet this Noah character. You know what he told me?"

My breakfast rumbled in my belly, threatening to come up. The tattooed man's voice was even and steady, too much so. The calmer he remained, the more nervous I grew. I didn't trust myself to answer, so I waited.

"Noah must've been a good friend to your grandson. He didn't want to tell me where he stole it from. That made me really suspicious because why would some junkie care about the guy he stole from?" He paused in his story and sneered. "You're just like everyone else. You look at me and think I'm some idiot. I'm actually pretty good at figuring things out. Just like I realized leaving my stuff behind when you stole my car meant you were the thief, I knew that Noah was trying to protect someone. Strange to see so much loyalty in someone like him. Took quite a bit of persuasion 'til I had the truth."

I gasped. "You beat him up?"

The tattooed man burst out laughing, a hacking, guttural sound. "I was going to, but it only took a couple of hits. Yeah, he was coughing up blood when he started jabbering about how this Wyatt fellow is his old buddy, and he told him where to find the car."

"He gave you my address."

"Better than that. He gave me your registration. He kept it. Seems he thought your grandson might help get him clean someday. Because they were buddies. And suddenly everything made sense. Noah, that little lying piece of shit, stole your car and used it to pay off his debt, but then he turns around and tells you how to get it back. Very cute."

I trembled under his glare as I swallowed down bile.

"Now, let this be an important lesson for you for the rest of our time together. I don't like cute."

I had to ask. "What'd you do to Noah?"

The tattooed man looked up at the mountains. "Let's just say Noah's habit will never bother him again."

My stomach clenched in fear. "Did you k-k-kill him?"

He turned his icy eyes back on me. "Don't ask me questions you don't want the answer to, you feel me?"

Oh, I felt that.

"Now that we've reached an understanding about what I do to people who cause me problems, this should go fast. I want what's mine." The tattooed man leaned in close to my face. "Now!"

26

I pulled the keys out of my pocket and dangled them in front of the tattooed man. "The car's all yours."

He swatted my hand away. The keys went flying into the grass. "I don't want the car. I want what was in it."

I licked my lips and opened my mouth to speak. Only a squeak slipped out. I swallowed hard and tried again, my voice strained and warbling. It didn't sound like me at all. "We ate the pizza."

"Oh, you're a funny man." The smile drained off the man's face. He pointed at the car and demanded, "Open the trunk."

Earlier, I had dreaded the arrival of the sheriff or one of his deputies. Now, I was praying for them. I wanted to hear a car approaching, but nothing crunched on the gravel behind me. My knees felt weak as I answered, "There's nothing in there."

"There better be."

I didn't know what else to do. I retrieved the keys, unlocked the trunk, and let the lid float open. The man stepped forward and looked inside. His eyes grew wide, and color ebbed from his face. He bent over and reached behind the spare tire. His hand flopped around in the shadows before pulling back and reaching in from the other side. He straightened and turned slowly, inches away from my face. His breath reeked. Spittle from his lips landed on my nose. "Where's the bag?"

"What bag?"

The man's face flamed red. He grabbed my shirt front and slammed me against the car. I hadn't been in a fight since—I don't know, since almost ever. Maybe middle school. Jimmy Kinston had bloodied my nose in eighth grade. That was nothing like this. The man was wiry but strong, and he easily pinned me against the hot metal. "Where's the damn bag?"

I gasped for breath and struggled to speak. My voice squeaked as I said, "I don't have it."

He picked me up by my shirt. My feet left the ground. My heart raced. Then I was flying backward toward the car. I slammed into the metal, and my neck snapped backward. Pain fired down through my legs. My head slammed against the roof. I slid down the side of the car as my legs gave out, but he grabbed the collar of my shirt. I felt blood trickle down the back of my neck and under my T-shirt. "Last chance, old man. Where is it?"

I struggled to stand, but my legs were rubbery. He was so much stronger than me. I couldn't move. My breath wheezed out of my lungs. I choked out the words. "It's gone."

The man released his grip and took two steps back. I slid down the side of the car and crumpled to the ground. He kicked me in the gut, and all the air in my lungs raced out. I vomited on the gravel and cradled my stomach with my arms. All I could see were his shoes, but I felt his presence lean over me. "Don't play around, old man. I want... I need... it back. Every last cent." He emphasized the three words, pausing between each one. His teeth grated in anger. "Start talking."

I figured I was going to die, so I had nothing to lose. I told the truth. "I gave it away."

I heard the rustle of a cigarette pack and the flick of the lighter. The smell of tobacco smoke drifted down to me. I struggled to focus on an ant walking across the gravel. The ground swayed in my vision. His voice sounded far away. "Then we have us a real problem."

My head swirled, fear paralyzing my brain. I needed time to think. Anything. "I'll get your money back. I swear."

"My money?" A harsh laugh. "You're scared of me, aren't you?"

I tried to nod, but I wasn't sure if I did or not. The world swooned.

"I'm not the one you should fear. That money belongs to Rudy the Roach, not me."

I spit into the dirt, surprised to see a bright-red glob on the ground. I stuttered, "R-R-Rudy the Roach? That's a name? Why do you have his money?"

He looked at me as if it was none of my business, but he answered anyway. "I'm a collector. I gather money from people who owe him and deliver it."

I lay on the ground, sucking in desperately needed air. My mind swirled in confusion, trying to come up with something to say, something to get me out of this, but instead it kept picking at a detail. My former job where I managed inventory came to my mind. "But why do you still have it? Driving around with it hidden in a car? You weren't collecting when we followed you."

He spun and glared at me. The answer was obvious to me, and I couldn't stop the thought from slipping out of my mouth. "You were stealing that money."

"Watch it, old man." Then his glare faded into a resigned look, and he shrugged. "I'm tired. I've got kids. You don't retire from what I do."

"And you had a car he didn't know about." I wondered aloud as everything became clearer to me. "You planned to disappear with your family before he figured out you were late turning in the money."

He squatted so that we were on the same level. "Great plan, until you came along. That dude will put a bullet in my brain himself. Do you feel me?"

I nodded.

"In case you think this gives you some big advantage, ask yourself if I'll tell him you took it if that gives me just the slightest chance I might live? Or do you think I'll keep my mouth shut and take your bullet? I'm probably dead either way, but I'll take you to hell with me, old man."

I was too paralyzed with fear to answer.

"Now you understand the situation. I need to know who has the money. We're going to pay him a visit."

I tried to sit up, but the man stood and placed his foot on my shoulder. He shoved.

I fell backward and looked up at the towering opponent. "The sheriff."

"The... Why does the..." The man cursed under his breath and walked several steps away. "Don't tell me. I don't care. How're you going to go get it back?"

I sat up and leaned my back against the car. My head pounded, and blood soaked my collar. Even though he had removed his foot, I wasn't sure I could stand. I was sure I couldn't handle any more beating. If I died, this man would just wait on Wyatt to come home. I needed to get him out of here before that happened. The only way I could do that was to agree. "I can. I'll have to convince the preacher it's mine, then he'll call the sheriff and get it back. It's the only way."

"The preacher? What...?" The man clenched his fists and looked toward the sky. "Never mind. Just go do it. I'll wait here."

"No." I swallowed and licked my lips. "I've got to clean up. He'll be suspicious of the blood, and he can't think anything weird is going on. I'll meet you with it."

The man thought about it. "Okay, I'll give you until three o'clock, but I don't want to come all the way out here again. You live in the damned boondocks. We meet out by the interstate, but not the truck stop. Too many cameras."

"Three? I need more time. Tomorrow."

"Tonight. My clock's ticking. I can't let Rudy figure things out. I've got to be on the road with my family far away from Knoxville before that happens." He pointed his finger. "Tonight."

I knew asking the preacher was a long shot. The man would ask lots of questions, and then he would still need to convince the sheriff to give back the money. If he failed, I was dead. Shelby would be alone. I needed to have one last dinner with her. I needed to hug Wyatt goodbye and tell him to disappear. I forced myself to look the tattooed man in the eye. "Nine o'clock."

"Nine?" The man screamed.

"The picnic area at Coogan's Cove. No cameras. And it's right off the interstate, so you can get home easily."

"A picnic area? Tourists will be there."

"Not at sunset. There's a trail in the back fishermen use to get down to the Pigeon River. No one will be back there that late."

The man chewed on his thumb. He appeared to be calculating in his mind. "Okay. See you at nine. Bring the money." He shoved me hard, knocking me flat on my back. The clouds above me spun, and the ground became wavy. I watched the tattooed man's shoes walk away from me, his words floating through the buzz in my brain. "Don't even think about not showing. Do you understand? If you don't show up, remember I know where you live. I'll tell Rudy the Roach even if it's the last thing I ever do. If you think you're scared of me, you ain't seen nothing. That man will kill you, but he'll do it slow. And he'll do that grandson of yours and your Cody friend. Do you feel me, old man?"

I coughed and muttered, "I feel you."

27

"Hey, buddy, you okay?"

A hand slid under my back and lifted me to a sitting position. I leaned against my kitchen cabinets, though that confused me because I didn't remember coming inside. I tried to open my eyes to make sense of what I was seeing and feeling but slammed them shut as the light pounded into my brain. The floor wobbled underneath me. The memory of some danger flickered in my mind, but I couldn't quite place it. "Is Belle okay?"

"She's fine. Was lying in the floor with you when I got here."

I tried to reach out to stroke her fur, but my hand didn't seem to be fully under control. I could see it, sense it, but I couldn't make it move the way I wanted. It flailed about at the end of my arm until a raspy tongue licked my fingers. Knowing she was fine lifted a weight of fear off me. The tension melted from my muscles and allowed me to focus on me.

I took a deep breath and steadied my nerves. With trepidation, I peeled my eyes open again until a sliver of daylight slid in. It didn't burn into my head the way it had a moment earlier. The spinning of the room slowed. My vision focused on the larger man squatted in front of me. I didn't understand how, but C.J. had known I was in trouble and came for me.

When I tried to speak my gratitude, nothing came out. My throat burned. My mouth was parched. Saliva had abandoned me. Nothing allowed me to swallow and soothe the pain. I coughed, winced, and choked out the words, "I must have passed out or something."

The concerned look on his face amplified. "Passed out? More like knocked out. Someone kicked in your door. Was it a burglar? Did you get a look at them? Do you know who it was?"

"Not a burglar. Not exactly." I raised a shaking hand and wiped my forehead. With some relief, I looked at it and realized it was wet with sweat, not blood.

"Doesn't matter. I'm calling an ambulance." C.J. crossed the room to the telephone on the wall, an old-fashioned rotary that made Wyatt chuckle.

Cell phones worked better than they used to in the rural parts of the county. I carried one, but I couldn't give up my old landline. Storms knocked out power, and weather disrupted cell towers, but the phone line always worked. If the nursing home needed to get through in the middle of the night, I needed to be reachable.

Why buy a cheap, Chinese-made piece of plastic to replace my rotary phone just because it had buttons? It might be faster to punch numbers rather than wait on a rotary to spin back into position, but you couldn't destroy that old Ma Bell hunk of machinery. It would be working long after I was gone.

C.J. lifted the handset, stuck a finger into the nine on the dial and spun. Upon his release, the receiver clicked as it returned to position, a sound reminding me of the crinkling of the cigarette pack. The tattooed man's visit flooded back into my mind. So did his threat and the looming deadline.

I couldn't go to the hospital. They would keep me all day— probably overnight. I wouldn't get the money back. I would miss the meeting at Coogan's Cove. Wyatt would be here in the house all alone when the tattooed man came back.

"Hang up."

With his hand on the dial to spin the last one, C.J. turned with an incredulous look on his face. "Why?"

"I don't need an ambulance. I'm okay."

"No, you're not. I don't know what happened here, but you need a doc. Your head's busted open and needs stitches. You've got blood on the back of your shirt. You can try to tell me all day that you fell, but I don't buy it. You need to go to the hospital, and we need to call the sheriff."

"I didn't fall." I shook my head and instantly regretted it. Pain flared up along my neck. I rested my face in my hands. The room grayed. I fought to stay conscious. "I was pushed."

"Pushed? So it was a burglar. Did you recognize him?"

"Wasn't a burglar. It was the tattooed man."

C.J. looked at the phone on the wall. I could see his internal debate, the way his eyes flickered back and forth and his lips moved. "The who?"

"From yesterday. The guy we took the car from."

I could only pray he would hang up since I couldn't stop him. I couldn't even stand up. Reluctantly, he lowered the handset into the cradle. He rested his hand on the phone and stood still. I held my breath until he pushed away from the wall and crouched beside me.

"He was in the house?"

Careful not to move too fast, I nodded. My stomach flopped. I closed my eyes and swallowed back the bile that rose in my throat, begging myself not to vomit again. When I thought I could continue, I reopened my eyes. C.J.'s worried face loomed. "Waiting for me. He shoved me against the car. My head hit. Then he pushed me to the ground. He left me lying in the driveway."

C.J. looked out the screen door at my car parked in the drive. "How did you get inside?"

"I... I don't remember. I guess I crawled."

He chewed his lip in thought. "The man assaulted you. He needs to be arrested. Tell me why I shouldn't call the sheriff."

"We can't. He wants his money back. Tonight. If I don't meet him with it, he's going to come back."

"All the more reason to get the law involved. Once he's arrested, it's over."

I shook my head and instantly regretted it. My vision clouded over as pain pulsed around my skull. "It wasn't his money. Belongs to some guy called Rudy the Roach."

"What a stupid name."

"Feel free to tell him that. You'll get the chance because the sheriff can't arrest the roach monster because he's got nothing on him. He will come looking for his money even if the tattooed man is locked up."

He sat back on his haunches. The only sound in the room was Belle's panting as C.J. studied the wood planks on the floor. "How did he find you?"

"Noah. The guy who stole the car, the guy who called Wyatt, he kept the registration. Gave him the address. And then the tattooed man killed Noah. That's the people we're dealing with."

C.J. stood and crossed to the kitchen sink. He soaked a rag under the tap and dabbed the back of my head. I caught glimpses of the bright-red blood soaking into the cloth as he cleaned the wound as best he could, tsking as he went. When he was done, I gingerly touched the knot and winced. I withdrew my hand and stared at the spots of blood on my fingertips. It hurt, but my mind was clearing.

"How did you know to come out here?"

He leaned against the wall. "After you drove off this morning, I started thinking about you giving that money to Brawley. I wanted you to know I understood why you did it. That I wasn't mad or nothing. I called, both your cell and your home, and when you didn't answer…" He shrugged as his voice faded away.

We'd talked about it before when we were in a melancholy mood—the horror of dying alone. Maybe that was why we all gathered around that Liars' Table every morning, a sort of a senior citizen roll call to ensure we had all made it through the night. If someone didn't show, we would make light of it, but someone would inevitably swing by their house. Just to visit, of course, at least officially. If they needed help, calls would be made. If they were already beyond help, different calls would be made. It was the least we could do for each other.

But I wasn't dead yet. Right now, I wanted to get off the floor. I motioned with my arm, and C.J. helped me to my feet and over to the kitchen table. He got me settled in a chair and poured a glass of ice water. When he joined me at the table, I wrapped my hand around his wrist and said, "Thanks."

He dismissed my gratitude with a flip of his wrist and asked, "What's the plan?"

"Only thing I can think of is to go see Preacher Brawley and see if he can get the money back from the sheriff. What else can we do?"

He scratched the side of his head. "Maybe your grandson has got a better idea."

I didn't want Wyatt involved. He had worked too hard to extract himself from that life. He didn't need to be forced back into it. The tattooed man, and whoever this Roach was, were exactly what he needed to avoid. "Let's keep him out of it."

"Too late. He's on his way."

"But—"

"When you didn't answer, I panicked. I called him to see if you were with him. When he said no, I said I'd come out here and check. He said he would meet me."

"Call him back. Tell him it's nothing. He shouldn't miss work."

"You and Shelby are all the family that boy has. I couldn't stop him if I tried."

I wiped my hand across my mouth. My mind, already fuzzy from the assault, raced for a story that would convince Wyatt to go back to work and stay out of this mess. "Let's just tell him I fell. Maybe something I ate made me weak. I'll promise to schedule a doctor's appointment. You're here, so no need for him to stay."

C.J. gestured to the door. "How do you explain that? Or the blood on your shirt? He's going to take one look at you and probably carry you over his shoulder to the hospital."

I struggled for a plausible explanation that might work, but the sound of gravel crunching under tires floated through the screen door. C.J. looked outside and confirmed it was too late. "He's here."

28

A car door slammed. Boots clomped up the front steps and across the porch. The screen door squeaked open. Wyatt stepped into the shadows of the kitchen. His eyes locked onto mine. I tried to sit up straight in the kitchen chair, my best effort to convince him everything was fine.

"Grandpa—"

"I'm fine."

He crossed the room, chattering with relief. "Thank God. When you didn't answer your phone, and C.J. said he couldn't reach you, I had the worst thoughts. Pictured you face down in the yard with a heart attack or something."

"I'm fine, really. I must've been out in the yard when you called the home phone. I left my cell in the bathroom, never heard it ring. Sorry to scare you like that. Go back to work."

He looked over at the sink and the wet washcloth stained with my blood. His eyes grew wide, and he walked around me, examining my wounds. He gently touched the back of my head and stared at the tacky blood on the tips of his fingers. The color drained out of his face. His voice was low and serious. "What happened?"

I focused on getting him out of the house so C.J. and I could figure out a solution, so I tried to wave him off. "Wasn't feeling real good. Maybe it was something I ate. I passed out and must've hit my head. Not a big deal."

"Passing out isn't a big deal?"

That sounded weak. "Maybe it's a little bit of a big deal, but I'll call the doctor and make an appointment. Have him run all those blasted tests those vampires like to do."

He looked at C.J. for answers, but my friend was doing his best to find something on the ceiling to study. "What did you hit your head on?"

I stammered with an answer. "I don't know. Don't remember. Maybe the counter."

Wyatt's eyes flicked around the room. In his hurry to make sure I was okay, he hadn't taken in the details, but now he saw everything. His mouth opened into a little o as his gaze settled on the crack running up the middle of the front door. The thud of his boots on the kitchen floor echoed in my head as he crossed the room and ran his hand across the shattered door frame at the latch. He dragged the toe of his work boots through the pieces of wood scattered about the kitchen floor. The sunlight highlighted the clear outline of a boot print beside the doorknob, the tread sharp against the faded white paint. He traced it with his finger. His face clouded with fury as he asked, "Did you fall against the door too? Are you going to tell me you had a shoe on your head, and it made this print?"

I exchanged a glance with C.J., hoping for inspiration for a better story, but nothing came from him. I opened my mouth, closed it, and then shrugged.

Wyatt covered the gap between us and leaned over the kitchen table until his nose was only inches from mine, like a parent scolding a wayward child. "Out with it. What really happened?" When I started to answer, he issued a stern warning. "Don't even try one of your cockamamie stories on me. No more lies. I want the truth. Who was it?"

What choice did I have? I let the whole story flow. About searching the car at the rest area and finding the money. About debating with myself what the right thing to do was. About dropping the money in the church's donation box. About the sheriff telling us about the reverend turning the money over to the police. About coming home and the confrontation with the tattooed man. About my plan to get the money back and deliver it at Coogan's Cove.

I left out only one detail, about giving the money for supplies at the nursing home. The rest of the tale sounded innocent. Stupid, but innocent. If I could get the money back from Bobby, then neither Wyatt nor C.J. would ever have to know about that part. Bobby had said he would go slow to not attract attention, so he probably still had the money locked up there in the shop. I would get it back when I went to the nursing home to have dinner with Shelby and add it to the pile.

When I finished with my tale, I leaned back in my chair and listened to the silence in the kitchen. C.J. remained as still as a statue. Wyatt stared at the ceiling, what he normally did when he was thinking through things. When he lowered his gaze, he asked, "And Noah?"

I shook my head.

Wyatt clenched his hand into a fist and squeezed his eyes shut. When he opened them again, he said, "It's not safe for you to go alone tonight."

My gut clenched. This was why I hadn't wanted to include Wyatt in the first place. "No. I don't want you involved."

"Too late. I already am. I was the second I met Noah at the truck stop."

C.J.'s chair squeaked as he shifted his weight. "So we call the sheriff, right?"

Wyatt looked down at his hands. "I don't think we should.

These guys are dangerous. If we don't give them the money, they won't stop looking. They won't just go away. And they won't be bothered by some small-town sheriff. That would just buy us some time before they killed us."

An eyebrow shot up on C.J.'s face. "I thought you said drug dealers didn't really kill anybody. That was just in the movies."

Wyatt sighed and raised his head. "I said the dealers, the guys on the street, don't usually kill their customers. Debts there are so small, it's not worth it." Wyatt pointed at the shattered door. "But this ain't a couple hundred dollars. A hundred grand is killing money."

I rested my head in my hands. "He'll kill me if I don't give it back."

"Not just you." Wyatt leaned across the table. "Everybody who helped you. He'll kill C.J. He'll kill me. He might just kill the preacher and the sheriff."

"The preacher?" Numbness crept through my body. "You really think the tattooed man would kill that many people?"

"I don't know him." Wyatt turned his head to look out the screen door. "But Rudy the Roach would. And he'd sleep like a baby after doing it."

I touched Wyatt's hand with a trembling finger. "You know who that is?"

Wyatt's tongue ran along his lips. "Never met him, but I sure as hell heard of him. That's enough."

29

"Purvis Webb and Cody Joe Duncan. Now there's two faces I haven't seen inside this church in way too long." The imposing figure of Reverend Jacob Brawley leaned back in his chair and cupped his hands behind his head. The tall, solid man with close-cropped black hair sprinkled with gray wore a jet-black suit, a crisp white shirt, and a bright-red tie. His voice boomed in the office, just a hint of the power it had from the pulpit on Sunday mornings.

The office was simple. A desk, a couple of mismatched chairs for visitors, and a modest chair for him. A pair of degrees hung slightly askew on one of the few sections of exposed wall. The rest of the room was taken up by a variety of bookcases of different sizes and colors filled to overflowing with books. I scanned the titles and noticed they were primarily scholarly religious texts, though some were in languages I didn't recognize. Maybe some were Latin, though I certainly wouldn't have any way of knowing for sure.

When C.J. had called the church earlier to ask for a meeting, the minister was doing rounds at the hospital and wasn't expected back for the day. Only after begging the secretary had we secured an appointment, but not until four in the afternoon, leaving us a narrow window for success.

C.J. and Wyatt asked me repeatedly what I planned to say, how I planned to convince Brawley to get the money back, but my head hurt too much to talk. I lay in the hammock with an ice pack as the two of them nervously paced the yard. Belle wasn't happy with any of us for disturbing her afternoon nap as we waited for the time to pass.

We arrived at the church a few minutes before four, but the minister was running late. We waited for a nerve-wracking half hour but were finally face-to-face with the preacher. We didn't have time for small talk, so I jumped straight to the issue at hand. "I need to confess."

"Confession is good for the soul, my son."

"More than that, Preacher." I took a deep breath and plunged ahead. "The money in your donation box last night— I'm the one who dropped that off."

The minister's chair squeaked as he leaned forward. "Is that right?"

"Yes, sir, and I need it back."

The reverend's piercing blue eyes bored through me, searching my face for the truth. He leaned forward, placed his elbows on the broad desk, and folded his hands together as if in prayer. He touched one finger to his lips and spoke quietly. "You can imagine the wonder I have about how you came into such an impressive sum of money." He snapped his fingers. "Now how much was it?"

"One hundred nineteen thousand five hundred dollars." Out of the corner of my eye, I saw the questioning look from C.J. I had never mentioned the money I used at the nursing home, so he had expected a different answer.

"A number the sheriff no doubt said to all you fellows sitting around Abe's store, swapping gossip like you do every morning."

"No, sir, he only said over a hundred grand. And we don't gossip." I shook it off. Didn't matter right now. My only job was to convince Brawley to help us. "The money was in a black trash bag. The bills were bundled in those color bands the banks use. Three of the bundles were ten thousand each, made up of hundreds."

"Still details the sheriff might have said in his desire to court votes from you fellows."

"Except if you ask, you will find he never said that." I looked over at C.J. to make sure he was still backing me up. I was about to reveal another detail I hadn't shared with him. "A handwritten note was included, scribbled on the back of an envelope from the electric company. I told you to make sure the money went to those who needed it most. If you want, I can write that out so you can see it was my chicken scratch."

Brawley nodded slowly and leaned back in his chair, apparently satisfied with my answers. C.J.'s glare burned into the side of my head, so I guessed he wasn't satisfied, but I could deal with that later. The minister asked, "Do you want to tell me how you came into that kind of money? That's a lot of hard-earned dollars to stuff into your mattress or bury in your backyard."

"It wasn't hard-earned, which is why I didn't want it. I…" I nodded my head toward C.J. "We found it, and it would've been wrong of us to keep it."

"I see." He steepled his hands again, tapping the index fingers together in thought. "If it's wrong of you to keep it, why do you want it back?"

"We don't. The owner does. When I dropped it in that box out front, I didn't know who it belonged to. Now I do. I need to give it back to him."

"I see," he repeated, still tapping those impossibly long fingers. "And did he earn this money in a respectable manner?

My experience is people who carry large sums of cash are rarely the most godlike people."

I had expected this question and planned to lie in my answer, but I couldn't bring myself to do it. If Brawley didn't trust me, he wouldn't give me the money. "I wish it wasn't true, but he is decidedly not a godlike person."

"And would that have anything to do with the fresh bruises on your face?"

I paused and touched my cheeks and nose. I hadn't thought about how I looked and wasn't sure how to answer. "He was persuasive."

"Hmmmm." Tap. Tap. Tap. "So the money came from devilish means?"

I shrugged. "I don't actually know, but I suspect so. But it's not my job to judge, right, Reverend?"

"No, of course not. But it is my job to protect my flock from all sorts of dangers. Is this man here in Miller County? Do his money-making opportunities tempt our citizens?"

"No, sir, he's from out of state. If I give him the money, he goes back to where he came from and leaves us alone. That's all I want."

"Fair enough." Tap. Tap. Tap. "How much of this should I tell our good sheriff in order to get the money back? The whole reason I gave it to him was because I was afraid it was tainted by evil. Now you are telling me my worst fears are true. You can surely see my quandary."

"Yes, sir, but I think you can see my quandary as well. I gave you money that wasn't mine to give, so you could say I stole it. Unintentionally, but it happened, and I need to return it. The sheriff's involvement could complicate things, so I would appreciate it if you would tell the sheriff as little as possible."

"You want me to lie?"

"No, sir. Just maybe not tell him everything."

"Mr. Webb, I'm sure you understand how a man in my position might consider withholding information akin to lying."

I couldn't argue the definition of sin with a man of the cloth, but nor could I afford the delay that involving the sheriff would mean. I looked Brawley in the eye. "Isn't something said in confession sacred? You can't just share it with the police?"

"Not quite." He smiled. "But I work hard to keep my confidences and try to do the right thing at the same time."

"When I give this man his money, he will leave the sheriff's jurisdiction—and our community—and not come back. That seems to be the right thing for us. The sooner we get that done, the sooner we can all relax."

Tap. Tap. Tap. Brawley's eyes twinkled as he leaned forward. "I tell the sheriff the true owner has been found, and I will see to it the money is returned. By doing so, I help you absolve yourself of your sin. But that, Mr. Webb, does require a penance from you."

I was dumbfounded. "A what?"

"A penance. An act you commit to repent from your sin." He nodded toward C.J. "And from you as well, Mr. Duncan. I suspect you are mightily involved despite your silence, despite your occasional looks of shock that I can only assume implies Mr. Webb knows a bit more than you. If you didn't have a role in this, you wouldn't be sitting here."

C.J. and I exchanged glances and shrugged shoulders. What else could we do? I asked, "And what would our penance be?"

"The only way you can truly repent is to be here in the house of our Lord, am I right? Something the two of you have been most lacking in the last few years. Both of you used to be quite regular in attendance, I suspect because your wives cared more about your souls than you do. When your wife died, Mr. Duncan, and your wife fell ill, Mr. Webb, your attendance—oh, let's say—slipped. Quite dramatically. That needs to change."

"You want us to come to church?"

C.J. spoke up. "Both of us?"

"All three of you, because young Wyatt needs guidance, too, I am sure. Each and every Sunday. And not in the back, but down toward the front, so I can see your eager faces." He placed his hand on the desk telephone. "Do we have a deal?"

At that point, I would have promised anything, so I nodded.

Brawley smiled and dialed the phone. "Sheriff Newman, I have excellent news. The donor of that money has come forward and identified himself, though he wishes to remain anonymous to the community. He has provided me explicit instructions on its dispensation. I've become convinced his plan is to the benefit of the community—therefore I would like to get those funds back forthwith."

For a man who didn't approve of lying, his explanation was about the smoothest thing I had ever heard.

The preacher listened intently on the phone and smiled. "No, sir, you know I can't do that. A man trying to do the right thing doesn't need everyone knowing his business."

After listening a bit longer, he said, "I understand. I'll be by your office then and pick it up."

He hung up the phone and spread his hands wide. "You can relax. It's all arranged."

I leaned back in my chair and exhaled. Relief flowed through my body. "Thank you. That's such good news."

"Now, if you'll stop by around ten tomorrow morning, I'll have it ready for you."

All the air in the room evaporated. I struggled to find my voice. "Tomorrow? Can't it happen today?"

"Oh, no, gentlemen. The sheriff secured the money in the evidence lockers."

"He can't just get it out of there?"

"No. First of all, you're assuming he's at the office, which he isn't. That was his cell phone I called. But second, he must manage the property records carefully because the lawyers eat that chain of custody stuff up, so they have strict rules for access. He will direct his team to prepare the proper paperwork, but it's the end of the workday. He will pull it first thing tomorrow. Keeps it all neat and legal, which I'm sure is quite important to all of us."

30

"Now what?"

C.J.'s question echoed in my head as I stood next to Wyatt in my driveway, my hands shoved in the pockets of my jeans while I stared at the range of mountains surrounding the valley. Those looming peaks had smothered me as a child, a barrier preventing me from escaping to the wider world. Adventure and opportunity waited beyond them, at least it seemed like it until I left home. Once the military was done with me and I returned to Millerton, though, I began to see those barriers as keeping the bad out and our valley safe.

Like I had, Jessica left our safe haven as a teenager. Rather than being repelled by the bad in the world, though, she wallowed in it until it killed her. Bringing Wyatt back to live with us had protected the boy from some of the bad in the world and allowed him to become a decent young man. We were safe until evil, unfortunately, had slipped back into Miller County with Noah. I made the mistake of following his trail back across those ranges and brought the bad back to us again.

I needed a way to chase it away permanently. Returning the money that night would have worked, but now I was empty-handed. I could see only one path forward. To miss the meeting in Coogan's Cove would only invite the villainy to stay in our peaceful valley. To go without the money would probably result in disaster, but what choice did I have? It was the only option. "I go to Coogan's Cove. I tell the tattooed man the truth."

C.J. replied, "The truth never entertained anyone. I'd rather make up a good lie."

"You're the storyteller. If you have a suggestion that might work, I'm all ears."

He kicked the gravel in the driveway with the toe of his boot. "I'm working on it."

"When he realizes I don't have his money, he won't care about any story. The only chance I have is to convince him we'll pay it back."

Wyatt leaned against the car. "Then you can't go empty-handed. You've got to give him something."

I reached into my front pocket and pulled out a money clip. I counted the attached bills and announced, "I've got forty-three dollars. Probably have as much in change in a Mason jar in the house." I scratched the side of my head. "Got a couple of hundred in my rainy-day fund stuck inside Shelby's old Bible too."

C.J. dug into his overalls and extracted a well-worn leather wallet as thick as his hands. Papers overflowed from the sides. From hundreds of viewings over the years, I knew the plastic sleeves contained well-worn photographs of fish, trophy deer, and Wanda. He might talk as if those three held an equal place with him, but the wallet flopped open on its own to Wanda photos. His fingers pushed aside the receipts and notes and counted the bills. "Twenty-seven dollars, but it's all yours. We can stop by my house too. I've got a few hundred dollars in an old coffee can in my kitchen."

Wyatt slung his arm over my shoulders. "I don't hide my

money in coffee cans or books, so I'll go to the ATM in town. Take out whatever they allow. If we pile everything together, maybe we have a grand or two to offer him tonight."

I looked down at my feet. "I can add another four." My throat felt thick as I confessed what I had done with the money for the nursing home. Their response surprised me because I expected shock or even anger. Spending that money for Shelby's comfort felt like using it for myself, but they didn't see it that way. Wyatt's eyes even teared up as he said, "We'll get her a TV when this is done, Grandpa."

C.J. asked, "Do you think it'll be enough to convince him to wait another day?"

"Who knows? I'll do what I can."

"We… We'll do what we can," Wyatt said.

"No. Me alone." I stepped back, creating space between us. "I can't put the two of you at any more risk."

"He might kill you," C.J. said.

My knees weakened to hear my fears said out loud. "Better than him killing all three of us."

Wyatt shook his head. "He wouldn't do that."

"I thought you said he would kill for this kind of money."

"Of course he would." He looked up and smiled. "But he knows he can't kill us all."

I ran my fingers through my hair as I tried to figure out his logic. "Why not? What stops him?"

The grin on his face widened. "You've got to think like he thinks. What's his biggest fear?"

"Same as ours. Some weirdo called Rudy the Roach might kill him."

"Exactly. If he kills us, he signs his own death warrant. Think about it. Is Reverend Brawley going to give the tattooed man the money? Would the sheriff? If he kills us, he has to explain to Rudy that he killed the last chance to get the money back."

I nodded slowly, processing the logic. "But once he has the money, what stops him from killing us then?"

"Nothing, except I don't think that's who he is."

"He killed Noah."

"Are you sure? Maybe he just said that. Like I said earlier, things like that make you fear him more." Wyatt looked wistfully to the west, in the direction of Knoxville. "I think it takes a lot out of a man to murder. He's trying to escape, and I can't imagine what killing three people would do to him. Once he has the money, we don't matter anymore."

I walked across the lawn and sat in a chair under the shade tree. Belle rested her head in my lap. I dutifully scratched behind her ears. "Say you're right. Why don't I go alone? Doesn't it accomplish the same thing?"

Wyatt settled into the grass beside me and crossed his legs. "He's already proven he can lose his temper and hurt you, right? And if he does, he still has us to come after. But if we're all three there, he can't. It makes it all or nothing, and he can't play that game."

He was right, as a group we were all safer, but was that worth the risk to Wyatt and my best friend? "I don't like it."

"There's nothing to like about it, Grandpa, but here's the deal. I do know these types of people. I know what they care about. The money. That's it. We go see him tonight. We tell him exactly what's going on. He'll be mad, but my bet is he goes back home because he doesn't really have any other choice."

"Why wouldn't he stay?"

"Right now, Rudy trusts him." Wyatt shrugged. "Well, trusts him as much as he trusts anyone. But if he's gone overnight, away from his family, maybe Rudy starts wondering why he's disappearing so much. Figures out there's missing money. The tattooed man has to keep up appearances, so he's got to go home. He can always come back if we don't show, and we all know it."

"He's going to believe we'll get the money in the morning, drive to Knoxville, and deliver it right to him?"

"I think he will. He won't like it, but he'd rather do that than risk going to jail on a murder charge or get killed by Rudy the Roach."

"How can you be sure?"

"I can't, of course, but what's one day more or less? As long as his boss doesn't find out, he'll end up okay. When we give him the money tomorrow, it's all over."

I looked across the field and sighed. After thinking for several minutes, I nodded and stood. As I reached into my pocket for my keys, Wyatt grabbed my arm. "Where are you going?"

"To have dinner with your grandmother. I never miss. And I'm certainly not going to skip tonight just in case it's the last time I ever see her."

31

I paused at the front door of the nursing home to calm my shaking nerves. With a deep breath, I plastered a smile on my face and entered the building. I nodded at the same faces I saw every night, warmed by the smiles and waves sent in my direction.

The building hummed with late-afternoon activity. Residents were returning from events to get ready for dinner. The low ringing of a telephone at a nursing station echoed in the hall. The canned laughter from a sitcom floated from the dayroom, the seated residents chuckling along with the characters. The click of keyboards from the computer room echoed their symphony.

I froze midstride. Why was I hearing so much noise from a normally quiet facility?

I stuck my head into the dayroom and looked at the half-dozen smiling residents scattered about the room in the glow of the TV. The day before, people had been sitting in here reading. Had that TV been working yesterday? I thought it wasn't, but I couldn't be sure. Maybe it had just been turned off.

Coincidence.

I leaned my back against the hallway wall as my nerves tingled with anxiety. Across the way, the glass-walled computer room hummed with activity. A half dozen residents sat in front of computer screens, happily typing away in the glow of the monitors. A spare computer waited for the next visitor. No one stood in line at the door. The machines didn't look new, but they were all working. The day before, there had only been three.

Breathe. Don't forget to breathe.

Bobby had assured me he couldn't move this fast. There had to be some other explanation. A government grant. A generous donor.

But that didn't make sense. Bobby would have known about that and told me when I handed him the money.

I walked briskly down the hallway, doing my best to look and feel calm, though panic exploded inside. My pulse raced.

As I moved deeper into the wings with bedridden patients, my pace quickened. I passed the secured entrance to the dementia unit in a near jog to the rear of the building. Before I reached it, the employee access door opened as a pair of clerical staff members exited with their purses under their arms and headed for the parking lot and home. They didn't say a word to me as I barged past them and into the hallway beyond. Out of breath, I arrived at the maintenance room door, rapped my knuckles on it in two quick bursts, and pushed it open.

Bobby was closing up his tool cabinets for the day and startled at the sudden noise. When he saw me, a grin broke across his face. "Our unsung hero. I have the best news ever."

My stomach tightened, fearing his best news was my worst news. I collapsed into the chair Bobby indicated. "The TV in the dayroom? The computers? Is that...?"

"Yeah, isn't it awesome?"

"Awesome?"

Bobby's smile faltered. He cocked his head. He probably expected me to be dancing a jig. He continued, caution in his voice, "I got to thinking last night and reached out to a buddy of mine who runs a couple of consignment stores down in Asheville."

"Like one of those places people take their old furniture to?"

"Yeah, but wait until you hear the cool part. One of the businesses he owns buys stuff from those companies that clean out old motels and apartment buildings." He pushed tools to the side of his workbench, planted his elbows on the cleared surface, and leaned toward me. "These big motel chains do a refresh every few years. They rip out the old carpet and put down new. They paint the walls. Put in new towels, sheets, and comforters. Then they install new furniture—beds, chairs, desks, everything."

"I'm not following."

"The first thing they have to do is get rid of all the old furnishings. Instead of paying dump fees, they sell it. My buddy buys it by the truckload and resells it through his stores. Couches, chairs, desks, bed frames, lamps, everything. Neat, huh?"

Cold fingers of dread threaded their way through my gut. "Neat."

"When he's down to stuff he can't sell, he donates it to homeless shelters, halfway houses, places like that. Very little of it ever goes to the dump. It's like he's the master recycler, and he makes money doing it." When I didn't celebrate his friend's ingenuity, Bobby's smile slipped again, but he plowed ahead with his story. "Every motel room has a TV. It sounds crazy that they get rid of working electronics, but they aren't buying high-end equipment. They buy them in bulk and want them all exactly the same to make it easy for their maintenance staff." Bobby rolled his eyes. "I wish we could afford to do that."

"Where does he get computers?"

"From the little business centers motels have. No one wants those machines because they aren't very powerful, but they're perfect for doing email."

"You bought it all from him." I leaned back in my chair and ran my hand through my hair. "But so fast? I thought you had to go slow."

"That's the coolest part. I told you he donates his leftover stuff to homeless shelters. So as far as the bosses know, because they don't know about your little gift, he donated everything. They think he's Mr. Citizen. Even had a reporter out here. They're going to do a big article about it."

"But you gave him the money."

"Yeah, but look at what we got. All the TVs are working. I even have spares when one goes on the fritz. We have new computers. We got some chairs, tables, and lamps for the dayrooms. We got a good deal. He did us right." Bobby paused and cocked his head. "You don't seem happy. Isn't this what you wanted?"

"I'm just shocked." I did my best to smile. He'd done better than I ever imagined. And faster. Much faster. "I couldn't be happier. It's great. You did really well."

Bobby shook his head. "No, you've done good. Too bad no one will ever know, but your secret's safe with me."

We chatted for a few more minutes, though I couldn't remember what about. My head buzzed the whole time. I was not sure if that was from getting banged around earlier or from my ever-growing panic. Now, even when I finally got the money back from the sheriff and added in what Wyatt, C.J., and I rounded up, I still might be short.

What a mess.

32

The electronic lock clicked shut behind me as I entered the dementia unit. Teresa was beaming from the nurses' desk. "Did you hear? Bobby got some guy to donate TVs."

I think I smiled. I tried to. Can't say if I succeeded or not. "That's great."

Teresa didn't pick up on my tense mood. She tilted her head toward Shelby, who was sitting with some other residents in front of the flickering TV screen. "Look how happy she is. They've all been so good this afternoon."

I tried to be happy for them despite the gnawing of doom deep in my belly. The patients seemed to be in a better mood. My crossing of the dayroom went smoothly—simple nods and hellos to the residents. No one stopped me to tell me about a conspiracy or a planned escape or some other creation. No one argued with inanimate objects.

I came to the couch as a burst of canned laughter erupted from the tinny speaker. The people on the screen zinged one-liners at each other in some sitcom that seemed vaguely familiar. The child actors were neat and clean-cut. Their problems could be solved in a half hour. The residents gathered around smiled as if they understood every double entendre.

When the action on the screen faded to commercial, Shelby looked up at me and said, "How was work today, Purvis? Dinner's almost ready, so wash up. I was just watching a little TV as it cooked."

A warmth spread through me, calming my jittery nerves. I needed a pleasant surprise after a day of bad ones, and having Shelby call me by name meant the world to me. She might not be in the current year, but at least she knew who I was. I'd take whatever I could get and was determined to push the impending meeting out of my mind for the next hour. I just wanted a few good moments with her.

I sat beside her on the couch and took her offered hand. "Did you have a good day today, dear?"

She sighed. "Work was fine, but the school called. Jessica skipped classes again. I tried to talk to her about it, but you know how that goes. I'm worried what's she going to do next."

I squeezed her hand gently. "Me too, dear, me too."

JESSICA HAD BEEN, to put it mildly, a surprising child.

News of Shelby's pregnancy got out quickly in our small town, and congratulations poured in. The women at church gathered for a baby shower, helping us with the baby supplies we suddenly needed. C.J. showed up unannounced one day with paint and brushes to get a nursery together. We began to think we would be prepared when Jessica surprised us again by coming three weeks before her due date.

The contractions hit in the middle of night with little warning. By the time we realized it wasn't a false alarm, they were coming fast and furious. We barely made it to the hospital before Jessica made a grand entrance before Shelby's doctor even arrived.

We were expecting Jeffrey, not Jessica. We were told such things are rare—even rarer nowadays, but this was forty years ago. Sometimes a boy was born when the parents expected a girl because important body parts had been hidden during the ultrasound. In our case, though, the technician mistook a shadow, or maybe the umbilical cord, and declared we were having a boy. Those baby shower clothes and the light-blue paint C.J. had spread on the nursery walls needed some updating.

Not that we should have bothered. Jessica never cared the least for girly things. She preferred riding a dirt bike or an ATV on the backwoods trails to dresses and dolls. Despite Shelby's efforts to entice her with old family recipes, Jessica never wanted to be in the kitchen.

That should have made it easier for me. I could have taken her fishing and camping. Spent time teaching her how to build a campfire, how to handle a gun, how to whittle a stick, how to tie a knot, and how to care for animals. Those were the things I could have taught her.

I tried, but I couldn't help but notice her eyes, her chin, her nose, and the shape of her mouth. The older she grew, the more obvious it became. She was going to be taller than her mother or me with a heavier frame. It challenged me, every day, to see how much Jessica resembled Horace. She looked like what she was—his daughter, not mine.

Shelby and I avoided any mention of it, doing our best not to open old wounds. We certainly never mentioned it to Jessica. What was the point of burdening a little girl with the dirty secret of her conception?

That didn't keep the details from her, though. She figured things out. Maybe on her own. Maybe through the curse of small-town gossip. You don't keep something like an affair a secret in Millerton. Women whispered about it during book club meetings or civic fundraisers. Old men discussed it over breakfast with their buddies. Maybe a child overheard it, shared it at school, and it got back to the target. Accidentally. Or maliciously.

She was eleven the day she marched into my little workshop behind the house and demanded to know if I was her real dad. I've replayed that moment a thousand times. I should've gotten up from my stool and wrapped her up in my arms.

But when I heard her voice, I heard Horace. When I looked at the fierceness in her eyes, I saw Horace glaring back at me. When I saw the way she set her jaw as she demanded to know the truth, I saw Horace commanding a room like he always had. The pain of Shelby's betrayal burned, and it paralyzed me. Instead of going to her, I hesitated.

I'd give anything to have that moment over. I've agonized over that conversation, thought of all the different ways it could have gone.

Things grew more difficult in her teen years. Jessica had always had perfect grades and eagerly did her homework, but she lost interest in school, and her grades plummeted. She snuck out her window and hung out with boys, drinking beer and smoking pot. We tried to enforce curfews but only succeeded in escalating conflicts.

Shortly after she turned sixteen, she and Shelby were in a terrible fight. I came home from work and felt the tension, but neither one of them would talk about it. Jessica went to her room, barricaded the door, and threw things against the wall. Shelby locked herself in the bathroom and cried. I bounced between their doors, up and down the stairs, trying to find out what it was about, but ended up eating dinner alone and confused.

That was, I now realize, the end. A few days later, Jessica was gone.

I had never forgiven myself for not loving her enough. I vowed when she came home, it would be different. I would love her unconditionally. I would tell her that none of it mattered. I would tell her she was my daughter, no matter we didn't share genetics.

I never got the chance. When we received the phone call that she had died, it crushed me to the core. I knew that moment in my workshop, that small piece of time that only Jessica and I knew about, was the root of everything that happened afterward.

When we were told she had left a son, we were shocked. I had a chance to redeem myself. I didn't know how I would ever be able to explain to him how I had failed his mother. I vowed to Jessica in a silent prayer that I would make up for all my failings to her. I would start by telling him the whole story. Then he could judge me as he wished.

When I met him for the first time, I knew I would never do that. Under the shaggy hair and dirty skin, the face of Horace Pearson stared back at me. The boy was the spitting image of his grandfather.

In the years since, I had never told him what happened before his mother left Millerton. I had never apologized for chasing her away. I had never explained why I didn't treat her as my daughter.

Worst of all, I had never called him my grandson.

33

Dusk settled over the mountains as C.J., Wyatt and I arrived at the nearly empty parking lot of the Coogan's Cove picnic area. C.J. and I had spent many days fishing here, but we were usually long gone before the sun dropped. The road to the cove was narrow and winding with rock outcroppings rising along the edge of one side and steep drop-offs on the other. It wasn't an easy drive in the daylight but became downright perilous at night.

A scattering of cars remained after a summer day of hiking and fishing. A few people would be down by the river, packing up their fishing gear. Others would be completing day hikes. Only two small groups of people used the picnic area as far as we noticed.

A family at the nearest picnic table packed the remnants of their dinner. A boy of maybe ten gripped a red Kentucky Fried Chicken bucket overflowing with debris. He managed to carry it without losing any contents to the nearest bear-proof trash can and waited for a teenaged girl. She bobbed her head, dancing to music I guessed streamed through her white earbuds, though I never understood how people enjoyed walking around with noisy Q-tips shoved in their ears all day. She rolled her eyes in response to her little brother's pleas for help. With an exaggerated sigh, she opened the metal door and waited while he dumped the contents. Dad slipped his arm around Mom and whispered to her, the two of them giggling as they followed the kids to a shiny sedan with an overflowing luggage carrier strapped to the top. Minutes later, they left for their hotel or to complete their journey home or wherever they were headed.

At a far picnic table in a shadowy corner, a young couple kissed and groped each other. Probably high schoolers enjoying the last evenings of their summer break, they ignored their untouched and cooling food on the table, far more intent on tasting each other. They didn't react to the arrival of a car containing three nervous men. I doubted they knew we were there at all.

After I shut off the ignition, only the sound of the ticking of the cooling engine filled the air. I glanced at my watch. "Ten minutes early."

C.J. said, "Maybe he isn't here yet."

"That's the car he was driving yesterday." I pointed to a space occupied by an Explorer a dozen slots away in the parking lot.

Wyatt's head swiveled as he surveyed the woods. "He would've wanted to get here early, familiarize himself with the area. Make sure you didn't set him up somehow."

C.J. groaned. "So he's watching us."

I pushed open the driver's door and winced at the creak of the hinges echoing in the silence of the parking lot. The female half of the couple broke away from her partner and looked at me.

I leaned against the hood of the car, doing my best to appear braver than I felt. "Let's get this over with."

Together, we climbed the wood-chip-covered path to the

rear of the picnic area. The young couple glared in irritation at the interruption. Apparently, they had come up for enough air to recognize this wasn't their bedroom or the back seat of their car.

When we reached the top of the hill, the forest thickened into shadows so dense we couldn't see if anyone waited. A small wooden sign with an arrow pointed down a dark trail weaving to the river below. We huddled and debated what to do.

I couldn't see the tattooed man but assumed he was watching us. "His move."

We didn't have to wait long until a voice came from the shadows. "Who are they?"

I turned in the direction it came from but couldn't find the source. "My friends."

"The young one... Is that your grandson?"

Wyatt nodded but didn't speak.

"And the big old dude. I'm guessing that's Cody."

C.J. replied, "Cody Joe."

"Cody Joe? How quaint." A twig snapped in the woods. I thought a shadow shifted, but I wasn't sure. "Cute how you left out the Joe part. Thought maybe if I went looking for Cody, no one would realize who I was asking about?"

I could only shrug in defense. I had been protecting my friend and wasn't ashamed about that. No sense in arguing.

"Why did all three of you come? You could've brought the money by yourself and not put them at risk."

I didn't like him thinking of risk in the same way I did. That made it all too real. It also confirmed we had made the right decision. "They wouldn't let me."

Wyatt spoke up. "We thought it would be safer this way."

"For him, maybe. Not for me. And sure not for you, Grandson."

The gurgling of the rushing water of the river had muffled

our ability to pinpoint the man's location. The metallic sound of the slide being pulled back on a pistol clanged through the woods. My heart skipped a beat. I held my breath and braced myself for a shot, but none came.

The tattooed man materialized from the shadows with a pistol held to his side. "Thought I would even the odds. Three on one didn't seem fair."

My bladder felt full. I wouldn't have been surprised to feel a stream running down my leg. Fortunately, I was an old man. I only dribbled. No one noticed. "No need for a gun."

"As long as no one does anything stupid, you're right."

I swallowed, trying to lubricate my throat to keep my voice from cracking, but I didn't have any saliva.

The tattooed man motioned with his free hand to the nearby picnic table. "Put the money there and back up. If it's all there, this'll be over."

The moment of truth. "I wish I could."

His eyes narrowed, the gun clenched in one hand as the open hand slowly fell to his side. "What's wrong?"

"I don't have it yet."

The tattooed man stood stock still, puzzlement spreading across his face. "Why would you come without it?"

"What would you have done if I hadn't shown up?"

"Gone to your house and killed you."

"That was my guess. I'm trying to avoid that." I spread my arms wide, my best "we've come in peace" look. I doubted it worked. "I'm getting your money back. I'll have it tomorrow morning. As soon as it's in my hands, I'll drive over to Knoxville and deliver it to you. Promise."

"Promise?" The tattooed man stared into the woods at the spot he had come from. Through gritted teeth, he said, "You promised you'd have it tonight."

"No, actually, I didn't."

The man closed the distance between us in a flash and

jammed his pistol against my head, the cold metal digging into his skin. "You calling me a liar?" he yelled.

I've always been told your life flashes before your eyes in moments like that. It didn't for me. I only saw the potential future. The tattooed man pulling the trigger and everything being over in a flash. Wyatt leaping forward to defend me and taking the bullet instead. C.J. trying to use his bulk to wrestle the gun away and failing. I needed to calm things before any of those things happened. "No. Never. I just meant…"

"Talk fast, old man."

"We talked to the preacher. He called the sheriff and told him to give it back."

"The sheriff said no?"

"No! I mean yes. I mean…" Sweat ran down my back. My legs quaked. I dribbled a little more and no longer cared who noticed. "He agreed. He's giving it back. We're picking it up at ten tomorrow morning."

"Why tomorrow?"

"Something about evidence lockers and chain of custody and… I don't know. He said tomorrow."

The tattooed man glowered, and his eyes flicked back and forth across my face as if he was trying to decide whether to believe me. Then he pushed away and screamed, "Arrrrrrrrgh!"

The young couple that had been making out jumped. With a startled glance in our direction, they gathered their loosened clothing and ran toward their car. A minute later, they peeled out of the parking lot, nearly clipping a large SUV that was entering. The tattooed man paced back and forth, talking to himself. "Tomorrow is not fast enough. I need it now. Now. I need it now. Not tomorrow. Too late. Too late. It's not fast enough."

The SUV parked, and two men exited. They began the climb up the hill to the river trail. Must be tourists, I thought, because you left the woods at night. You didn't enter them. I prayed, though, that their presence might save us. The tattooed man wasn't deterred by them because he never seemed to notice them at all. Instead, he screamed in frustration, grabbed my shirt, and pushed me flat on my back on the picnic table. I felt my head wound open up and blood trickle down. He shoved the pistol against my cheek. Spittle flew from his lips. "Why shouldn't I just shoot all three of you right now?"

My heart pounded in my chest. I grasped for Wyatt's words from earlier. "Because then you'd never get the money. You need us to get it."

"But tomorrow's not fast enough."

"It's all I've got to offer. You can't get blood from a stone."

"He can't," said the smaller of the two approaching men. "But I can."

Wyatt gasped.

The stranger stepped in front of him and smiled. "You must be the legendary Wyatt Earp."

34

The tattooed man released his grip on me and backed away, allowing me to stand. I felt blood drip down my neck. My mind swirled in confusion. I touched Wyatt's elbow with my hand. "Who is this?"

The man smiled broadly, a toothy grin that held more menace than warmth. "Wyatt would know me as Rudy the Roach, an unfortunate nickname, but let's stick with it, shall we?"

Wyatt attempted to shake loose my hand, but I gripped his elbow harder. "How do you know... each other?"

Before Wyatt could answer, Rudy—or was it Mr. Roach—laughed. "Better question, old man, how do you know our little Wyatt?"

I tried to answer, but I felt dizzy. As much as I had feared the tattooed man, this new character froze my blood. He was neatly dressed—khakis and a golf shirt—as though he was just coming off the course. His hair was closely cropped, his face clean shaven, and his skin absent of any tattoos. At first glance, he looked like nothing but a businessman. His eyes, though, were cold and dark. His voice was equally icy. Menace filled his aura.

The big ape who came up the hill with him hadn't said a word. He stood two steps behind Rudy, like a dog waiting on instructions. I really didn't want to know what those might be.

My legs threatened to let go. I leaned against a tree to keep from falling to the ground and tried to speak, but nothing came out.

Wyatt looked worried and reached out. "Grandpa. Are you okay?"

Laughter erupted from Rudy, a cold, harsh sound. "Grandpa? Oh, this is rich."

Wyatt clenched his fist and took a step forward. The large, silent man slid between him and Rudy. He didn't threaten. He didn't need to. He was built like a granite boulder—broad shoulders, thick arms, massive hands. He could snap me in half without breaking a sweat.

The interaction between them only brought more laughter from Rudy. "I heard Wyatt had a temper."

I pulled Wyatt back. "The past doesn't matter."

"Ah, but it does. I always heard good things about him—until he disappeared. Reputation was Wyatt was quite the little hustler. I'd been told he had some potential for moving up. He was quite skilled at moving inventory into the schools. Got to get a customer young, so you can have them for life."

I sneered in disgust. "You're okay selling drugs to kids?"

"Oh no. I never did anything like that. Never even met Wyatt. I tend to stay a healthy distance from specifics." That sly grin crossed his face. "I'm more executive level. I only get into details to resolve business problems." He aimed that wicked grin at Wyatt. "Sadly, though, your grandson had the same weakness for the product his mother had."

Wyatt snarled and stepped toward him, but the ape moved

lightning fast for such a big man. He didn't strike but positioned his body between his master and the threat.

Rudy ignored the conflict with a shrug, confident his attack dog had things under control. He returned his attention to me. "Now tell me why you didn't bring Gene my money."

I looked at the shrinking tattooed man. "His name is Gene?"

Rudy raised an eyebrow. "What did you think it was?"

"I didn't know… We just called him the tattooed man."

Rudy's eyes moved over Gene's ink-filled arms. "That works." With a dismissive shrug, he turned back to me. "You're stalling, old man."

"No, I'm not. I've already explained. I'll bring all the money to him tomorrow as soon as I get it."

"No, you'll bring it to me. Gene won't be available tomorrow." He turned his focus on the tattooed man. "He has issues to atone for."

The confident Gene who had pushed me around earlier in the day was gone. He had been replaced by a nervous, jittery man who tried to shrink into the shadows. His voice quivered. "I'll fix this. I promise."

Rudy ignored him, that slimy smile broadening. "Do you know what Gene's issues are?" When I didn't answer, he continued. "He has such a simple job. He collects payments from, shall we say, retailers with a need to stock up their inventory. Our terms are payments in advance—saves that messy collection business. He counts it to ensure we have payment in full—never trust the front line, Grandpa, a key rule of business. Then he places a phone call. The retailer receives his shipment from a package delivery specialist. Do you know why those jobs are separate?"

I didn't know and didn't care, but I wasn't about to say that. Whatever the man was trying to communicate, I just wanted out of the situation.

Seeing we had nothing to contribute, Rudy continued. "Keeping product and cash separate keeps things running smoothly. Makes it much harder for those boys in blue to interfere in business."

I didn't know how to react. Congratulate the man on his brilliance? Discuss legal strategy? No reaction seemed wise, so I stayed quiet.

"But there's a side benefit, one my employees don't really think about. You might be surprised to discover dishonest people are attracted to this business. Shocking, right?" He smiled, but no one laughed. "By having the product and the cash separate, I can spot skimming. If the two of them want to pull off something creative, they must work together, and that always fails. Trust me, there really is no honor among thieves."

He turned his attention away from me and over to Gene. "When this one was late, I asked around. Discovered he had bought a stolen car. Had a chat with the guy he bought it from, who introduced me to the punks who stole it."

Wyatt's head popped up in shock. "Noah's alive."

Rudy cocked his head, an eyebrow raised in surprise. "A little bruised but very much alive. Did this one tell you different? Gene doesn't have killer in him. Acts tough, but he's too soft. Too bad because Noah was quite helpful. Told me all about the car."

Rudy focused on Wyatt. "He told me all about you as well. I had heard about you years ago. Heard you had potential back then. Thought it might be fun to get to know you again, but first I need to handle some business."

The tattooed man shivered in fear as Rudy spun back around to him and said, "People who lie to me don't work for me for very long. Nor do people who steal from me."

Gene backed away, but the gorilla was on him before he made it two steps. He pinned those tattooed arms behind his back and forced him to his knees. Rudy approached and tapped Gene's forehead with his finger in cadence with his next sentence. "This idiot decides to carry the cash in a stolen car. My money. Money that should already have been turned in."

He looked back at me, and I realized his smile was gone. As chilling as it was, now I missed it. His face was contorted and snarling. "He made it worse. You know how, old man?"

I didn't know what the right answer was, so I slowly shook my head, not trusting myself to speak.

"He didn't tell me. He kept information from me. That's the same as lying. Wouldn't you agree?"

He grabbed Gene's chin in his hand. "Why hide something like that? Makes me wonder why he wouldn't tell me. Why he needed a stolen car. Maybe he had plans for that money that didn't involve me. Maybe he was taking his lovely bride and sweet little children on a vacation. A very long vacation."

He raised his hand high in the air and roared, "*With my money!*" He backhanded the tattooed man across the face. The sickening snap of a breaking nose filled the air. Gene cried out, and the gorilla let him fall to the ground. He whimpered and sniveled, which only infuriated Rudy further.

"Sit up."

"Please," Gene sobbed, his voice muffled through his shattered nose.

Rudy reached down, wrapped his hand around Gene's throat, and pulled him upward until he was on his knees. "Why didn't you tell me you lost the money?"

"Because you would've killed me."

"Did you think I wouldn't have found out?"

"I-I-I…"

"If you'd gotten the money back, you never would've told me?"

Gene looked up, tears running down his face mingling with the blood from his nose.

Rudy began speaking rapidly, ignoring Gene's pitiful pleas. "Were you planning to steal from me, Gene?"

"Please—"

"Are you lying to me, Gene?"

"I'm begging you—"

He pointed at us. "Tell them what happens to liars and thieves."

"Please—"

Rudy sighed and looked up to the stars. "I always have to do things myself."

"Please—"

He stepped to the side of Gene and kept his eyes on him, but he spoke to me. "You promised me you'd bring the money tomorrow. If you don't, I'll know you lied. And I'll know you're a thief. Here's what happens to people like that in my world."

The pistol appeared in Rudy's hands like magic. I didn't know if it had always been there or if the man was that fast on the draw. But it was there. Crammed against the side of Gene's head. The tattooed man had been reduced to a mess of begging, over and over. "Please. Please. Please."

I squeezed my eyes shut as Rudy pulled the trigger. The roar of the gun filled my ears.

35

We were on the interstate, headed back to Millerton, when a sheriff's car passed in the other direction, blue lights flashing. We hadn't spoken since Rudy had left us standing dumbfounded around the body as he calmly walked away with his gorilla in tow. We hadn't spoken, even as I shuffled C.J. and Wyatt back to the car and drove away from Coogan's Cove.

Wyatt shifted in his seat. "I'm sorry."

I was still trying to get the ringing out of my ears. "For what?"

"The drugs."

"I knew you used drugs."

"But you didn't know I delivered them."

I whispered my reply, "No."

Wyatt hung his head and stared at his feet. "He told you how he split collections from distribution, right? The collectors were fairly safe because they only handled cash. If the cops stopped them, they weren't really guilty of anything. But the distributors had drugs on them, so if they were arrested, they would at least get charged with possession. Usually with intent because that's based on quantity."

"Okay."

"The trick was that the distributors had to be dumb about the organization in case the cops swooped in. We didn't know anything other than where we picked up a package and where we delivered it. Even if you were stupid enough to talk, you didn't have much to give. And, trust me, you just kept your mouth shut. You weren't facing much time anyway."

"The judges just need to give the distributors long sentences."

"The distributors... were kids."

"Kids?"

"Yeah. Like me. The younger, the better. If we got caught, we didn't have a record, so we'd just get probation or something. Even once you had a record, it didn't matter because you just went to juvie for a few months."

"And that was okay?"

"You know Rudy the Roach said he resolved business problems?" Wyatt looked out the window and licked his lips. "He didn't care if the problem was only thirteen or fourteen years old. I knew better than to ever be a problem."

We rode in silence for a few minutes. I asked, "Jessica knew about this?"

"What was she going to do? She needed her fix. She'd beg me not to work for them, but someone had to bring home the money."

I wiped the back of my hand across my face. "I understand."

"No, I don't think you do." Wyatt took a deep breath. "I will always regret it. I should've found another way. Social workers. Churches. Teachers. I just didn't take their help."

"You can't blame yourself. You didn't have any choice."

"I used to believe that lie too."

The tires hummed on the pavement. "This is on me, Wyatt. I chased your mother away. She hated me, and I don't blame her."

Wyatt sat up straight and squeezed the steering wheel. "Mom didn't hate you. Why would she? You raised her like she was your daughter, unlike Horace Pearson, who never gave her the time of day."

I glanced in the rearview mirror to see C.J.'s reaction. He knew about the affair—the rumor mill in our little town made sure everyone knew—but we didn't talk about it a lot. He wasn't paying attention, though, and was staring blankly out the window. I said quietly, "We tried to keep that quiet. Tried to hide it from her."

"Some kids teased her about it. They even had some rhyme about Horace and his whore."

I flinched. Poor Jessica, having to suffer for the sins of her parents. "I don't like your grandmother being called that. If I had been a better husband, the affair would never have happened."

Wyatt shrugged. "You were upset because you were shooting blanks. It happens."

I jumped. "You knew all this?"

"Sure. Mom and I didn't keep many secrets. I mean, we kind of knew the worst about each other anyway, so what was left?"

I blinked back tears. "I'm so sorry I made you go through everything. If only I had protected her more, loved her more, she wouldn't have left."

Wyatt's hand wrapped over my shoulder, his fingers squeezing. "She didn't leave because of you. She regretted hurting you with her decision, but she left because of Grandma."

I focused on the reflectors embedded in the pavement flashing by and tried to make sense of what he was saying. "Because of the affair?"

"Because of the letters." He let go of me and leaned his head against the passenger window. He sighed so deeply, a cloud of fog formed on the window. "You really don't know."

I shook my head.

He hesitated before plunging ahead. "Mom skipped school one day, but it was colder than she expected. She needed a jacket. She snuck home to get it, but the house was nice and warm, so she wasn't in any hurry to leave. She didn't really have anywhere to be. She just didn't want to be at school, listening to those girls talk about her. To kill time, she poked around some, looking in drawers and boxes. Not really looking for anything, but just looking. She found a shoebox full of letters. She sat there for hours and read them until Mom pulled in the drive after work."

"The ones we wrote while I was in the air force."

There was silence from beside me until I heard a sniffle. "The ones from Horace."

The air evaporated from the car. I struggled to catch my breath. When I spoke, only a wheeze came out. "Horace?"

"Yes."

"They had letters? She kept them?"

"I wish I hadn't told you."

I gripped the steering wheel. A tear rolled down my face. "Do you know where they are?"

"Gone. Mom piled them in the fireplace, squirted lighter fluid on them, and burned them. Grandma caught her, and they had a huge fight about it. Mom said she demanded Grandma tell you everything, but she refused. A few days later, Mom left."

TUESDAY

36

C J. took a handkerchief from his overalls' pocket and mopped his sweaty face. His hair was unkempt. Puffy dark circles hung under his eyes. I hadn't slept well myself. What had happened at Coogan's Cove bothered me, of course, but what Wyatt had revealed unsettled me even more.

I had searched the drawers and closet of our bedroom late into the night but never found any of the Horace letters. Jessica burned the ones that existed before she left, of course, but were there newer ones? Perhaps Shelby had stopped corresponding with Horace long before Jessica left. If I found letters, they would break my already broken heart. If I didn't find any, I would never be sure.

I asked C.J., "Did you sleep at all?"

He folded his handkerchief and stuffed it back in his pocket. He wouldn't look me in the eyes but stared westward toward the mountains instead. Coogan's Cove was nestled between them in that direction. "How could I? We watched a man get murdered."

We stood in the parking lot of Abe's Market. Through the window, we could see our friends gathered around the Liars'

Table. They were sipping coffee, eating breakfast, and laughing at each other's corny jokes. We had debated the night before about skipping breakfast but realized our friends would be worried about us. If they came out to our houses to check on us, they might get sucked into this nightmare. That, we wouldn't allow.

C.J. hung his head, his voice barely above a whisper. "He didn't deserve to die like that."

"Look at me."

His head rose slowly until I could see his bloodshot eyes.

"He was a drug dealer and a thief. He threatened to kill me if I didn't get the money back. He beat me up yesterday. I'm sorry he's dead, but I'm not going to mourn him."

His eyes were glassy and out of focus. "He had kids."

I stuck my hands in my pockets and hung my head. "Yeah, he did. But what are we supposed to do about it?"

C.J. leaned against his truck. He fidgeted with the buttons on his overalls. "I don't know. If we tell the sheriff…"

"The Roach killed a man for stealing from him. What do you think he does to people who rat him out?" I gently squeezed his arm until he looked up at me. "The guy he killed didn't deserve it, but he was a bad guy. This Rudy is a worse guy, someone who uses kids like Wyatt to deliver drugs. If we keep this secret, maybe Wyatt has a chance at a normal life. Isn't that worth it?"

C.J. tilted his head back and studied the sky. His answer was a whisper. "Okay."

"As soon as the reverend gets the money, we deliver it, and then this is all over. Until then, we just have to act normal."

"Normal?" C.J. grimaced. "Normal is I eat a whole mess of eggs with some bacon, grits, and biscuits. I down three or four cups of coffee. If I tried to do that this morning, I'd throw it up. I might do it anyway."

I stepped back and looked at my friend. "Okay, you're

right. We probably shouldn't have come. I'll tell them we're both feeling under the weather. They'll take one look at us and believe it. Give me just a minute, and then we're gone."

"Too late."

I followed his gaze to see a car turning into the parking lot from Broad Street. The sheriff's unmarked SUV pulled up beside the store. Hearing C.J.'s groan, I knew we didn't dare chat with the law without our friends around us. I grabbed his elbow and guided him into the store.

Colette was busy with a customer at the cash register, and Martha wasn't in sight, so we made it quickly to the back of the store. We headed for our normal seats when Danny spoke up. "Morning, guys. Want me to whip up the usual?"

C.J.'s face was pale. Sweat dribbled down the sides of his cheeks. His eyes were wide and darting around the room. He breathed rapidly, panting like Belle did in the summer heat. I thought of a panicked rabbit I had seen racing from a stalking coyote. Realizing C.J. had been right—he really would get sick if he attempted to eat any food—I called out to Danny, "Just coffee for now. We might order something later."

Danny's mouth dropped open. "Now I've heard every-thing." Instead of arguing, he spun around and rolled his wheelchair into the kitchen for the coffeepot and a couple of mugs.

As we settled into our customary chairs, Abe greeted us. "Both of you are late. I've never seen C.J. pass up a meal. I saw you conspiring outside. Can't wait to hear this tale."

My heart leapt into my throat. I feared C.J. wouldn't resist the bait and would weave a convoluted story. I feared more he wouldn't say a word, and I would be forced to come up with something. I tried to deflect attention. "Just late. No story."

The faces around the table told me it wasn't going to be that easy. They exchanged glances with each other as Danny placed full coffee cups in front of us. Chip opened his mouth to lead the questioning, but the bell over the front door jingled, announcing a new arrival.

Sheriff Newman entered, greeted Colette behind the cash register with a quick nod, and strode purposefully to the rear of the store. Like C.J., his face was tired, the sign of a man who hadn't slept all night.

As the sheriff retrieved an offered coffee from Danny, Levi hollered out a greeting. "Sounds like you're having a busy morning."

Chip, at least temporarily diverted from his interrogation, gestured at the scanner propped up on the table. He leaned over and whispered, "While you were oversleeping, we got ourselves a dead body. Haven't had a murder in Miller County in a long time."

My heart skipped a beat. C.J. groaned. Out of the corner of my eye, I saw he was even paler than when we entered. Visions of him fainting passed through my mind. I elbowed him to keep him focused. He turned to me in slow motion, like he was treading water. Without his help, I pretended to be clueless. I hoped I looked shocked and not scared. "Murder?"

The sheriff stumbled up to the table, sipping from his coffee cup. He ran his hand across the stubble on his face. "You know I can't tell you gents everything, but I also realize much of it has already been broadcast on that blasted radio. So, yeah, a man got himself shot up in Coogan's Cove."

Ronnie leaned forward. "Thought the Cove was forest service territory. Don't the feds handle that?"

Newman shook his head. "If it had happened in the woods, the rangers would have it, but the picnic area is county. Once they saw where the body was, they gladly handed it over to us, but they did get the first shots-fired call."

No one had been around. Who had reported it? "Someone heard the shots?"

"Better than that. Someone saw it."

"Saw?"

"Well, sort of saw." The sheriff gripped the coffee and drank like he was drawing energy from it. "A young couple was in their car in the parking lot. They heard the shot, looked up, and saw a group of men."

I had forgotten about them. I thought they had left. "They get a good look?"

The sheriff grimaced. "Unfortunately, the young couple was paying more attention to each other than what was happening, if you know what I mean."

Abe laughed and nodded knowingly. "I can guess exactly what they were doing."

The men around the table all chuckled.

The sheriff shrugged. "They said a group of men had been arguing about something, but they never heard about what and moved to their car to get away from them. When they heard the shot, they were pretty scared and hid until everyone was gone. Then they called 911. They couldn't describe very much, but at least they told us what the men were wearing."

Abe snickered again. "Considerably more than what those two were wearing, I'm sure."

Ignoring Abe, Ronnie asked, "Think it was tourists fighting over something? Maybe a family dispute?"

"Doesn't look like it." The sheriff hesitated but continued, "We're thinking it was a drug deal gone bad."

"You find drugs?"

The sheriff sipped his coffee again before answering, looking like he was deciding how much to share. Everyone, especially the sheriff, understood anything he said would be news in the county within minutes. He was talking to the unofficial press corps of Miller County. "The dead man has a record over in Knox County and Sevier County, mostly drugs and related crimes. Nothing was found on him or the Explorer he apparently arrived in, but it doesn't take a big leap to assume drugs were involved."

Ronnie said, "Well, at least it wasn't a local boy. That's good news."

"He wasn't, but we think the people he was meeting might have been local."

I choked on my coffee. I coughed and sputtered while they looked at me. Finally getting it under control, I croaked, "Why?"

"The way they were dressed. The way they talked. The car they were driving."

"Could the kids see the license plate?" I tried to sound nonchalant. Since I hadn't been to the DMV to report it stolen, my license plate was still missing. I had taped a hand-written sign in my back window that listed the lost plate and the number. Besides, it wasn't like my car wasn't unique enough. If the kids had noticed many details, I was toast.

"One of them. Two men left in a black SUV with Tennessee plates. Unfortunately, that turned into a dead end. The plate had been stolen off some old lady's car who rarely drives anywhere, much less into Coogan's Cove. She had nothing to do with it."

"That's it?"

The sheriff chortled. "The other group left in some old clunker. The kids tried to get the license plate, but they said they couldn't find it. Maybe the light was out, but the bigger issue was a cloud of blue smoke blocked their view. Apparently, the car was burning oil. All they saw was the shadow of three men."

My shoulder muscles relaxed. Maybe, just maybe, we were in the clear.

I studied an old stain on the table. The sheriff startled me out of my thoughts when he asked, "You okay?"

I sat upright and looked at him, but he wasn't looking at

me. His gaze was on the man next to me, and concern was on his face. "C.J.?"

C.J.'s face had gone from pale to as white as a freshly bleached sheet. His jaw twitched. His mouth opened and closed. He tried to speak but nothing came out.

I placed a hand on his arm. It was clammy and cold. "You okay, buddy?"

C.J. turned to me, his eyes glassy. His lips were tinted blue. His hands slid up his overalls and clutched at the center of his chest. With a gasp, he collapsed forward onto the table.

37

"How are you doing, my son?"

I jumped at the sound of Reverend Brawley's voice. Normally the man boomed, projecting across wide open space to his congregation, but now he spoke in hushed tones, so he didn't draw any more attention than he was already receiving.

All eyes in the emergency department waiting room were on us. His navy-blue suit, white shirt, light-blue tie, and silver cross tie tack stood out in the sea of jeans, overalls, and T-shirts. His uniform announced his role. Perhaps the other people waiting thought he was delivering bad news. Perhaps, I realized with a start, he was.

"Have you heard…?"

The minister gestured at the empty chair beside me. "May I sit with you?"

Once the man settled beside me, I asked, "Do you know anything? They keep telling me a doctor will come talk to me, but no one's told me anything."

"They have to attend to the sick before the well. Don't fret, though, because I asked before coming over to see you. He's had a heart attack, a major one from the looks of it."

I tugged at my shirt. "Is he going to live?"

"Unfortunately, though I pray every day, I'm not privy to all His plans. We can only pray for C.J.'s recovery."

I shifted in the plastic waiting room chair, my butt numb from hours of sitting. Since arriving, I had stood only to ask the nurse at the desk for information. She patiently explained each time that she didn't know, that the doctor would come out and talk as soon as possible. The longer I waited, the more my panic grew. The words came out my mouth in a jumbled rush. "Seeing him lying on that floor at Abe's… The look on the paramedics' faces as they worked on him… The firefighters straining to lift him off the floor and onto the gurney… Their rush to get him into the ambulance… I…"

The reverend draped his arm over my shoulder. "I know the doctors and nurses here well. They're excellent at their jobs."

"But…" I couldn't finish the sentence as the tears flowed. We sat like that for several minutes. The fear would have over-whelmed me without the comfort of his arm around me. With Jessica gone and Shelby in the nursing home, all but gone mentally, my life revolved around Wyatt, C.J., Belle, and breakfast at the Liars' Table. Losing a piece of that was my greatest fear.

I didn't know how long I cried, but when the tears finally slowed, I realized I had been babbling. The minister quietly listened until I was calm again. He nodded his head toward the glass doors of the emergency room entrance and the men from the Liars' Table gathered outside on the sidewalk. "They all care for you, don't they?"

They had followed the ambulance and had stayed throughout the day, going into the fresh air only for breaks. "Yes, they're good friends."

"And your grandson?"

"Wyatt took off work early when he heard. He stopped by for a few minutes and then went home to take care of Belle." I looked around. "He should be back soon."

"He'll get comfort sitting with you."

"Yes."

"Even the sheriff cares about you. I saw him earlier asking about C.J., though he's got a busy day going."

I sat up straight. The sheriff. The murder. The money. In the panic over C.J., I had forgotten everything.

The reverend shifted in his seat. "Do you think the man who was murdered might have anything to do with what we discussed last night?"

"I..."

"I ask because the sheriff thinks there is a connection, though he's confused what it might be. The dead man is quite well known to police over in Tennessee. They suspect he is a moneyman, a collector of sorts, who might have tens of thousands of dollars on him at any moment."

"Really?" I tried to act shocked and clueless, but my voice didn't sound genuine to me.

"Our good sheriff thinks it's possible it was a robbery gone bad."

I felt my chest tighten. The air in the room grew thick.

The reverend didn't seem to notice my discomfort. "But, see, that's where the sheriff is confused. If the money that 'appeared' in the church donation booth"—the minister indicated quotes with his fingers—"was stolen from him, how come it showed up before the man was killed?"

My mind grasped for any possible explanation that wouldn't sound insane spoken aloud. Nothing came to me. "That means it can't be connected, right?"

"Maybe not." Brawley leaned back in his chair, squinting. "But until the sheriff can get comfortable that there's no connection, you can see he would be reluctant to release the money. And I would be reluctant to ask for it."

I swallowed hard.

Brawley leaned forward and shifted gears. "I saw Shelby this morning."

"You did?" I sat up, startled. "I mean, I appreciate you visiting her."

"I do the Tuesday morning chapel service for the residents. We ministers rotate the days. I enjoy it." Brawley looked around the room. "Attendance was down, though. Seems I had a little competition for the residents' attention."

My mind was still grappling with the reality that we weren't going to have the money for Rudy. We were already late, so I couldn't see any good outcome. I tried to stay in the conversation. "Competition?"

"The nursing home was blessed with a donation from a consignment company down in Asheville. Got some new TVs and computers. Used but new to them."

I swallowed hard.

"Sadly, many patients prefer to watch game shows rather than come to chapel." Brawley shrugged. "I guess it's good. They need the entertainment. And it is wonderful such generous people want to help our community, though I admit to some confusion."

"Confusion?"

"I'm careful about suggesting something may not be quite on the up and up, but the man who made the donation is not known for such generosity. His track record of donations tends more along the line of items of limited monetary value. In fact, shall we say, they are worth less than the cost of disposing of them in a landfill. Thus, the benefit to him is that the items are out of his hair. But TVs and computers aren't really the same thing. He could have made some money off them and isn't the type to normally pass up such an opportunity."

I opened my mouth, but nothing came out.

"The administrators aren't going to look a gift horse in the mouth, but I find it quite the change in heart."

I stammered, "T-t-that's good, right?"

"Perhaps." Brawley studied me carefully, his eyes twitching. "I just want you to know, if you need some help, I'm here."

He was right. I was drowning in trouble. We were dealing with evil people, and I didn't know how to make them go away. When I tried to do the right thing, things got worse. My best friend was sick, maybe dying. Wyatt was in real danger. This wasn't going to end well. I needed the help. Telling the truth seemed the only remaining option. I started my confession, "I—"

"Mr. Webb?" A thin man in blue scrubs approached us from the double doors leading back into the bowels of the emergency room. He nodded at the minister. "Good morning, Reverend."

"Good morning, Dr. Queen. Do you have news on Cody Joe Duncan?"

The doctor hesitated and tilted his head toward me. "Are you Mr. Duncan's next of kin?"

Brawley smiled kindly at me and once more extended his arm over my shoulders. "Mr. Duncan's wife passed away a few years ago. Mr. Webb here is his best friend, the closest thing he has to kin."

The doctor hesitated. "Children? Siblings?"

"No kids. Had a brother who passed away. No one else I'm aware of. How about you, Purvis?"

I shook my head, fear gripping my body as I waited on the news.

The doctor nodded and leaned forward. "Mr. Webb, we did everything we could. I'm so sorry."

38

I drove home in a haze, barely remembering telling the others about C.J.'s death. They stood at the entrance to the hospital, swapping stories about his antics over the years, but I couldn't bring myself to laugh.

Brawley, however, encouraged the men to share the tales at a memorial service at the church. They mapped out plans, arranged for a mortician, and drafted an obituary. The mechanics of death marched forward long after I found a way to extricate myself from the group.

C.J. and I had long bantered about his potential for a heart attack. I had tried to get him to pay more attention to his doctor's warnings about his high blood pressure and terrible cholesterol level. I had chided him about his weight and the need to eat better. He complained the medicine made him feel funny. He liked food too much to lose weight.

Had I not tried hard enough?

And why had I allowed him to go to Knoxville with me to retrieve the car? Why did I even care so much about the car in the first place?

If we hadn't gone, we never would've met the tattooed man. We never would've found the money.

And then I'd made everything worse by foolishly giving the money to the nursing home and the church. If I hadn't done that, I could have returned it to the tattooed man. He would still be alive. And maybe C.J. would be too.

Everything was my fault.

I blinked back the tears in my eyes, bringing the yellow lines on the road back into focus. A farmer waved from his seat in his tractor as he worked his field of late-summer corn. A murder of crows settled onto a power line above my head and cawed to each other.

Rudy the Roach was coming. I had missed the meeting with him, so he would kill me. If that put an end to this mess, then fine. The men of the Liars' Table would be sad for a few days, but they would continue without me. Our empty seats would be filled by others. Bobby would be retiring soon.

And Shelby? Teresa and the rest of the staff at the nursing home would take care of her. She would probably never realize I stopped coming. She probably didn't know I came now.

That left Wyatt. He was my responsibility. His life had been such a mess, all because of my own issues years ago. Whatever Shelby had done, she did because of my weakness. He had grown into a good man, had a whole life to look forward to, and the strength to do it.

He needed to pack his few belongings and leave. Right now. Disappear. He could start his life over somewhere else. The money we had pooled to give to the tattooed man would provide him with a start. Wyatt's ability to work with his hands would give him everything else.

His roots weren't in Millerton anyway. He'd never lived here before his mother died. He would be better off some-where else. At least he would be alive.

I was resolved. I would help Wyatt pack and leave. I'd drive out to the nursing home for one last dinner with Shelby. I would distract Rudy the Roach long enough to give Wyatt a head start. Then I would die.

The church came into view. A couple of days hence, mourners would gather to say goodbye to C.J. I hated to miss it. But maybe I wouldn't. Maybe there would be a double funeral. My own casket could be beside my friend's.

WYATT'S CAR waited in its familiar space in the driveway. The rocking chairs and hammock sat empty. Belle stretched in her usual spot in the shade under the tree, napping in the afternoon heat.

I shut off the engine and looked around the yard. I wanted to cry for C.J., but I didn't have the time. Wyatt would resist, but he had to leave. We could have him packed in fifteen minutes.

I paused. He should have heard me pull in. Dread settled over me, though I told myself I was overreacting. My hand shook as I opened the door and got out of my car.

"Wyatt?"

The wind rattled the maple tree's branches, hinting of a possible thunderstorm to rumble over the ridge later in the evening. An eagle screeched as it soared over the field, searching for an errant mouse or rabbit. Smaller birds chirped as they flitted through the air. Belle's snores provided a rhythmic undertone. But no reply came from Wyatt. Concern mounting, I cupped my hands around my mouth and hollered, "Wyatt!"

Belle started at the noise. She raised her head. Her tail thumped the ground. When I didn't go to her, she stood and stretched, a yawn spreading across her face. She waddled across the yard in her unsteady, old-dog gait. She nuzzled my leg and pawed my foot for attention. I reached down and scratched behind her ears. "Where's Wyatt, girl?"

She padded across the yard and squatted to pee in a grassy patch. She climbed the steps to the porch and took a drink from the bucket of water filled fresh daily. With a glance over her shoulder to see if I was following, she wandered through the open front door and disappeared inside.

Wyatt wouldn't leave the door ajar. He often griped about the gnats and flies of summer living. His tools, though, were stacked neatly on the porch. He had promised to repair the door when he got home from work. Maybe, I told myself, he just hadn't heard me yet.

With fear clenching my stomach, I crossed the yard and stood at the front door. Only silence emanated from the house. With a trembling voice, I called out, "Wyatt?"

Belle flopped down on her bed, but no other sound came back. I couldn't see any movement in the shadows. I knew what it meant but refused to accept it. Instead, I stepped through the doorway into the stuffy interior. Wyatt's cell phone, wallet, and keys sat on the small kitchen table. The recliner and couch in the den were empty. The TV was off.

Desperate to deny the reality, I climbed the steps to the second floor, glancing into the bedrooms we had never used as I went down the quiet hallway. His door at the end of the hall was open. The room was dark and vacant. In his bathroom, the shower curtain hung open. Nothing was big enough to hide in, not that he was likely to be playing hide-and-seek.

"Wyatt?"

The curtain flapped in the open window, the loudest sound in the room. I spun on my heel and returned to the kitchen. The search was useless, but I walked through the empty house again anyway. Denial is powerful. Only a loud ringing stopped me.

Wyatt's phone vibrated on the kitchen table. I waited for

him to race into the room and snatch up the device, but I knew he wouldn't. When he didn't appear, I inched over and looked at the lighted screen. Unknown caller.

The ringing stopped before I could pick it up. The screen went dark. I waited, unsure what to do. My mind raced. I wanted to call C.J. for help, but that was impossible.

The phone bounced again. The ringing had returned. Unknown Caller announced itself. I picked up the phone, pressed the answer button, and stuck it to my ear. "Hello?"

"Purvis Webb." The voice was flat, emotionless. Rudy. "You missed our meeting."

The world slipped under my feet. Unable to remain standing, I sat down hard in a chair. "I'm sorry."

"You promised. I told you what happened to people who lie to me."

"But C.J.—"

"Croaked. Yeah, I heard. Wyatt told me you had called him from the hospital with the unsettling news. We've been having such a nice little chat."

My throat went dry. The words were stuck. "Please don't hurt him."

"Where's my money?" The voice was cold, lifeless.

"I don't have it."

"Well, that's a big problem."

The hum on the line echoed in my brain. I grasped any hope. "I'll get it. I don't know how, but I'll get it. I need time."

"That's one thing you don't have." A humorless chuckle came over the phone. "Well, maybe you do. But Wyatt doesn't."

"Please." I hated the sound of my voice begging. It reminded me too much of Gene the night before, but what else could I do?

"I had hoped to convince young Wyatt to come work for me once we got this unfortunate matter resolved. I have an opening, you know. I was always told he had such talent." The line hissed and popped. "But there's no room in my organization for someone I don't trust. If you don't have the money, I might as well get this over with."

"No! Wait!"

I closed my eyes and waited on the sound of a gun. Instead, Rudy's voice replied, "Why?"

"I'll get it. Somehow. Give me a week."

"Tonight."

"More time. Please."

"Same as last night. Coogan's Cove. Nice private place you have there. Nine o'clock. You can join Gene. If you don't show up, Wyatt will die."

I inhaled, my mind racing. I started to protest, but the line went dead.

IMPOSSIBLE. I would never get my hands on the money that fast. Without it, my choices were limited.

Rudy knew it too. He only wanted a meeting for one reason. If I went to Coogan's Cove empty-handed and tried to reason for more time, he would kill me. And then he would kill Wyatt. The only other scenario was that he killed Wyatt before I got there, but I thought he would wait.

If I didn't go? If I got into my car and disappeared? Wyatt would die. I would spend the rest of my days thinking of him and missing Shelby.

I sat at the kitchen table with my head in my hands, thinking through my limited options.

If I went to the meeting empty-handed, Rudy would kill me and then kill Wyatt.

If I didn't go to the meeting and ran instead, he would kill Wyatt.

If I called the sheriff and Rudy figured out police were coming, he would kill Wyatt, disappear, and then hunt me down when I least expected it.

I closed my eyes and leaned my head against the wall. Every scenario in my head ended with Wyatt's death.

How do I solve the impossible? How do I get out of this alive? Answer? I don't. I have to somehow trade my life for his.

I looked at the clock above the kitchen stove. I had time. A strange thought considering I would die before midnight, but I realized how few loose ends were left in my life. If I did this right, Wyatt would be alive and free. He had his whole life in front of him. I was an old man. The choice between us was simple.

Every kitchen has a junk drawer. My house was no exception. Scissors. Tape. Paper clips. Rubber bands. Clothes pins. A screwdriver. An old key that went to something, but I could never remember what.

I removed a roll of Scotch tape, a pad of paper, and a pen. I sat down at the kitchen table and wrote:

Dear Wyatt,

If you're reading this note, it means my plan worked. You're sitting in my car and wondering what to do.

Start the car. Drive away. Now. Go anywhere you want except Millerton. Don't go home. Ever. Start a new life. Disappear so Rudy can't find you.

All your clothes and everything else from your room are in the trunk. I signed the title to my car. You can sell it if you need the money. Or keep it. It's yours to do with it as you want.

I stopped at the ATM and took out all the money I could. I added it to the money we pooled last night. It's in the glove compartment. I figured the bank has cameras. The police will see you didn't rob me or anything.

I'm sorry I didn't know you when you were growing up. I wish I

*could've patched things up with your mother. I should never have let it fall
apart so badly.*

*At least we got a chance to spend the last few years together. You're a
strong man, and I'm proud of you. I hope you have a good, long life.
You've earned it.*

Now, go. Please.

Love,

Purvis

The paper in my hands shook as I reread the letter. I
wanted to say so much more, but my whole plan hinged on
Wyatt driving away. Otherwise, we would both die for nothing.

I wanted to rewrite it until it was perfect, but time didn't
allow it. I made only one change. I crossed out my name and
scribbled:

Grandpa

I folded the letter and slipped it into my pocket along with
the tape I would use to affix it to my steering wheel. With the
first task done, I leaned back in my chair and surveyed my
small house. I loved the place and hated to think of it abandoned, but it had done its job. Shelby and I had years of
cooking together in the kitchen. Jessica had run around the
small den and swung from a tire hanging from the maple tree.
For the last few years, I had built a bond with the young man I
hadn't known existed.

Now it was just a house. Shelby would never get well
enough to come home. Jessica was long dead. Wyatt needed to
leave. No one else was here except for Belle.

Sensing my thoughts, the dog stood from her bed beside
the fireplace, shook, and stretched. She wandered over and
settled her big head onto my lap, looking at me with those big
brown eyes. I scratched her ears as I debated with myself

whether to put her in the car so Wyatt could take her with him. But a dog would make Rudy suspicious. And worse, he might hurt her. "Don't worry, girl. I have a plan to take care of you too."

I took her out to the yard for her bathroom break. Once back inside, I poured several days of food into her bowl and made sure she had plenty of water, just in case my plan failed and no one checked on her for a couple of days. The guys at the Liars' Table would soon enough.

While she was eating, I retrieved my old duffel bag from my closet. I went into Wyatt's room and began emptying drawers and removing clothes from hangers. There wasn't much. I stuffed all Wyatt's worldly possessions into the duffel bag and took another look around the room.

On the dresser was a picture frame holding the single photo of Jessica and Wyatt. The boy was little, only three or four, and the image was faded. It was the only picture he had of his mother. I gently put it on top of his clothes and closed the duffel. I slung it over my shoulder and walked to the door, taking one last look around the den. I hoped the next family had lots of children.

Belle settled onto her blanket beside the empty fireplace as if it was any other night.

"Goodbye, old girl," I said and pulled the door closed behind me as I left.

39

When I arrived at the nursing home, I wanted to go straight inside and sit with Shelby. I had no illusions I would ever get another chance after tonight, so I yearned to spend as much time as possible with her before I had to leave. She probably wouldn't know who I was. Even if she did, she wouldn't remember it tomorrow. She wouldn't remember it an hour after I left.

But I would. When Rudy did the inevitable, I would be thinking of holding her hand, listening to her talk, kissing her head, and saying goodnight. Whether she heard it or remembered it, I wanted to go to my grave having told her one more time that I loved her.

I had obligations to take care of all my loved ones. So few were left in my life, but I had to take care of the ones that were. Because I had to think of the others, I sat fidgeting in my car in the parking lot of the nursing home, watching the day-shift employees come out of the side entrance of the building in twos and threes, laughing and joking as they walked to their cars. Each time the door swung open, I held my breath, waiting on the right one, wondering if my target had the day off or was working late. I should have called first, but I wanted our conversation to appear accidental, almost an afterthought.

To my relief, Bobby appeared at the exit door with a satchel in his hand, whistling as he walked across the asphalt. When he was only a few car lengths away, I got out of my car, trying to look as casual as possible. Our eyes met, and I acted surprised to bump into him.

"Headed in for your dinner date?" Bobby asked.

"Yeah. Never miss."

"Almost did. Food carts are already making their rounds. You're running later than normal."

"Got busy and lost track of time." The lie slipped easily from my lips.

"Busy?" Bobby raised an eyebrow. "I can't wait until I retire. Sitting around with the rest of you, shooting the breeze at Abe's and then fishing all day." His eyes went wide, and his face paled. "Oh my God. I'm such an idiot. I heard this afternoon about what happened to C.J. I'm so sorry."

"It's okay. Don't worry about it." I waved my hand in dismissal. "I have a favor to ask of you."

"More money to give away?"

"No. Nothing like that." I kicked at a pebble in the parking lot, nervous about his reaction to my question. "You have a couple of old hounds, right?"

Puzzlement spread across Bobby's face. "Yeah?"

"You know I have one too."

"Belle? She's not sick, is she?"

"No. She's fine. Just old, but she's a good dog. I was just wondering…" I swallowed and raised my eyes. Time to plunge ahead. "C.J. and I had a deal. If anything ever happened to me, he'd take her and make sure she lived a good life. With him gone…"

"You want me to take her if something happens to you?"

"Yeah."

Bobby cocked his head. "What about Wyatt? Wouldn't it be easier on her to stay in the house with him?"

Good question. I had been so focused on my plan, I hadn't even thought about others not understanding everything. Maybe this gave me an opportunity to plant seeds to explain Wyatt's pending disappearance. Lemonade out of lemons. "He's finished with his apprenticeship and has his electrician's license. Lots of building going on, and he's had job offers. Out of town. Since he didn't grow up here, those bigger cities appeal to him. Anyway, we've talked a lot about it, and he's probably moving soon. Might even happen this week."

"Isn't he going to C.J.'s funeral?"

So many questions. So many good ones. Why hadn't I planned out this conversation better? "You know how jobs go. If he doesn't take it right away, it might not be there."

"Yeah, I understand." Bobby nodded, but his eyes were clouded with doubt. "Of course I'll take Belle if Wyatt isn't around. I love dogs. You know that."

"I do. That's why I asked. Thanks."

I turned to walk away, but Bobby's hand on my elbow stopped me. "You're okay, aren't you? You look kind of tired. You aren't sick or something?"

"I'm fine."

Bobby looked around the parking lot to make sure we were alone. He lowered his voice. "It's just asking me to take care of Belle and then giving away the money the other day. Those are the kinds of things someone does if they think they aren't going to be around long."

"No, nothing like that."

"We see that here. People come and just give up. Some even try to speed things along. With C.J. dying and Wyatt leaving, I know that's a lot on you. If you need something…"

He thought I was suicidal, and I wanted to protest how untrue that was, but wasn't I? I was going to offer to trade my life for Wyatt's. What else would you call that but suicide? The lying was getting complicated. I put on my best smile and hoped it look real. "I'm fine. Tired, yeah, and sad, but I'm okay. With C.J. dying and Wyatt moving, just made me realize I needed to make sure Belle was okay if something happened to me."

Bobby studied me for a minute and then nodded. "I'll take her if something happens."

"Thanks. You're a good friend." We shook hands, and I walked toward the nursing home entrance.

Teresa offered her condolences about C.J. the moment I entered the dementia unit. In small towns, news travels fast. Bad news travels faster.

The nurse then gave me something positive. "Shelby is having one of her better days. She's been engaging with others, good spirits, and lots of memories."

Finally, some good news, though I kept my excitement in check as I crossed the large room. We had noticed early on her dementia path the curse of sundowners, the declining of a person as the day turned to evening. She was more likely to forget things or to be easily upset late in the day. Our years-long habit of sitting on the porch, watching the sunset, had been increasingly curtailed in her last years at home as she had often forgotten who I was during that time. I'd lost count of the number of times she was my wife while the sun was in the sky but a complete stranger by the time it was dark.

Fearing the moment of clarity had already faded for the day, I approached the couch with some trepidation. She looked up from her seat in front of the TV, confusion clouding her face. I swallowed my disappointment and said, "Good evening, darling."

She cocked her head to the side and opened her mouth, but then she hesitated. She studied me as her mouth drew closed again. Her face brightened as the fog lifted and her smile spread. She patted the couch beside her and said, "Purvis, it's good to see you, hon."

Her recognition of me drove warmth through my body. It was hard to describe to someone who hadn't dealt with this disease how much it meant that she knew who I was. Moments like this were a rebirth of sorts, a resurrection of a loved one you thought had been lost. I settled beside her and tucked her hair behind her ear. "You're looking good today."

She blushed, her eyes twinkling. "You're so sweet. I know better, but thank you. Not exactly a beauty parlor here in the nursing home."

"I think you're gorgeous."

"And I think you have a silver tongue." She playfully pushed against my arm. "You remember talking your way past my father to ask me to the movies that first time."

I squeezed her hand. "You asked me what movie was showing, and I had no idea."

Her melodic laugh floated to my ears. "That's how I knew you liked me. And the way you always treated me like a queen, holding the door for me in that old car of yours."

"You are my queen. And that old car was your limo."

"Some limo." She laughed again, the sound healthy and strong. "But it's all I ever needed. That, and you, of course."

I knew that was a lie. Maybe she didn't remember her affair with Horace. Maybe she didn't remember keeping his letters long after the affair was over—or, at least, long after I thought it was over.

But sometimes a lie is okay. We may have started out more as friends than lovers. We'd certainly had our rough patches. We'd made mistakes. We certainly could have done better for Jessica. But I couldn't change any of that.

I threaded my fingers through hers and held her hand as she rested her head on my shoulder. I kissed the top of her head and said, "I love you."

She looked up at me and gave me a quick kiss on the lips. "I love you too, Purvis Webb."

40

The parking lot of Coogan's Cove looked much the same as it had the night before—a scattering of cars and an absence of people. I knew Rudy the Roach was there, somewhere, watching me, but I couldn't find him. His gorilla was probably beside him. I didn't see the dark SUV, but maybe he changed cars regularly. No shadows moved in the forest. Not even any young lovers sat at a picnic table, fondling each other. As far as I could tell, I was alone.

I pulled Gene's pistol out from underneath the seat and checked it for the dozenth time since putting my plan into play. I didn't think I would get a chance to use it. Even if I did, I had never been a good shot, but I chambered a round to be ready. It was as good a plan as I had.

I got out of the car and stretched in the fading light. Thunder rumbled in the distance, a storm working its way over the mountains. I would miss the smell of approaching rain in the mountain air and the feel of a cool breeze rolling down the hill.

I expected to hear my name, but only the sounds of nature

reached me. If he was waiting, he would be at the top of the hill, watching me.

Showtime.

I walked to the rear of the car and opened the trunk. I wanted him to see me clearly. I hoped he was watching. I pulled out a shovel with fresh mud crusted around its blade.

What was he thinking as he spied from the shadows? He expected a garbage bag of cash. When he saw the shovel, would he be curious or mad? He might shoot Wyatt and run right now. Then I would have to wait until he showed up at the house one night to slit my throat. I was counting on his curiosity, though.

I rested the shovel on my shoulder, the blade pointed skyward to catch the maximum light. He needed to see the mud. I tried to appear calm but doubted it worked because my guts were a tangled mess of nerves. I fought the urge to vomit and did the only thing I could—traipsed to the top of the picnic grounds.

Once there, I leaned the shovel against a tree. I wanted it to draw his attention.

And then I waited. Was he already here? Or would a car pull into the parking lot?

Five minutes. The place was eerily quiet. No one moved.

Ten minutes. I heard a twig snap. Wyatt stumbled into view, pushed from behind. His hands were tied together, and a gag was stuffed in his mouth. Rudy emerged with a pistol raised and pointed at Wyatt's head. "What do you think you're doing, old man?"

"What I promised. Giving you your money."

His face was squinted in confusion. His eyes showed doubt. I wanted to keep him talking but knew I needed to draw him out. I forced myself to wait on his question. Wyatt looked back and forth, concern in his eyes.

After two minutes ticked by, Rudy finally asked, "Where is it?"

"Buried."

He cocked his head and circled the barrel of the pistol, an indication he wanted me to continue. Instead, I waited in silence until he asked, "Now why would you do a fool thing like that?"

"Bargaining chip."

He looked incredulous and waved his arm wide to indicate the empty picnic area. "What do you want? A last meal or something?"

"Let Wyatt go."

Wyatt's eyes grew wide, and he shook his head, but I avoided looking at him. I needed to concentrate.

Rudy laughed, a hearty but evil sound. It tapered off into a chuckle as he shook his head. "Why would I do that?"

"Because then I'll give you your money."

"I'm not sure what you're thinking, old man, but Wyatt here is *my* bargaining chip. You don't give me my money, and I kill him. And then I'll kill you."

"I figured that much out." I smiled. I didn't mean to. I wasn't even sure why I did because I didn't find anything funny. And yet I smiled. And that smile might have unnerved Rudy. "The problem is you're going to kill me anyway. Right after I give you the money, I'm dead."

"The second you give me my money, you go home."

I wanted to believe that. I really did. But only a fool would. "I don't think so."

"Why would I kill you? What reason do I have?"

"A couple. First, revenge. I stole your money. I didn't mean to. I tried to explain that, but I did steal it. You killed Gene because you suspected the same thing without an iota of proof."

Rudy looked around the picnic area. Maybe he thought I

was wired and was looking for a confession. I wasn't. That would have been a good idea.

"Like you said, it was an accident. That's different."

"That's the other reason. I watched you kill a man. And that is, as you would probably say, a loose end."

Rudy squinted and stared me hard in the face. I could see he was thinking. He knew what I was saying was true. "If that were true, wouldn't I kill your grandson too? He saw the same thing you did."

"Yep. That's exactly what I'm thinking."

"Then I might as well get it over with."

He didn't pull back the slide or thumb the hammer down like the bad guy would in a movie to make his point and ratchet up the drama. He just jammed the pistol against the back of Wyatt's head. I had the time it takes to pull the trigger to stop him.

"Just one problem."

He kept the gun hard against Wyatt's skull, pushing his head forward. Wyatt had his eyes squeezed shut. I could see his lips moving. I figured he was praying.

The tide turned. Rudy cocked an eyebrow at me. "What problem would that be?"

"You kill him, you're out a hundred grand."

He shook his head. "You'll dig it up for me."

"Once you kill Wyatt, I have nothing left in this world. All I have is my own life, and we've already established you're going to kill me whether I give you the money or not."

"I can make it fast or slow."

"True. I've thought of that. You could beat me, shoot me, torture me, but I'll have nothing to live for, so I don't care." Sure, I cared. I tried my best to make it sound like I didn't. "But if you let Wyatt go, then I'll give you the money."

Rudy flexed his hand that was gripping the pistol. My heart leapt, thinking he was pulling the trigger, but he didn't. His eyes went back and forth from the back of Wyatt's head to my face. I hadn't sold him yet, but I had him thinking. Time to close the deal.

"Here's what you're thinking. Once Wyatt's gone, what keeps me from just refusing?"

His eyes told me that was exactly what he was thinking, so I kept pushing. "Here's why. You'll still kill me, but I don't think you'll care as much about killing Wyatt once you have your money."

Wyatt's head popped up. Our eyes locked. I knew he wanted to protest, but what I was saying was as much for him as it was for Rudy. I needed to convince them both. "You'll look for him, of course, but he won't be in Millerton. There's nothing here for him once I'm dead. I loaded all his clothes in the car. I even left him a note taped to the steering wheel. Go read it if you want. It tells him to simply disappear. You'll never find him. After a while, you'll decide you have other things to deal with. Wyatt will become an afterthought."

I could see he was almost there. One last push. "Your choice is simple. You kill us both and never see your money. Or Wyatt goes free, you get your money, and then you kill me or you let me go, though we both know what the real answer to that is."

Ever so slowly, Rudy lowered the pistol to his side. With a wave of his other hand, he dismissed Wyatt. "Get out of here. I'll find you someday no matter what your grandpa thinks."

I untied the knot holding Wyatt's hands together and removed the gag. Wyatt tried to speak, but I hugged him instead. "I love you. Now go."

41

We watched Wyatt as he headed down the trail to the parking lot. I wanted to see him in the car and gone, but Rudy wasn't waiting that long. He shoved me to get my attention and said, "Okay, old man. Where's my money?"

I gripped the shovel and pointed to the trail snaking down to the river. "It's buried at my favorite fishing hole down there. C.J. and I have fished at it since we were little kids, so that makes it easy for me to remember where to find it even in the dark."

Without looking to see if he would follow, I marched into the blackness. I figured Rudy debated whether to pursue Wyatt or follow me. The problem for him was simple. Retrieving Wyatt wouldn't change anything. He didn't know where our favorite fishing hole was or which spots on the river we used. Even if he could figure it out, he wouldn't know where at the spot to look. He could dig for years and not find it. I was counting on that money meaning more to Rudy than revenge.

After a minute, I heard Rudy's footsteps behind me, scrambling to catch up. He had chosen to let Wyatt go. He'd have to pursue him some other day. I hoped Wyatt had read the note, took it to heart, and really took off. He could never return to Millerton.

The fading daylight made it difficult to avoid tripping over rocks and roots on the trail. Rudy stumbled behind me several times, much to my amusement. Each time, I debated trying to draw the pistol hidden in my waistband and shoot him, but he never holstered his own gun. I doubted I'd be fast enough. Besides, the longer I waited, the farther away Wyatt was. If I failed, he needed to be far away.

To entertain myself, I imagined the challenge Rudy would have leaving here later. I doubted I would get the joy of witnessing it, but he'd have to fight his way back up this trail in the dark of night. Maybe he'd get lost. That would be poetic justice.

We made it to the bottom of the gorge and reached the river. I sucked in a lungful of the cool, fresh air. I looked at the gentle rapids and debated making a run for it across the shallow water. He would just shoot me in the back, though, as I slipped on the wet rocks. Wyatt needed more time. I wanted him a hundred miles away before Rudy could start his pursuit.

I pointed upstream and began pushing aside the thick growth of rhododendrons that clogged the banks. On our walk down, we had passed a smooth trail just twenty yards behind us. It made the entrance to our fishing area easy, but my goal wasn't ease. As exhausting as this path was for me, I wanted it to be worse for Rudy.

What he didn't know was C.J. and I knew this area like our own backyards. We'd spent many a day since grade school knee-deep in these waters, casting our lines for trout. It was our happy place. I also realized there were far worse places to die.

A few hundred yards upstream, we stumbled into a small clearing centered by a fire ring built from river rock. Many a day, we had grilled our catch over that fire, sat against those boulders, and drunk beer cooled in the river water.

The flat boulder on the far side was our table we used for gutting and filleting fish. It was also my marker that indicated where I wanted to dig. I pointed at the ground. A flash of lightning illuminated the clearing as Rudy stepped up beside me and said, "Start digging, old man. I don't want to be here all night."

I jammed the blade of the shovel into the ground, the metal clanking against the rock under the surface. With a slam of my boot, I was able to drive it a few inches below the surface. I lifted the weight and dumped it in the pile. Slow and methodical, I repeated the process, digging and struggling to pull the rocks out of the ground. My muscles burned. Sweat dribbled down my back. My heart pounded in my chest. Mother Earth fought every step of the way as I worked my way deeper. The lightning overhead became more frequent and the thunder louder.

Maybe twenty minutes passed—could've been thirty—before Rudy realized what I was doing. He came up behind me and said, "You've never dug here before."

I jabbed the shovel in the ground and leaned against its handle, panting to catch my breath. "What do you mean?"

He gestured at the pile of dirt and rock I had extracted. "If you'd buried the money here earlier today, the ground would be softer. You wouldn't be digging up all these rocks."

How far had Wyatt driven? Had I given him enough time? I could only hope he was far away. Doing my best to gain a few more minutes, I looked at the ground with my best puzzled expression. "I think this is the spot."

Rudy growled and yanked the shovel out of my hands. "You didn't bury the money. I don't even think you have it."

I shrugged. My time on earth was short. No sense delaying it anymore. "Nope," I said as I reached for the pistol tucked in my pants.

In the movies, drawing a gun looks easy. Two cowboys, one

in a white hat and one in black, face each other on a dirt street. A clock ticks. The guns come out smooth as silk. Gun smoke rises. The bad guy falls to the ground.

What they don't show you is that it takes practice, something I had never done. I'd managed paperwork in the air force. I wasn't CIA or some other nonsense. I'd barely qualified with a rifle. I certainly didn't know how to smoothly draw a pistol.

I didn't lift my shirt fast enough. The gun caught on my pants. I didn't have my hand in the right position. I gave Rudy the Roach all the time he needed to swing that shovel. He knocked me to the ground. The gun bounced out of my hand, skipped across the rocks, and splashed into the river.

Kerplunk.

I looked up to a pistol in my face. Rudy glared at me with fire in his eyes. "Time to die, old man."

42

"Last chance. Where's my money?"

I lay on the ground beside the shovel, staring at the river. The storm was building, and the lighting was frequent. I could see clearly in the flashes of light. The lies were done. All I had left was the truth. "The sheriff still has it."

Rudy stood near the center of the clearing, the gun in his hand dangling at his side. His calm demeanor scared me. His voice came out cold as ice. "You lied to me."

I pushed myself up into a sitting position and met his eyes. I didn't want to die a coward. "Yep."

"I showed you what I do to liars."

The water gurgled peacefully past us. I thought of it rolling down to the Pigeon River, over to the Tennessee River in Knoxville, and down the Mississippi to the Gulf and the ocean beyond. My blood would soon join that flow.

With a glance at the wet stones, I wondered if the pistol I'd dropped would still fire if I pulled it out of the water. Not that it mattered. Rudy would shoot me long before I reached it. Even if he missed on his first shot, I wouldn't be able to find the gun on the bottom of the river. I rested my arms on my knees and stared him in the eyes. "Same thing you were going to do to me anyway."

He smiled, and it chilled me. "Oh, I'm going to kill you, old man, but not yet. I've got a far better idea."

The shovel lay five feet away from me, right where he dropped it. Could I reach it? Stand. Swing. How many bullets would he put in me before I slammed the shovel into his face? Three? Four? I suspected I was still quite low in my estimate.

"I can't get you the money no matter how much you torture me."

"I believe you. For once, I think you aren't lying."

I took a deep breath of fresh mountain air. I didn't know how many more breaths I had remaining, and I wanted to savor each one. I was stalling, but so was he. "What's your plan?"

Rudy smiled broader, menace on his face. "You're going to watch me kill your grandson."

"First, you're going to have to catch him. He's three counties away by now, and you don't even know which direction he went."

"You wish."

The sound was soft at first, like the first drops of rain falling from the sky, but it became unmistakably clearer in the quiet of the night. Footsteps came down the trail. The more Rudy smiled, the bigger grew the pit of dread in my stomach. A minute later, my worst fears were realized. Wyatt came marching into the campsite. Duct tape covered his mouth and bound his wrists. The gorilla was behind him, pistol in hand. When they reached the center of the clearing, the gorilla shoved Wyatt to the ground and placed a foot on his back. He squirmed, but he couldn't push back against all that weight.

Rudy turned to me and said, "How rude of me. I never introduced Ian the other night, did I?"

I was numb. Couldn't think. I could only shake my head.

"Ian has been my right-hand man for a very long time. He's big, of course, but people underestimate him. He's wicked smart too, which is why I trust him." Rudy held up his phone. "Desperate men always try something, but I didn't know what you might do. Before we met, I called Ian and left the line open. He's been listening the whole time. As soon as we were out of sight, he scooped up young Wyatt before he reached your car and escaped. Then he tracked my phone to find us down here."

Ian spoke, his voice a deep bass that bored into my soul. "Found a note, too, boss." He handed across my scribblings I had left taped to the steering wheel for Wyatt.

Rudy read it hurriedly and then mocked me. "Love, Grandpa. How sweet."

Ian stepped back as Rudy walked to Wyatt, grabbed him by the hair, and pulled him up onto his knees. He shoved the sheet of paper in front of his face and asked, "Do you want to read it? See what Grandpa had to say?"

"Please," I begged. "I'll get your money."

Rudy walked to the edge of the river and looked up to the sky as the rain began to fall steadily. His sigh was barely audible. "You're lying again."

"I don't know how I'll get it, but I'll figure it out. Somehow. Some way."

"Time is up. Money is gone. Cost of doing business, I guess."

"Please."

He spun on his heel, pointed across the clearing at Wyatt, and said to his gorilla, "Shoot the boy."

Lightning flashed across the sky, illuminating Wyatt's face as he squeezed his eyes shut in terror. Behind him, Ian leveled the pistol against the back of his head. I had nothing left to lose, so I dove for the shovel as a tremendous crack of thunder rattled the trees. My only chance was to connect the shovel against that pistol without knocking out Wyatt's brains.

I had never been much of an athlete in school. I wasn't big enough for football, fast enough for track, or agile enough for basketball. Most importantly, at least to my shovel-wielding plan, was the fact that I could never hit a baseball.

I was that kid. When I'd come up to bat in some captain's choice baseball game during PE class in middle school, the defense collapsed from the outfield almost to the bases. The infield closed to near the pitcher's mound. I had never, in all my years, managed to make them regret that move. There was no risk I would hit it over their heads. If I connected with the baseball, something that rarely happened, it dribbled across the field until someone scooped it up and tossed it to the first baseman. The only time I ever got on base was if a wild pitch beaned me.

I was the strikeout king. I swung at slow pitches. I swung at fast pitches. I sometimes hit a pop fly, a foul ball, or an unintentional bunt that dribbled impotently across the grass. Mostly, though, I struck out.

I was doomed the second I went for the shovel. Like every other plan I had ever made, I hadn't thought it through. I didn't have the skill. If I was telling this story as some tall tale, I would describe how I swung low and level. How I connected perfectly. How Wyatt's hair flopped in the breeze created by the shovel while the pistol flew across the river. Wouldn't that make a great story? What a great ending.

It didn't happen.

The wet shovel handle slipped in my grip. My swing was off. Way off. At least a foot high. More like two. Way outside the strike zone. It was a swinging strike. I wasn't in any danger of hitting Wyatt's head. Unfortunately, I missed the pistol wide too.

As bad as my aim was, though, I couldn't have asked for a

better result. The flat edge of the shovel blade whistled through the air high above its target and slammed into Ian's nose instead. The one thing I got right was the force of my swing. I wasn't swinging for my life. I was swinging for Wyatt's.

If I ever told this story at the Liars' Table—and I never would—I would describe how his nose flew out the back of his head and landed in the fire circle. Maybe I would have an eagle swoop down and snatch it from midair.

The nose didn't leave his head, though. It stopped somewhere deep in his brain. I doubt he even knew what happened. All I heard was his grunt as he crumpled, the pistol falling from his hand and clattering to the ground a few feet away.

I stood in shock, looking at the collapsed giant and Wyatt's stunned face. I couldn't believe my luck. The sound of a shot ripped through the air behind me, cutting my celebration short. Rudy, witnessing the death of his monster, had drawn and fired at me. Fortunately for me, he wasn't as good a shot from twenty feet away as he was from point-blank range. The bullet smacked into a tree, off target by more than my shovel swing. It was just a matter of time, though, until he connected with a bullet.

Wyatt was still on his knees in the center of the open area. I needed to drag him into the woods before Rudy took out one of us. I ran toward him, hunched over to make a smaller target, but slipped in the mud and tripped over one of the rocks surrounding the fire ring. A bullet whizzed over my head as I sprawled to the ground, scraping my chin. The next bullet splashed through a growing puddle two feet to my right.

I scrambled toward Wyatt, clawing the ground to stay as low as possible. My hands wrapped around roots for leverage. Rudy screamed in frustration, and I realized his gun had jammed. He raised it above his head like a hammer and launched himself at me. The butt of the pistol caught me between my shoulder blades. I collapsed to the ground and flailed with my arms. Another bolt of lightning lit up Wyatt's stunned face, frozen in terror. Off to his side, metal reflected in the sudden light. Ian's pistol.

I bucked Rudy off my back and crawled through the mud. He jumped on me again, pounding my back with his fists. I did my best to ignore him as I pulled myself forward, inch by inch, until my right hand wrapped around the gun. With the last of my strength, I twisted my body and shoved the barrel of Ian's pistol under Rudy's jaw. His eyes grew wide as I pulled the trigger.

Lightning struck a tree fifty feet away, creating a giant flash of light that was simultaneous with an explosion of sound. I could see Rudy atop me, his fist drawn back to plunge into my face, and a spray of blood exploding behind his head. He hands fluttered to his neck and grasped the wound. A gurgling noise testified to his fight for air. He rolled off me, hit the ground, and went motionless a few seconds later.

I struggled to my feet, shocked to still be alive. Wyatt scrambled to his feet, his hands trembling with fright. His teeth chattered despite the warm evening air.

I didn't know if anyone was left in the parking lot during the storm or if they could even have heard the gunshots, but we needed to climb back up the gorge to our car and leave before the police arrived. I wiped the pistols clean with my shirt. With my best throw, which wasn't much, I sent them sailing through the air and into the river with a splash. They joined the other gun that was already there.

I slipped the tape off Wyatt's mouth and hugged him. Then I grabbed the shovel with one hand and placed the other on Wyatt's elbow. Gently but firmly, I guided him to the trail and out of the gorge, with only a glance over my shoulder at the two bodies left behind in the driving rain.

FRIDAY

43

"C J. would've liked what you said."

I jumped. For such an imposing man, Reverend Brawley could sure sneak up on a guy. "You think it was okay? I'm not much on public speaking."

"You were a natural up there. The best eulogies come from the heart. I'm sure he loved the stories you told."

Harlow chortled, twisting that mustache between his fingers. "That old wild boar chasing him up around Soco Gap... I had forgotten that one. I haven't laughed so hard in a church in ages."

Ronnie smiled broadly. "The eagle flying away with the fish was his best story ever. That has been legend ever since he first told it. I loved that you shared it again for him."

Chip's eyes misted over. "The way you talked about Wanda always griping about his overalls. She always wanted him to dress better when he went to town. The silver-tongued devil would tell her he didn't want to distract anyone from her beauty. You could tell how much those two were meant for each other."

The sheriff brushed a speck of dust off his glistening

badge. "He and Wanda sipping moonshine on their back porch... Let's just say, I'll pretend like I didn't hear that one, though I admit it did make me smile."

"Now they're back together, just like they were always meant to be." Brawley rested his hand on my shoulder and squeezed.

"Glad you were able to make it, Sheriff," I said. "I know you've had a busy week."

Miller County went most years without a murder at all. Three in a week was unheard of. With an election coming up, the sheriff wouldn't have missed a chance to be around voters for anything.

"The two killed Tuesday night were on national forest property, so that makes it federal anyway. The Fibbies who showed up on Wednesday weren't all that worried about juris-diction, but then it turned out those two were part of the same drug organization as the guy killed Monday night. A squadron of FBI and DEA joined them yesterday. Technically, that first one is still our case, but it makes sense to let them run with it. Probably all goes back into Tennessee anyway. Doesn't look like locals were involved."

I swore the corner of the sheriff's mouth twitched upward like he was smiling at the mess they'd taken from him, but he was smart enough to put his serious face back on.

Abe raised an eyebrow. "I thought some locals were seen there on Monday?"

"The Fibbies think it was probably just witnesses who skedaddled. Doesn't fit their profile. They're big believers in that profiling crap."

"Do they have any leads?"

"Not much. They're pretty sure it's some drug war, maybe even the cartels or something, but it doesn't sound to me like they got anything solid. Lots of boot prints, but you'd expect that from all the fishermen along the river. By the time we found the bodies, that blasted thunderstorm had washed away most of the evidence. Found pistols in the water, but they're mostly useless. Plus, their bodies had lain there overnight and been gnawed on long before those hikers found them. Probably coyotes."

Levi snickered. "Maybe it's that big old mountain lion C.J. always swore he saw up there."

Tommy rolled his eyes. "Ain't no mountain lions. How many times have I got to tell you that? If he saw anything, it was a bobcat."

Harlow groaned. "There are at least two mountain lions. My daughter's boyfriend's cousin's pa saw one up there. Had pictures and everything."

Tommy laughed. "I saw those photos. So blurry you couldn't make out nothing. Looked like a regular old barn cat to me, not that a barn cat would be opposed to taking a chunk out of some human who offended it."

People had been debating for decades whether mountain lions roamed our woods. I didn't know who was right. Nor did I care. I just wanted to put the past week behind me. I was thankful when Wyatt came up to the group and asked me, "You ready to go home?"

"Yeah, it's about that time."

Levi asked, "What's your hurry?"

"Dinner date with my wife. I never miss."

Reverend Brawley asked, "We'll see you both at church Sunday morning?"

Wyatt looked a little unsure, but a promise was a promise. We had a whole lot of penance to make. "We'll be here."

Abe asked, "You coming for breakfast tomorrow? We've missed you this week."

Everyone had given me space to mourn the death of my best friend. Other than going to have dinner with Shelby, I hadn't left the house the last few days. I missed their stories and the camaraderie, so I would go back. Just maybe not every day. "Monday."

"You got big Saturday plans or something?"

I threw my arm around Wyatt's shoulders. "My grandson here has the day off. The two of us have a day of fishing planned." Yeah, I had finally been able to start calling him that. Seemed silly I had avoided it all these years.

"Coogan's Cove?"

Wyatt and I looked at each other. "Nah, we're tired of that place. Have to change things up some."

Abe shrugged. "Can't wait to hear about the fish that got away."

"I wouldn't want to do something as plain as that."

Their eyes grew wide. Mouths dropped open.

I waited, like a good storyteller does, until I knew I had my audience hooked. "I'll have a much better story for you."

They begged me to give them a hint, but I didn't. I hadn't made the story up yet, but I had time. It would be a doozy.

D.K. WALL NEWSLETTER

If you enjoyed *Liars Table*, please subscribe to my monthly newsletter to learn about upcoming projects and to receive FREE subscriber-only bonus stories.

If you decide it's not for you, simply unsubscribe. No questions. No fuss.

ACKNOWLEDGMENTS

Growing up in the Carolinas, I thought every town had at least one Liars' Table. It might be a table in a diner or fast food restaurant, a bench in front of a gas station or general store, or men leaning against pickup trucks in front of the feed and seed store, but the key element is always the same—stories the teller swears to be true but no one really accepts at face value.

I spent many nights as a teenager at a campfire with other Boy Scouts honing my storytelling skills and listening to others do the same. In my responsible adulthood period in the corporate world, I traveled the globe and learned how similar people everywhere are—including the love of tall tales.

Now I'm blessed beyond belief to be settled back into my beloved Carolina mountains spinning yarns again. I hope you enjoyed meeting Purvis, C.J., and Wyatt.

As always, I have to thank the amazing editing team at Red Adept—Lynn McNamee, Sara Gardiner, Darlene Gardner, and Irene Steiger. They help me get the story in my head down on to paper which is no easy task. And, of course, they get to corral my creative use of commas, an even harder job.

The incredibly talented Glendon Haddix of Streetlight Graphics takes my story and captures it in the beauty of his cover designs. He outdid himself again with the *Liars' Table*.

None of this would be possible without the cheerleading and coaching of Todd Fulbright. He's always the first to hear my ideas for the next story and is my sounding board when I get stuck.

And, yes, we've already had hours of conversations about the next novel and the early drafts are coming together.

Finally, Dear Reader, I thank you as well—not only for reading my tales but for your emails, social media posts, and letters. You don't know how much your kind words inspire me to write the next book.

D.K. Wall

ABOUT THE AUTHOR

D.K. has lived his entire life in the Carolinas and Tennessee— from the highest elevations of the Great Smoky Mountains near Maggie Valley to the industrial towns of Gastonia and Hickory, the cities of Charlotte and Nashville, and the coastal salt marsh of Murrells Inlet.

Over the years, he's watched the textile and furniture industries wither and the banking and service industries explode, changing the face of the region. He uses his love of storytelling to share tales about the people and places affected.

Today he's married and living in Asheville. Surrounded by his family of rescued Siberian Huskies known as *The Thundering Herd*, D.K. is hard at work on his next novel.

For more information and to enjoy his short stories and photographs, please visit the author's website:

dkwall.com

ALSO BY D. K. WALL

The Lottery

Jaxon With An X

Liars' Table

Sour Notes

FOLLOW D.K. WALL ON SOCIAL MEDIA

f facebook.com/DKWallAuthor